THIS
BOOK IS
NOT
GOOD
FOR
YOU

THIS BOOK IS NOT GOOD FOR YOU

CHEF DE CUISINE

pseudonymous bosch

NEW YORK TIMES **BESTSELLING AUTHOR OF**
THE NAME OF THIS BOOK IS SECRET

Illustrations by Gilbert Ford

LITTLE, BROWN AND COMPANY
New York   Boston

Little, Brown and Company

Hachette Book Group • 237 Park Avenue, New York, NY 10017
Visit our website at www.lb-kids.com

Little, Brown and Company is a division of Hachette Book Group, Inc.
The Little, Brown name and logo are trademarks of Hachette Book Group, Inc.

First Paperback Edition: September 2010
First published in hardcover in September 2009 by Little, Brown and Company

ISBN 978-0-316-04086-0 (hc) / ISBN 978-0-316-04085-3 (pb)

10 9 8 7 6 5 4 3

RRD-C

Printed in the United States of America

FOR
INDIA AND NATALIA
WHEN THEY'RE OLD ENOUGH

M m m m m . . .

. . . good snap . . . melts

a hint of blackberry . . .

mmm . . . yes . . . strong

is it cardamom?

velvety mouth-feel . . .

finish . . . mmm . . .

AAAAAAAA
AAAAAAAAA

m m m m m . . .

smoothly on the tongue . . .

yet earthy underneath . . .

note of . . . cinnamon and—

or maybe licorice? . . .

not too sweet . . . lovely

must have another . . .

**AAAAAAAA
AAAAK . . !**

4 Oh. It's you.

Thank Goodness.

For a second, I thought it was — well, never mind what I thought.

The question is: what am I going to do with you?

You see, I'm — nbot quhgbite rlaaeady —

Sorry, my mouth was full. What I was trying to say was: I'm not quite ready for you. I'm very busy. Didn't you see the **DO NOT DISTURB** sign?

What am I doing? Something important. That's what.

Well, if you must know, I'm eating chocolate. But it's not like it sounds! Trust me. It's work. Research.

This book is all about chocolate. And — ykuh wounbrldbnt wrannt — sorry, I couldn't resist another bite — you wouldn't want me to write about something I didn't know about, would you?

What's that? You wouldn't expect anything else from me?

Great. Thanks for the vote of confidence.

Let me tell you something: I'm not the same scared writer I used to be, and I'm not going to take any guff from you. I have other readers now. Grateful readers. Readers who know how to treat an author.

Take this extra-large box of extra-dark, extra-expensive, extra-delicious chocolates that I'm eating right now. Not to toot my own horn but a fan sent it to me as a present.

For P.B. - the best writer in the world, said the note.

What? It must be a trick? Nobody would say that about me and mean it?

OK, out — now! There's no way I'm going to write this book with you sitting there insulting me.

I'll tell you what: on my desk, there's a chapter I just finished. It's supposed to come much later in the book, but you might as well read it now while I continue . . . researching.

It will be like a prologue, an *amuse-bouche*, if you will — something to tickle your palate before the real meal arrives.*

Speaking of meals, which chocolate shall I have next? The caramel nougat or the raspberry *ganache* . . . ?

Eeny meeny miny moe . . .

*At a fancy restaurant, a chef will often send an *AMUSE-BOUCHE* to your table before he or she serves the main meal. Translated from French, it means *amuse the mouth*. I don't know about you, but my mouth has a great sense of humor.

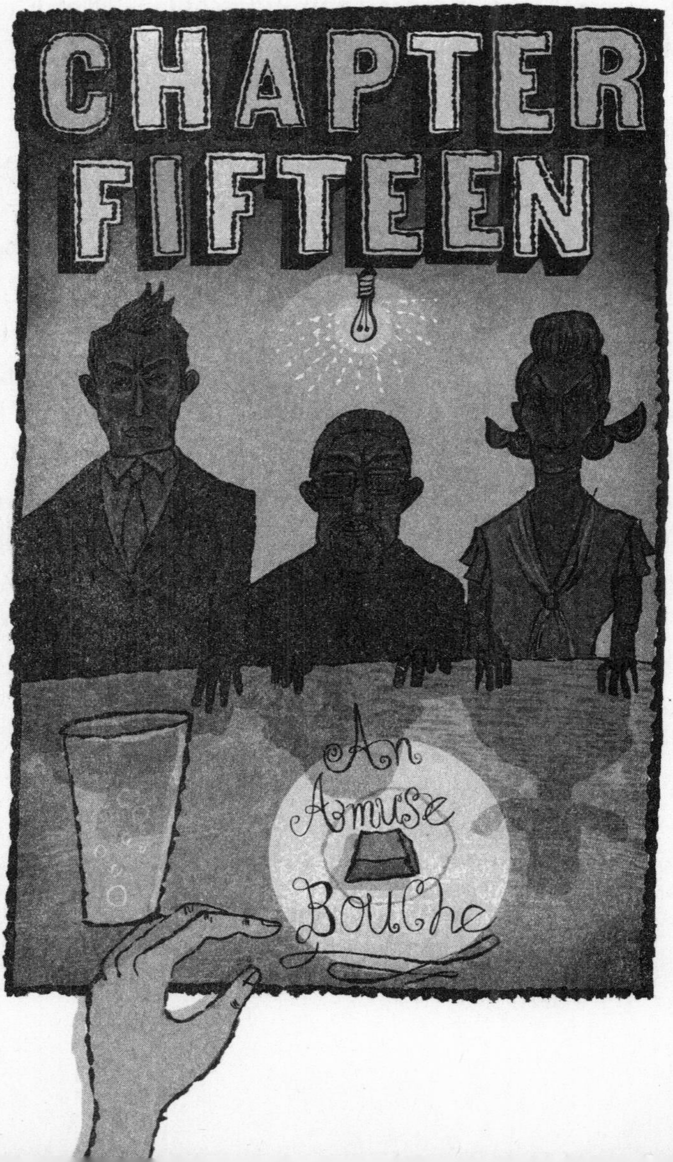
CHAPTER
FIFTEEN
An
Amuse
Bouche

A bird poked his head through the iron bars and nudged the arm of the girl on the other side. The bird was bright green with a red chest, yellow crest, and big, begging eyes.

"Patience, my friend!" said the girl. "My gosh, you are a greedy bird!"

(In reality, she was speaking French and what she said was: *"Patience, mon ami! Zut alors, tu es un oiseau avide!"* But the French version is a little less polite.)

Laughing, the girl opened her hand and revealed a small broken piece of chocolate — the same color as her delicate skin.

The bird swallowed it whole, then looked at her beseechingly.

"Sorry, that's all I could get today."

The bird squawked — whether in thanks or in protest, it was hard to tell — and then flew away, his long tail waving in the wind.

"*You* should be bringing *me* food. I'm the one in the birdcage!" the girl called after him as he disappeared into the dense jungle.

Glum, she sat down on the pile of old newspapers that served as her bed — and as the only source of entertainment in her cement cell. The bird was a pest but his visits were the highlight of her day. There was nothing to look forward to now.

"Look alive, Simone!"

One of the guards, the large humorless woman named Daisy, stepped up to her cage. "They want you again."

Already? Simone wondered. It had only been an hour since the last time.

They were waiting for her in the Tasting Room.

The three of them, as always, sitting in those tall silver chairs behind that long marble table. In their bright white lab coats. And bright white gloves.

They'd never introduced themselves, but she had names for them: The tan man with the silver hair, she called him the Doctor. The beautiful blond woman with the frozen smile, she was the Barbie Doll. And the blind man behind the dark sunglasses, he was the Pirate.

They were like a tribunal. Like judges.

Only, weirdly, it was *her* judgment they were waiting for.

She sat down opposite them on the low stone bench. The one that made her feel about two feet tall.

Always the same routine. First, they made her drink a glass of water. Twice distilled water without any trace minerals, they'd explained. Absolutely tasteless. To cleanse her palate.

Then the Pirate placed in front of her a small square of chocolate on a plain white plate.

A *Palet d'Or*, he called it. A pillow of gold.*

And then they waited in silence for her response.

They said she was a *supertaster*. Somebody with double the usual number of taste buds in her tongue. But she knew it was more than that.**

For as long as she remembered she'd been able to detect subtle differences in flavors.

Was the honey made from orange blossoms or clover? Clover. *Blackberry or boysenberry?* Gooseberry. *Was that lemon thyme or lemon verbena?* Neither, it was lemongrass.

She was like one of those virtuosos who can play an entire symphony by ear the first time they sit at a piano. She had the taste equivalent of perfect pitch.

Now, in this cold room so far from home, she looked down at the *Palet d'Or*. It was dark to the point of blackness, and it had a silky sheen.

Carefully, she nibbled off a corner. And closed her eyes.

---

*PALET D'OR IS MORE PROPERLY TRANSLATED AS "PALETTE" OR "DISK OF GOLD." BUT I THINK "PILLOW OF GOLD" IS MUCH MORE ROMANTIC.

**TO DETERMINE WHETHER OR NOT *YOU* ARE A SUPERTASTER, TRY THE TEST IN THE APPENDIX OF THIS BOOK.

For weeks they'd been making her try darker and darker pieces. Some so chocolaty and dense they were like dirt. Some so intensely flavorful they were like a jolt.

But this was something else altogether. It was like ultra chocolate. The quintessence of chocolate.

It was the best thing she'd ever tasted.

And the worst.

Tears streamed down her face as she experienced a lifetime of emotions all at once.

The taste of the chocolate — the *tastes*, that is, because the chocolate tasted of so many things — took her back to her childhood. To her family's old cacao farm in the rainforest.

In flashes, she remembered the gnarled roots of the cacao trees and the damp, fragrant earth. . . .

She remembered the flowers . . . those little pink flowers that bloomed year-round . . . not on branches . . . but right on the trunks of the cacao trees . . . as if each tree had come down with a case of flowery measles . . .

And she remembered the pods . . . red and yellow . . . like fiery sunsets . . . they looked as if they might contain alien spores or perhaps hives of evil fairies . . . but inside was the sweet sticky pulp that she loved to squish and squeeze between her hands . . .

And the seeds . . . she couldn't believe people made something as wonderful as chocolate from those sour little seeds . . . but soon she could identify any variety at a glance . . . the fragile Criollos . . . the purple Forasteros . . .*

How happy she'd felt on the farm . . . ! How safe . . . !

And then came that terrible day . . . the arrival of the three glamorous strangers . . . asking how she knew so much about chocolate . . . praising her tasting powers . . . promising a better future . . .

And then the crying as she was taken from her parents . . .

The gradual realization that she was a prisoner . . .

That her life was not her own . . .

"It's working!" exulted the Barbie Doll. "Look at her face!"

"She does seem to be . . . reacting," said the Doctor more cautiously. "Simone, can you tell us what you are tasting? What you are seeing?"

*YOU SAY COCAO, I SAY CACAO . . . SINCE SIMONE GREW UP ON A CHOCOLATE PLANTATION, SHE UNDERSTANDS THAT CHOCOLATE IS MADE FROM SEEDS — CACAO SEEDS. HOWEVER, I THINK YOU'LL FIND THAT MOST PEOPLE REFER TO CACAO SEEDS AS COCOA BEANS. COCOA ESSENTIALLY BEING A MISSPELLING OF CACAO. FOR A FULLER LIST OF CHOCOLATE TERMINOLOGY, SEE THE CHOCOLOSSARY IN THE APPENDIX.

"Yes, tell us!" urged the Pirate, clenching his gloved fist. "Have I found my recipe at last? Is this my chocolate?"

Simone opened her mouth to respond but —

Suddenly, she couldn't see. She couldn't hear. She couldn't even feel her arm.

All her senses were gone.

She tried to scream but she made no sound.

What was happening to her?

What awful thing had she just eaten?

PART ONE

ONE

APPETIZERS

Ka-chew!"

Max-Ernest sneezed so violently his spiky hair quivered for a full five seconds after he was done.

"Hey, did you notice — did I blink?"

He looked down at his friend Cassandra, who was crouched next to him, her pointy ears sticking out above her long braids.

"I read that every time you sneeze, you blink. So I always try to see if I can keep my eyes open."

"Sorry, wasn't looking . . . ," Cass muttered.

She had long ago learned to ignore half of what Max-Ernest said. A necessary survival skill if you were going to be best friends with the most talkative boy in town.

"Now what do soup mix and pest control have to do with each other . . . ?"

She was trying to read words scrawled on a cardboard box, but most had been crossed out:

~~PLUMBING EQUIPMENT~~

~~TEDDY BEARS AND TOY MICE~~

~~Catchers mitt and opera glasses~~

~~Dried flowers, flies for fly fishing, dried flies (real)~~

~~PARKING TICKETS~~

Canned tuna/ soup mix/ pest control

"Uh-oh, I think I have to — ka-chew!" Max-Ernest sneezed again. "It's the dust mites, I'm allergic —"

Cass pushed the box aside — it wasn't the one she was looking for — and stood up. Suddenly, she was a good half foot taller than her companion.

"Oh right, how could I forget a single one of your hundred allergies?"

"What do you mean? There's only sixty-three — that I know of," Max-Ernest corrected, not picking up on her sarcasm. "Let's see, there's wheat, walnuts, peanuts, pecans, strawberries, shellfish . . . oh, and chocolate, of course!"

"C'mon," said Cass, moving on to a box behind the one she'd just been looking at. "Are you going to help me find this thing or what?"

It was summertime and Cass was working afternoons at her grandfathers' antiques store:

THE FIRE SALE
EVERYTHING YOU ~~EVER~~ *NEVER* WANTED!

as it was identified on the front door.

As readers of certain unmentionable books will recall, the store was housed on the bottom floor of an old redbrick fire station. Cass's grandfathers, Larry and Wayne, lived upstairs, and every day they crammed their store with more and more stuff. Last year, Cass remembered, the store had already seemed like a maze, but at least there'd been enough space to walk between the shelves. Now you had to climb over piles of junk just to get from one part of the room to another.

Cass had told her mother that she was working at the Fire Sale to save money for a new bicycle, but that wasn't exactly true. It wasn't her *only* reason for working anyway.

In fact, she had an ulterior motive.

She was looking for a box. A special box she knew to be somewhere in her grandfathers' store. And considering there were at least a thousand boxes in the store, not to mention all the things that were *un*-boxed, she figured she would need all summer to find the one she was looking for.

Today, her grandfathers had taken their dog, Sebastian, to the vet, and Cass was taking advantage of
the time to redouble her search. Max-Ernest had gra-
ciously agreed to assist.

Or more precisely, had reluctantly agreed to keep
her company.

He was used to his survivalist friend's quixotic
quests, whether she was searching for toxic waste
under the school yard or killer mold under the cafe-
teria sink.* But this particular search, he felt, was
particularly hopeless.

"What makes you think the box is still here?" he
asked, not moving from his perch on top of a pile of
old encyclopedias.

"You know my grandfathers — they never throw
anything away." She closed up the next box and
moved on to another.

Max-Ernest looked around the store and shook
his head. "I think they have an obsessive-compulsive
disorder. It's clinical."

Cass bristled. She loved her grandfathers and
couldn't stand anyone criticizing them — except possibly herself. "Does everybody have to have a condition? Can't they just like stuff?"

---

* QUIXOTIC MEANS SOMETHING LIKE: IDEALISTIC OR ROMANTIC TO THE
POINT OF BEING COMPLETELY IMPRACTICAL. IT REFERS TO THE MAIN
CHARACTER IN CERVANTES'S NOVEL, DON QUIXOTE. A CHARACTER WHO
WAS ALWAYS TAKING OFF ON IMPOSSIBLE QUESTS. WHAT AN HONOR TO
BE SO FAMOUS THAT YOUR NAME BECOMES A WORD! COME TO THINK OF
IT, MY NAME, PSEUDONYMOUS, APPEARS IN MOST DICTIONARIES . . .

"So why can't you just ask them where it is?"

"Are you crazy? They'd tell my mom for sure."

"But we don't even know what it looks like. This whole thing doesn't make any sense —"

"I know it says, 'Handle With Care.' And there's a hole cut in the cardboard."

"Like if you were carrying a cat?"

"Max-Ernest!"

"OK, OK."

Max-Ernest wasn't very good at feelings, whether his own or anybody else's. But he noticed that Cass's ears — always a reliable emotional thermometer — were turning bright red.

The box was obviously a sensitive subject.

Indeed, it had been less than six months since Cass had discovered her mother's secret:

That her mother had not given birth to her.

That she was adopted.

That she was a "foundling," as her grandfathers put it.

That Cassandra wasn't even her real name.*

The story went like this:

---

*OF COURSE, IF YOU'VE READ MY OTHER BOOKS, YOU ALREADY KNOW THAT CASSANDRA WASN'T HER REAL NAME. ALL THE NAMES OF MY CHARACTERS ARE MADE UP; THEY'RE CODE NAMES INTENDED TO PRO-TECT THE IDENTITIES OF THE PEOPLE INVOLVED. THE POINT HERE IS THAT THE NAME CASS *THOUGHT* WAS HER REAL NAME, THE NAME CASS WENT

SPECIAL DELIVERY

The Arrival of Baby Cassandra

A not-so-long-ish time ago in a place not-so-far-ish away, there lived two not-so-very-old-ish men.

These two men loved collecting things so much that their home filled to the brim with odds and ends and this and that and a lot of bric-a-brac, too.

Knowing the men's acquisitive habits, the neighboring townsfolk were always leaving boxes on their doorstep. Their home was the home of last resort.

Usually, the boxes contained broken musical instruments or mismatched china or outgrown clothing.

Objects. Things. Stuff.

One fateful day, however, the men opened a box on their doorstep and discovered something altogether different. Instead of baby clothing, they found a baby.

An actual. Living. Breathing. Baby.

The men didn't know what to do. Of course, of all things in the world, a baby is the one thing

---

BY IN HER DAILY LIFE, THE NAME HER FRIENDS CALLED HER AND THAT SHE CALLED HERSELF — A NAME I WILL NEVER *EVER* DIVULGE — THAT NAME WAS NOT CASS'S REAL NAME EITHER.

most people would want to keep. But as tender-hearted as these men were, they knew that their home was a difficult and dangerous place to raise a child. There were far too many things to pull and poke and break and burn and rip and ruin.

Luckily, a friend was visiting at the time. This friend, a very smart and successful but also very lonely woman, had just been telling them how very, very much she wanted a baby of her own. They decided that the baby was meant to be hers.

The friend was Mel, short for Melanie, the woman who would become Cass's mother. That same day, the two men, a certain Larry and a certain Wayne, declared themselves Cass's grandfathers.

And they all lived happily ever after.

Almost.

When Cass first learned the truth about her origins, she'd been inclined to forgive her mother for not telling her sooner. She knew her mother hadn't wanted even the littlest thing to come between them. And the fact that Cass was adopted was a pretty big thing.

But as the weeks wore on, instead of softening, Cass's feelings had grown increasingly hard. For most of her life, as the child of a single mom, Cass had wondered who her father was. Now she had to wonder who her mother was as well?

The worst part was that her mother didn't seem to have any sympathy for Cass wanting to know who her parents were. Her *birth parents*, Cass agreed to call them. Oh, her mother *said* she had sympathy. She *said* she understood. But she wouldn't *do* anything about it.

With a normal adoption, you could march over to the adoption agency and demand to know the names of your birth parents. ("Sure, *when* you turn eighteen," her mother repeatedly reminded her. "Until then, the records are sealed.") Because Cass had been dropped on a doorstep, there was no agency to consult.

To Cass the answer was simple: hire a detective. But her mother refused. Even when Cass said she'd give up her allowance for a year.

So, not for the first time, Cass decided to play detective herself.

"*Please* help me," said Cass. "You have no idea what it's like not to know who your parents are. *Your* parents fight over you every second of your life."

"I said OK, didn't I?"

Max-Ernest made a big show of examining a shoebox on the shelf in front of him. "You think a baby could fit in this —?"

"No."

"What if it was a midget baby —"

"You know what — why don't you just leave?"

Before Max-Ernest could respond:

Thunk!

It was the sound of something very heavy dropping on the ground. Followed by a loud insistent pounding on the front door.

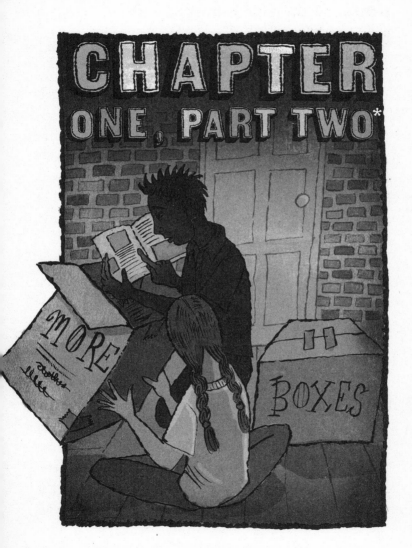

*I COULDN'T DECIDE WHETHER THE EVENTS THAT TRANSPIRED IN
CASS'S GRANDFATHERS' STORE SHOULD BE PRESENTED AS ONE
CHAPTER OR TWO. SO I MADE IT ONE CHAPTER IN TWO PARTS.
THAT'S WHAT'S KNOWN AS *SPLITTING THE DIFFERENCE*.

*T*hunk!

Again. And more pounding.

"Who *is* that?" Max-Ernest whispered, pale. "I thought the store was closed."

Cass shrugged, trying her best to look unconcerned. But she abandoned the box she'd been inspecting and stood up all the same. "Probably somebody unloading their old junk on my grandfathers, like usual."

Thunk!

Louder this time. They both flinched.

"Yeah, but what if it isn't?" said Max-Ernest, staring at the front door. "There's no time to get a message to the Terces Society."

Cass's ears tingled in alarm at the mention of their secret organization. "Shh! You never know who's listening."

"That's my point," Max-Ernest whispered. "The Midnight Sun could be right outside the door, for all we know. How 'bout that?"

Cass looked at him, her ears now turning cold.

Max-Ernest was right. The terrible truth was: they had done such a good job of driving away their enemies they no longer knew where their enemies were.

It had been months since they'd last seen the Midnight Sun's malevolent leaders, Ms. Mauvais

and Dr. L, flying away from a mountaintop graveyard
in a black helicopter, and despite the Terces Society's
best efforts, they'd been unable to determine where
that helicopter had gone.

Those insidious, invidious, and perfectly perfidious alchemists could be anywhere.

"Maybe they've been waiting all this time for
your grandfathers to leave," Max-Ernest continued.
"And now they're going to seize their chance to take
revenge on us."

Cass didn't say anything; she didn't have to.

They waited another minute or so — it felt much
longer — but there were no more *thunks*. Just the
usual *ticks* and *tocks* and *whirs* and *beeps* of the
many old clocks and assorted gizmos that cluttered
the store.

Then they started tiptoeing toward the front
door.

Bang! Crash!

They froze. This time the sounds came from
inside.

Had somebody broken in?

Grabbing each other's hands, they started turning around in slow circles (although whether they
were looking for the sources of the sounds or for
someplace to hide I'm not certain).

Finally, Max-Ernest pointed to the floor —

At his feet were the broken pieces of a ceramic rooster he'd knocked over. That was what had made all the noise. Well, those last noises. The bang and the crash. The thunking and pounding remained to be explained.

They waited another minute. Nothing.

Cass cracked the front door open —

And they breathed matching sighs of relief.

Cass's first guess had been correct: there were three cardboard boxes waiting for them on the landing.

They wouldn't have to battle the Midnight Sun, after all. Not right now anyway.

"Let's see," Cass said, expertly shaking the boxes one by one. "Shoes — hope they don't stink too bad . . . shirts — all stained probably . . . magazines . . ."

After struggling to find places in which to squeeze the new merchandise, Cass resumed searching for the cardboard box that had been her very first home.

Max-Ernest, meanwhile, sat back down on his encyclopedia pile and started flipping through the box of magazines. There were many kinds, some recent, some going back years. Sadly for Max-Ernest, there were no puzzle books or magic manuals or science magazines (the three things he was looking for in order of preference).

He was about to close up the box when he noticed a magazine that had been buried near the bottom.

"Hey, look at this — it's from last week."

"*We?* Since when do you care about *We?*" Cass laughed. "That's like all celebrity gossip and stuff. Have you even heard of the names in it?"

"I've heard of the Skelton Sisters —"

He walked over to Cass and thrust the magazine under her nose.

The cover of *We* showed two skinny blond girls — the twin teen superstars known as the Skelton Sisters — who just happened to be two of the youngest members of the Midnight Sun. (Most members were much older, as in hundreds of years older.) They were smiling dumbly at the camera, one of them holding an unhappy-looking baby — as far away from her body as possible.

Cass smirked. "She looks like the baby just peed on her or something."

She opened the magazine to an article headlined:

Twin ❤ Hearts IN AFRICA:
THE SKELTON SISTERS' LATEST ROCK TOUR IS A GOODWILL MISSION.

A two-page picture showed the twins standing with a nun in a white habit. Surrounding them were a dozen grinning children.

And in the background: a bright green bird with a long tail flying into the jungle.

Cass read the caption aloud:

Romi and Montana Skelton with Sister Antoinette at the Loving Heart Orphanage in the Cote d'Ivoire. The self-supporting orphanage runs a cacao plantation on which all the children lend a hand. "It's a wonderful learning experience, like an open-air classroom," says Sister Antoinette. "And of course at the end of the day there's always plenty of chocolate for everyone!"

Cass looked up from the magazine, shaking her head. "Can you believe they were at an orphanage? Probably they just went to have their photo taken . . . Hey, wait a second — we know this nun!"

"I doubt it," said Max-Ernest. "I don't know any nuns. I mean, unless I know a nun but I don't know I do —"

"Well, you know this one."

Max-Ernest stared. "Oh no, is that who I think it is?"

Cass nodded, excited. "Can you imagine anybody less likely to be a nun than Ms. Mauvais?"

"So we found the Midnight Sun? How 'bout that?"

Cass grinned. "How 'bout that? We have to tell everybody right away!"

"Tell us what? We're dying to know!"

They looked up from the magazine, startled.

Grandpa Wayne and Grandpa Larry had entered through the back, and were now standing over them, smiling.

It wasn't a very comforting sight.

Larry and Wayne had been competing with each other in a beard-growing contest for the last six months, and they were both looking slightly bedraggled, to put it mildly. (Larry brushed his beard religiously and Wayne braided his in two long strands — but neither approach really helped.)

Sebastian, their old, ailing, and blind basset hound, was sleeping in a baby sling around Grandpa Larry's neck. Dog drool dribbled down Larry's arm.

"So what's the big news?" asked Grandpa Larry.

"Oh, nothing," Cass stammered. "You know, gossip. It's a gossip magazine."

Grandpa Wayne eyed the magazine open on

Cass's lap. "Is that those girls — what are they called, the Skeleton Sisters?"

"Skelton, not *skeleton*. But ghoulish nonetheless," Larry sniffed. "Why a granddaughter of mine would be interested in girls like them, I'm sure I don't know."

Cass's first instinct was to defend herself, but instead she offered a rueful smile. "It's just so I know what the other kids are talking about. So I don't seem like a freak. Sorry, I know it's lame. . . ."

She would have to live with her grandfathers' disapproval. Today she and Max-Ernest had made a major discovery. Maybe it wasn't the discovery she'd been hoping for, but in a way it was much more important.

"How's Sebastian?" she asked, changing the subject.

"Oh, he'll be fine — won't you, Sebastian?" Larry patted the dog's head.

The dog barked halfheartedly, drooling onto Max-Ernest, who hastily wiped it away.

"Dander — it's in the saliva. I'm really allergic," he explained to no one in particular.

Late that night, five people — a retired magician, a certified public accountant, an out-of-work actor, and a violin teacher and her student — all received

the same e-mail message from somebody named
Miss Ardnassac:

LOOKING FOR SUN?
CHEAP VACATION!
ONE DAY ONLY!

Anybody reading over their shoulders would have assumed it was spam. Junk mail. The recipients knew it was anything but.

The message meant Cassandra had information about the Midnight Sun.

"Vacation" was the Terces Society's code word for meeting.

"Cheap" signaled that the meeting was urgent.

"One day only" meant the meeting would be the veryyyyyyyyyyyyyyyyyyyyyyyyyyyyyyyyyyyyyyyyyyyyyyyy
yyyyyyyyyyyyyyyyyyyyyyyyyyyyyyyyyyyyyyyyyyyyyyyyyyy
yyyyyyyyyyyyyyyyyyyyyyyyyyyyyyyyyyyyyyyyyyyyyyyyyyy
yyyyyyyyyyyyyyyyyyyy y y yy y y   y

CHAPTER TWO

Deceptively Sweet

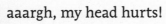aaargh, my head hurts!

What happened? Is it night already?

I must have dozed off in the middle of that last sentence.

Don't worry, there wasn't much left. Just "the very next day."

I wonder what could have made me pass out like that. Too much chocolate? I have to admit: it wouldn't be the first time.

Hmmm. I could have sworn I left those pages in a pile. What are they doing on the floor?

Has somebody else been here?

Hey, you don't suppose . . . ?

I wonder . . .

If a certain person or persons wanted to come in and read the pages on my desk while I was working, how would they do it? How would they get me out of the way? Might they slip me a sleeping pill — say, in a gift box full of chocolate?

What was that you said earlier? That the chocolate I received must be some kind of trick? Funny how positive you were about that. Almost like you knew something you weren't telling me.

Not that I'm accusing you.

Or am I?

You know, people always warn children about taking candy from strange adults. But they never warn us adults about taking candy from strange children.

All those sweet-looking kids who sell boxes of candy bars on the street to help pay for their schooling — how do we know what's in those bars? And don't get me started on that nefarious institution designed to lure unsuspecting customers into buying mysterious frosted goodies: the bake sale.

Adults, be warned: if a child wanted to poison you it would be a piece of cake! *Literally* a piece of cake.

As for you, you're showing yourself to be the worst kind of reader, aren't you? The kind that skips ahead to the end to find out what happens without reading the whole book. The kind that stops at nothing to get what he wants.

The kind that stoops even to *drugging the writer*!

I should have you arrested.

OK. Maybe I should calm down. I'm getting ahead of myself. After all, I have no proof that you are the culprit. Not yet.

And I should consider you innocent until proven guilty, right?

In the meantime, consider yourself warned: I
will get to the bottom of this. Whoever was in here
rifling through my papers, I'm going to sniff him or
her out if it's the last thing I do.

Until then, back to the book.

CHAPTER THREE

CLOWN CAMP

on't worry, Missus, we take great care of our campers here. Tightrope walking it is today, right Mickey?"

"Morrie, don't joke — you know that's too dangerous for the kiddies! Today, we're practicing . . . uh, squeezing into a Volkswagen. Or is it balloon-tying? Yeah, that's it . . . Balloons 101 — always the first course for us zanies."*

Clutching tight to her steering wheel, Cass's mother looked dubiously at the two clowns grinning down at her from outside her car window.

As with any self-respecting comic duo, one clown, Mickey, was tall and skinny, and the other, Morrie, was short and squat. But they were equally unkempt-looking; it was difficult to tell whether the color on their faces was clown makeup or leftover hot dog.

Mickey had Cass under his arm, Morrie had Max-Ernest under *his*. Not a very reassuring sight for a mother.

"OK, Mel — are you satisfied?" asked Cass. (Lately, Cass had taken to calling her mother by her first name, rather than calling her "Mom" or what her mother would have preferred, "Mommy.")

---

*ZANIES, IF YOU HAVEN'T GUESSED, ARE CLOWNS. FOR MORE CIRCUS LINGO, LOOK IN THE BACK OF MY FIRST BOOK. YOU KNOW, THAT BOOK WITH THE CONFUSING NAME.

Her mother sighed. "All right . . . but don't forget to meet me here right at two o'clock. We have that class this afternoon, remember?"

As soon as Cass's mother drove away, Cass and Max-Ernest disentangled themselves from the clowns.

Mickey shook his red wig in amazement. "*Clown Camp?* Who'd a thunk? I wonder if there's any money in it . . ."

"Hey, you guys better get going. Don't want to be late for balloon-tying," said Morrie with a wink.

"Um, do you know where?" asked Cass, slightly abashed.

It was the first time the Terces Society had met since Pietro had decided they should leave their longtime home, the Magic Museum (having the Midnight Sun break in once was enough!), and she and Max-Ernest weren't certain exactly where to go.

Mickey gestured to the far end of the dirt parking lot where a big striped circus tent flapped in the wind. A few smaller, more dilapidated tents stood next to it. They looked as if they might collapse at any moment.

"Farthest one from the Big Top. The Sideshow tent."

"Thanks," said Cass. She lowered her voice: "Keep your eyes open, OK? For anybody wearing gloves . . ."

"Don't worry," said Morrie. "No rotten old alchemist is going to get past this clown!"

Smiling mischievously, Morrie pulled a gun out of his baggy plaid pants and pointed it at an imaginary assailant.

A red flag popped out of the barrel: **BANG!**

Inside the sideshow tent, a row of old folding chairs sat on the dirt in front of a small stage that slanted steeply down on one side and was missing boards on the other.

For most of that morning, a tall boy with floppy hair had been standing on top of the stage taking a violin lesson. A long and hard violin lesson. He had been playing so long and hard his fingers were starting to bleed.

It felt like that anyway. At the very least, his fingers were red.

Raw. Definitely raw.

The worst part was he'd only been allowed to play scales. For three months. Even though he was an advanced student.

Yo-Yoji couldn't help feeling that he was being punished. His teacher, Lily — or Master Wei, as she insisted he call her — was angry that he'd quit playing violin the year before in favor of electric guitar, and now she was making him make up for lost time.

"You can run away from your talent, but you can't run away from me!" she said.

Master Wei was the toughest woman he'd ever met. Also, possibly, the most beautiful. But that was beside the point. You'd probably be killed if you ever mentioned it.

Apart from being a violin teacher, she was also the Terces Society's head of physical defense and a martial arts expert. It was partly for this reason that Yo-Yoji kept practicing the violin.

Yo-Yoji's main interests consisted of rock music and video games and collecting rare, brightly colored sneakers. But ever since spending a year in Japan he'd become more and more fascinated with Japanese history, especially the history of the samurai. He had memorized the samurai's Bushido ("way of the warrior") code, and he spent much of his free time watching old samurai movies on DVD.*

Master Wei was Chinese and specialized in judo and kung fu. But she was also well versed in most Japanese martial arts, including kenjutsu, the tradi-

*YO-YOJI RECOMMENDS THE FILMS OF AKIRA KUROSAWA, ESPECIALLY *THE SEVEN SAMURAI* AND *YOJIMBO*.

tional form of Japanese sword fighting practiced by the samurai. He hoped one day she would make him her kenjutsu apprentice.

It looked like he would be waiting a long time.

"Violin or kenjutsu, the philosophy is the same," she would say, whenever he asked about it. "As my father always said —"

"I know, *practice makes permanent*," Yo-Yoji would finish her sentence.

"You think you are too advanced for scales? There is no such thing!" she would respond. "As my father always said —"

"I know, *to go forward, you must first go back.*"

Today, though, was different. They'd be quitting their lesson early — after three hours, rather than the usual four. So they could attend the meeting.

The message from Cass had filled Yo-Yoji with excitement. At last, they had found the Midnight Sun! The Terces Society was back in business. And maybe, just maybe, Master Wei would let him stop practicing the violin and would teach him the skills he needed to face the Midnight Sun in combat.

But he was worried about seeing Cass again. They hadn't spoken all summer. Before that, they'd barely been on speaking terms. Ever since Cass learned that

44 Yo-Yoji had been hiding his membership in the Terces Society from her and Max-Ernest.

When was she going to forgive him?

Knowing he was going to see Cass, Yo-Yoji had put on his lucky sneakers that morning. The neon yellow vintage ones he bought in Japan.* They were a little too big for him then and a little too small now, but they were the coolest shoes he owned. Very rare and collectible. Usually, he only wore them when he was playing with his rock band, Alien Earache. Or when he was taking a test.

Not that Cass would notice his shoes anyway. She was always concerned with more serious things. Like tornadoes and floods and toxic sludge.

When Cass and Max-Ernest walked in carrying armloads of books, Yo-Yoji decided to play it as though nothing were wrong.

"Yo, dudes! What's up?"

He waved his violin bow in their direction.

Cass and Max-Ernest both took involuntary steps backward.

Yo-Yoji laughed. "Relax. There's no sword in this bow. It's just a normal violin. Like Master Wei would even let me use hers."

*SORRY, I DON'T REMEMBER THE BRAND. YOU'D PROBABLY KNOW IMMEDIATELY IF YOU SAW THEM. BUT AT MY AGE WE DON'T ALWAYS PAY THAT MUCH ATTENTION TO THE NAMES WRITTEN ON SNEAKERS.

"That's right. And you're not done practicing — you have three minutes to go," said Lily, crossing from the other side of the room to greet the newcomers.

"As for you two —"

She pulled a long, needlelike sword out of her violin bow and pointed it at Cass and Max-Ernest, who both tried (unsuccessfully) not to jump.

"You two are next — we have to work on your reflexes. Jumping in fright is not a good defensive posture." She smiled to show she was playing with them.

"Hi, Lily." Cass smiled back while sneaking a peek at the reluctant violin student.

The first thing Cass noticed: he was wearing his yellow shoes — her favorite ones, although she would never think of mentioning it to him.

"Where's everybody else?" she asked, turning away from Yo-Yoji before he could see where she was looking.

"Oh, they'll be here in a minute. Pietro's back in the archives with Mr. Wallace." Lily nodded toward an opening in the tent.

Through the opening, Cass and Max-Ernest could just make out the refrigerated trailer where the Terces Society Archives were now hidden. It was marked **CAT FOOD** in faded letters and had held the huge sides of meat that fed the "big cats" back when the circus was home to a team of hula hoop–jumping lions.

A man in an airplane pilot's uniform stepped out of the trailer and headed into the tent.

"Who's that?" whispered Cass, concerned. Strangers were unwelcome at Terces Society meetings, to say the least.

"Oh, a visitor," said Lily lightly. "He's Swiss, I think."

"*Guten Tag, Fraulein Cass,*" said the mysterious pilot.

"Um, *guten Tag . . .*"

"That means 'good day' in German," said Max-Ernest helpfully.

"You don't speak German," said Cass.

"Yeah, but I memorized how to say hello in a hundred languages."*

"Very wise, indeed," said the stranger, removing his hat.

Now Cass recognized him: "Owen?" Formerly a struggling actor/waiter, Owen was a master of disguise and frequently used his talents in the service of the Terces Society.

*TURN TO THE APPENDIX FOR MAX-ERNEST'S LIST OF A HUNDRED *HELLOS.*

"I didn't know you were a pilot," said Max-
Ernest, impressed.

Owen laughed. "I'm not really. But I *am* about to fly to Switzerland."

"So, did you learn to say hello in Italian?" Pietro, the old Italian magician, had entered the tent. He smiled at Cass and Max-Ernest. "How about a *buon giorno* for your old friend? Or do you prefer *ciao*?"

"*Buon giorno!*" Cass and Max-Ernest repeated, thrilled to see their pink-cheeked, gray-mustached, and almost always cheerful-looking leader.

He was followed closely by the tall, gaunt, and almost always pained-looking Mr. Wallace. The young Terces members waved halfheartedly at Mr. Wallace. He responded with a dry, raspy cough.

Pietro frowned, touching his wildly bushy mustache. "I think there is maybe a mustache hair out of place. It is annoying me and tickling my nose. Max-Ernest, can you please pull?"

Max-Ernest stared in surprise. "You want me to pull your mustache hair?"

"Yes, if you please." Pietro thrust out his nose, offering his mustache.

"Uh, OK," said Max-Ernest uneasily. Embarrassed, he reached forward and plucked an unruly hair. Pietro reeled backward.

"Ow! Not that one, this one!" He pointed to another hair, curling jauntily upward around his nostril. "And be careful!"

"Oh. Sorry." Max-Ernest carefully tugged on the offending tendril and pulled out a small gray —

mouse.

It dangled by its tail, clawing at the air.

"Eeek!" Max-Ernest dropped the mouse and it scurried across the dirt floor.

Pietro grinned. "It is my new trick. I call it the *Mouse-Stache.* You like?"

Max-Ernest guffawed loudly. "I think it's *great!*"

Nobody else said anything.

Cass and Yo-Yoji glanced at each other. Yo-Yoji raised his eyebrows slightly as if to say, *Can you believe them?*

Cass rolled her eyes as if to say, *I know, they're always like this.* And then she smiled. Maybe it was time to forgive him, she thought.

Maybe.

CHAPTER FOUR

BLOOD CHOCOLATE

Ten minutes later, Cass and Max-Ernest stood on the sideshow stage in front of a blackboard, drawing diagrams and writing down key points — just as if they were giving an oral report in school. (Not that they'd ever worked this hard on an actual oral report.)

They were so excited they kept tripping over each other's words:

Cass	*Max-Ernest*
"We found out where the Midnight Sun are hiding!"	
	"They're in the Cote d'Ivoire. That's *Ivory Coast* in French. That's what they speak there —"
"They're on a chocolate plantation. And —"	
	"The Cote d'Ivoire is in West Africa and that's where most of the cocoa beans in the world come from, although they're really *cacao seeds* —"
"They have an orphanage!"	

"Do you know how much chocolate is made with child labor?"

"But we think it's actually cover for a child labor camp —"

"Almost half the chocolate you buy! How 'bout that?"

"Some people call it *blood chocolate* —"

"Which is like *blood diamonds* — diamonds mined by slaves —"

"And after this is all over I'm going to organize a chocolate boycott —"

Now wait just a moment — a *chocolate boycott?*

The very idea makes me shudder.

With your permission, I will skip their lecture about the so-called evils of the chocolate trade and move on to the next part of their presentation.*

I'm afraid I'm going to have to cut-in in the middle of a sentence, but I'm confident you'll catch the drift:

---

*IF YOU'RE THE TYPE WHO CARES ABOUT THESE SORTS OF THINGS — AND BY *THINGS* I MEAN CHILDREN — YOU CAN FOLLOW CASS'S LEAD AND RE-SEARCH THE SUBJECT YOURSELF. TO BE ABSOLUTELY CERTAIN THE CHOC-OLATE YOU EAT IS NOT THE FRUIT OF CHILD LABOR, LOOK FOR A *FAIR TRADE* LABEL.

". . . and here it is," concluded Cass. She stepped off the stage and handed the magazine to Pietro.

"I agree — this picture, it is not right. Thank you for sharing it with us," said the old magician, studying the photo in *We*. "The reason Owen is going to Switzerland — it is because the Midnight Sun, through their business, Midnight Chocolate Incorporated, they are buying the chocolate companies all over the world. And now, we see, the chocolate plantations, too . . ."

"So what are we going to do?" Yo-Yoji asked, standing.

"Should we go to Africa to investigate?" asked Cass.

"Absolutely."

Cass lit up. "That's great! When do we go?"

Pietro chuckled. He leaned back in his folding chair. "I was thinking of Owen. He will be halfway there already."

Cass couldn't hide her disappointment. "But what about us?"

"And how would you explain to your mother?" asked Pietro.

"Then what can we do? There has to be something!"

Pietro smiled at the eager young Terces member. "With the Midnight Sun, there is never the accident. Why the interest in the chocolate? We have been wondering and wondering. Is there perhaps a history of using the chocolate in the alchemy?"

"Does it have something to do with the Secret?" asked Max-Ernest.

The tent went quiet for a moment.

Although the entire purpose of the Terces Society was to preserve and protect the Secret, the Secret was seldom mentioned aloud.

"Everything they do, it has to do with the Secret," Pietro said finally. "Nothing matters to the Midnight Sun except the immortality they think the Secret will give them. That's why this chocolate business is so confusing."

He stood, kicking his folding chair aside.

"What does the Midnight Sun want with the chocolate!? They never eat. They are like vampires. Is it for the money? But they have treasures going back centuries!"

He gesticulated with his hands, expressing the depth of his frustration. "I do not understand what they are after — that Ms. Mauvais and my Lucian . . . I mean, *Dr. L.*" He spit out the name as if it were dirty.

If Pietro was especially emotional on the subject of Dr. L, everyone in the tent knew why: Dr. L was Pietro's twin brother, Luciano. He had been kidnapped by Ms. Mauvais as a young boy and raised to be her partner. The hatred between Dr. L and Pietro was now as strong as their love once was.

Ending his long silence, Mr. Wallace held up a file stuffed with documents. Although he was an accountant by day, Mr. Wallace's true profession was that of Terces Society archivist. "Whatever the Midnight Sun is doing with all this chocolate, we think the Tuning Fork is involved somehow."

"Tuning fork? You mean like in music? To tune your instrument?" asked Yo-Yoji. "I have one at home."

Mr. Wallace gave him a withering look. "Not that kind of tuning fork, something much older. It is a cooking utensil, but according to the legends of the alchemists, much more."

He pulled a rumpled piece of paper out of the file and passed it around. It was an old drawing of a two-pronged instrument that looked something like a musical tuning fork (if you know what a musical tuning fork looks like), but it was longer and more rough-hewn.

"With the Tuning Fork in his hand, a Chef has the power to stir into being any taste in the world — as long as the eater has tasted it before," said Mr. Wallace as the others examined the drawing. "The food of the fork acts on a person's memory in a way that haunts him. And he wants it again and again."

"So what does it have to do with chocolate, Mr. Wallace?" Cass asked nervously. Mr. Wallace wasn't the easiest person to speak to.

"I was getting to that, if you would only wait a moment. As the story goes, the Tuning Fork was forged by an Aztec sorcerer and was first used to stir chocolate for the Aztec emperor. You know of course that chocolate came from the New World and was originally served only as a drink."

"Yeah, we knew that," said Max-Ernest, as if they'd known it for years and hadn't just read it on the Internet the night before.

"The Tuning Fork, I thought it was only the myth," said Pietro. "But who knows — Mr. Wallace, he may be right this time. Unlike the usual." He laughed at his own joke. "Cass, Max-Ernest, Yo-Yoji — I want you to learn what you can about this Tuning Fork. Is it real? Where is it? Let us hope we can find it before the Midnight Sun do."

"Well, where do you think it might be?" asked Max-Ernest. "Are there any clues?"

"Not many," said Mr. Wallace. "Supposedly, the fork traveled to Europe with a monk in the late fifteen hundreds —"

Rrrrring.

A loud and ill-timed telephone ring stopped Mr. Wallace in the middle of his sentence.

Her ears burning with embarrassment, Cass pulled her phone out of her pocket.

"You brought a cell phone into a Terces Society meeting?" Mr. Wallace stared in a way that would give the strictest grade school teacher a run for her money. "Never mind how rude that is — think of the danger. It could be bugged."

"Oh, do not be so hard on the girl," said Pietro. "Nobody has bugged her phone."

"It's my mom," said Cass sheepishly. "I'm supposed to meet her outside right now. She thinks this is . . . clown camp."

"Go on then," said Pietro. "Answer."

Miserable, Cass clicked on her phone. "Hello, Mel . . . No, no, don't get out of your car! It's all over. There's nothing to see . . . No, we aren't tightrope walking, I swear . . ."

Having a mother, even an adopted one, was terribly inconvenient when you were a member of a secret society. Perhaps, Cass thought, she didn't want more parents, after all.

CHAPTER FIVE

The CUISINE of the

SENSES

A real chef needs only one knife. It is his sword. It is his best friend. It is everything to him."

A man of the type often called dark and swarthy stood behind a stove holding a large knife in his gloved hand.

He wore a black chef's coat and, covering his bald scalp, a black scarf decorated with skulls and cross-bones. Adding to the pirate look: a hoop of gold in his left ear and a goatee ringing his mouth.

He also wore a pair of extremely dark sunglasses.

The glasses of a blind man.

He raised the knife higher so it gleamed in the light. "A real chef would as soon give up his knife as cut off his arm."

Then he sliced his knife through the air if he were about to cut off his arm in demonstration.

It was, in fact, a demonstration kitchen — a class-room clad in stainless steel — and facing him, on the other side of the stove, sat an audience of twelve.

His students gasped. Then let out a collective sigh of relief when the knife landed point-down in a cut-ting board.

"Other knives, like these here — bread knife, paring knife, boning knife —" He pulled the knives off a magnetic rack one by one, as easily as if he could see them. "They're for amateurs."

He smiled slyly, the stove's blue-flamed burners reflecting in his sunglasses. "Or for carnival tricks."

Without warning, he tossed the three knives into the air and juggled for a good thirty seconds. The knives spun so fast they were a blur.

Until he let them drop in quick succession, chopping an array of vegetables so they splayed on the counter in perfect rainbow formation.

An astonishing show, even if he hadn't been blind.

"Always keep your knives sharp. Contrary to popular belief, they're much more dangerous when they're dull."

The class burst into applause. Slightly muted applause because, like the chef, they all wore rubber surgical gloves. (He insisted that everyone keep their hands covered in the kitchen.)

But there was one person whose applause was mute for the simple reason that she was not clapping.

Yes, it was Cass. The pointy-eared and very grim-faced girl in the front row.

Her mother had received the brochure for the cooking class not long after Cass first confronted her about the adoption. It boasted a picture of the chef in his sunglasses, posing like a movie star.

"Look, Cass — what a great way for us to spend some time together!"

"Why would we want to do that? We already live together," Cass had pointed out.

"Cass . . . !"

"Well, why a cooking class?"

"How about so we can start having some home-cooked meals?"

"What's the matter with Thai takeout? That's what we used to always have."

"Exactly! I want to fill the house with the smells of cooking. The smells of childhood. The smells you will remember your entire life," her mother had answered.

But as far as Cass was concerned, her entire childhood had turned out to be a lie. She didn't care how it smelled.

And now here she was having to sit in class with her mother when she should have been hunting for the Tuning Fork with Max-Ernest and Yo-Yoji.

"I can't believe you like him. He's such a showoff," Cass whispered a few minutes later, when they were taking turns chopping zucchini.

"How could he be a showoff? — he's blind. Anyway, he has a right to be. Señor Hugo is one of the greatest chefs in the world. He invented the Cuisine

of the Senses," said her mother reverently. "And so
handsome, too," she added.

As if on cue, Señor Hugo stepped up behind them. "Oh, I wouldn't say invented. Maybe developed . . ."

He spoke with the lisping Spanish accent known as Catalan — the accent of his native city, Barcelona, or as the Catalans pronounce it, *Barthelona*.

"I'm sorry — may I . . . ? I can tell by the noise you make that you're not using the proper motion." The blind chef put his hand over Cass's mother's, gently correcting her chopping technique.

She blushed. Cass rolled her eyes. Her mother's crush was so obvious!

"All the senses are important to a chef — but luckily for me, sight is the least important," continued Señor Hugo.

Finally, he let go of Cass's mother's hand. (A little too late, in Cass's opinion.)

"I always wait to taste the food I cook," he said to the room at large. "Take a curry. First I dip my finger in and feel the texture. Is it too powdery? too foamy? I listen to the sounds. That hiss means it's not hot enough. That sizzle? Too hot. And at every stage I smell smell smell. Did you know that what we think of as taste is mostly scent? By itself the tongue only detects five flavors: sweet, sour, salt, bitter, and one other — have any of you heard of *umami?*"

"Yeah, it's the taste of fat," said Cass knowingly.

Señor Hugo nodded. "Yes, some people say that, although I prefer to call it savoriness or deliciousness."

He turned to the room. "Only when a dish is finished do I dare taste it. And when I do, I feel as if at last I can see, as if I have gained a kind of second sight. . . . Even so, there are some things I can taste only in my head."

"You mean, there are things you can't cook?" asked Cass's mother in surprise. "A master chef like you."

"All artists strive to greater heights, do they not?" the chef responded. "Take chocolate, which is my passion . . ."

"Oh, it's my passion, too!" said Cass's mother.

Cass groaned inwardly.

"My life's ambition is to make the ultimate bar of chocolate. The best, the purest, the darkest chocolate of all time. As close to one hundred percent cacao as possible."

It figures he would make chocolate, thought Cass, imagining the pirate chef commanding a ship full of child slaves.

"I keep trying to find the right equipment —"

He gestured toward the wall behind the audience. Sitting on a long steel shelf were dozens of cooking devices: narrow siphons, bulbous whisks, tall Bunsen burners, double, triple, and even quadruple boilers. They looked like they belonged in a chemistry lab rather than in a kitchen.

"I can taste it in my mind. But I have not yet made my chocolate a reality."

"Too bad you don't have the Tuning Fork," said Cass as snottily as she could.

Señor Hugo whipped his head around. "The what . . . ?"

"The Tuning Fork. The mythical cooking instrument made by the Aztecs. Anybody who had it could make any taste he wanted. Since you're such a great chef I just thought you would know what it was."

"Go on. I'm very interested in culinary history," said the chef, his attention fixed on Cass. She could almost have sworn he was staring at her.

"That's it. That's all I know about it . . ." She faltered, suddenly realizing the implications of what she'd just said.

Of what she'd just done.

"So how did you hear about this . . . Tuning Fork?" Señor Hugo persisted.

"I don't know. Maybe at school . . . ?" Her voice squeaked unconvincingly.

"You must go to a very interesting school," said Señor Hugo.

According to Mr. Wallace, the Tuning Fork might not even exist. But that wasn't the point.

Never talk about the Terces Society. Or anything to do with the Terces Society. It was the Society's first rule. Almost its only rule.

"Since you're such an expert in cuisine you must come to my restaurant as my guest!"

"Did you hear that, Cass? What an honor!" gushed her mother.

Their classmates nodded and clapped in envy.

"Señor Hugo's restaurant is famous," said one of the aspiring chefs. "Everybody eats in the dark — so you have to guess what your food is."

"People wait months for a reservation," said another. "It's like getting the golden ticket!"

"But we can't," said Cass. "Remember, I'm supposed to work on that report with Max-Ernest and Yo-Yoji? The one about chocolate and child slavery? It's due the first day of school."

(The three kids had all told their parents the same thing; their first "homework" session was scheduled for Saturday.)

"Well, then, your friends should come, too. On Saturday, we will be featuring a multi-course chocolate tasting menu. It will be research. For your report . . . oh, and don't forget your Tuning Fork!" joked Señor Hugo.

"Ha ha," said Cass, not laughing.

She tried to cheer herself up. As much as she disliked Señor Hugo, what real harm could it do that he knew about the Tuning Fork?

After all, she reasoned, he was a chef, not an alchemist. There was no way he could know Dr. L or Ms. Mauvais. It wasn't as if he were a member of the Midnight Sun.

But it was no use; she felt terrible.

At least the blind chef wouldn't see the tears of guilt welling in her eyes.

CHAPTER SIX

THE OTHER GLOVE

I must pause now to do something I hate: apologize.

Cherish these words because I doubt you will hear them from me again: *I'm sorry.*

You're not the conniving coward who sent me those chocolates. You're not the scurrilous scoundrel who trespassed on my property, who rifled through my personal papers.

I know that now.

You see, after an exhaustive search of my office, I found a glove. A white glove. It was caught in the clasp of a chest I keep beside my desk. The true intruder must have left it there.

Naturally, it is alarming to discover that the Midnight Sun has found me. In an odd way, though, it's a relief. It was inevitable, once I started telling these stories, that they would try to locate me. Now it's done. The other shoe has dropped.

Or rather, the other glove.

What I don't understand is why they left my book intact. Why did they leave *me* intact for that matter?

Are they simply toying with me? Biding their time until they strike again?

What strange plot is afoot?

Speaking of strange plots, I'd better continue with mine. Time, it is now clear, is of the essence.

Let's see: where were we? I'm afraid my close brush with the Midnight Sun has addled my brain just a little.

Oh, yes. Hugo's restaurant. That's what comes next. But I just had an awful realization: you're out of sync with the story.

Unlike Cass, you already know who Señor Hugo is, don't you?

If you haven't guessed yet, I will give you a moment to figure it out. Here's a hint: think back to Chapter Fifteen, the chapter I let you read at the beginning of this book . . .

That's right! Señor Hugo is one of the three villains in the Tasting Room — those people keeping Simone, the supertaster, prisoner. Hugo is the blind man. The one Simone calls the Pirate.

And who are Simone's other two captors, the ones she calls the Doctor and the Barbie Doll?

Correct. They're none other than that dread duo, Dr. L and Ms. Mauvais.

My question is this: have I ruined the suspense by clueing you in that the chef is a villain?

Or, on the contrary, have I made the meal the kids are about to have at his restaurant scarier?

Think about it: Cass and her friends will be eating in the dark. They will be entirely in Señor Hugo's power. He could poison them — or worse.

Alfred Hitchcock, the famous film director and master of suspense, always maintained that knowing something terrible was about to happen was scarier than not knowing.

Well, you know that something terrible is going to happen. (And believe me, it is!) Was Hitchcock right? Are you frightened? *How* frightened?

Please circle the face that best represents how you feel right now.

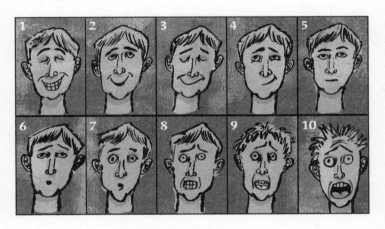

1. INSANELY UNSCARED — WOULD JUMP OUT OF AN AIRPLANE WITHOUT A PARACHUTE.

2. LAUGHING AT FEAR — WOULD JUMP OUT OF A PLANE *WITH* A PARACHUTE.

3. BRING IT ON — WOULD BUNGEE JUMP OFF A BRIDGE.

4. HAPPY AS A CLAM — WOULD BUNGEE JUMP IF PUSHED.

5. NORMAL — DON'T FEEL THE NEED TO TEST THE LAWS OF GRAVITY.

6. SLIGHTLY NERVOUS — THERE'S A CHILL IN THE BACK OF MY NECK.

7. SCARED — SHIVER DOWN MY SPINE, DOUBLE-CHECKING THE LOCKS.

8. VERY SCARED — TEETH CHATTERING, KNUCKLES WHITENING.

9. BEYOND TERRIFIED — FROZEN.

10. CATATONIC.

Thank you. That was very helpful.

CHAPTER SEVEN

A Stab in the Dark

EL CASTILLO DE LA NOCHE

From the outside, Hugo's restaurant, *El Castillo de La Noche*, looked as its name suggested it would. Like a *castillo*. A castle.

But a castle dipped in blue. Midnight blue.

The stone walls, the iron gates, even the turrets and the gargoyles — all were painted the same deep dark shade.

As Cass passed through the gates with her mother and Max-Ernest and Yo-Yoji, they all shivered involuntarily. The sun had not yet set but they seemed to be entering a kind of permanent twilight.

In front of them, a shadowy tunnel of oak trees led to the restaurant entrance.

"I hope there's at least one thing that doesn't have chocolate," said Max-Ernest. "I'm hungry."

"Too bad we haven't found the Tuning Fork yet," whispered Yo-Yoji. "Then you could turn your food into whatever you want."

"Yeah, but I wonder — even if I could change the taste, wouldn't I still be allergic? Or do you think —"

"Shh," whispered Cass, indicating her mother, who was only a few steps ahead of them.

The reminder about the Tuning Fork had made Cass slightly sick to her stomach. Although she'd planned on telling her friends about her little verbal slip, she hadn't yet found the right moment.

Or maybe it was that she hadn't yet found the courage.

The restaurant's tall front doors were shut and all the windows were shuttered. It looked as if the restaurant might be closed.

But as they stepped onto the portico the doors opened and Señor Hugo emerged from the dim interior.

"Cassandra," he said, smiling directly at her. "My guest of honor."

How, she wondered, did he know where she was? She hadn't uttered a word. Did he recognize her smell?

"Allow me to welcome the princess to her castle." He offered his arm.

Cass had no more a desire to take his arm than she had a desire to be called "princess," but her mother gave her a nudge, so Cass allowed the chef to escort her inside.

The entry room was dark and very plain, save for a candelabra sitting on a small table in the center. The flickering candles reflected on the glass surface.

Mismatched bouquets of color-clashing flowers were spread around the room apparently at random. But as she examined them more closely, Cass realized that the flowers were in fact very carefully arranged:

"They're scent bouquets," she said to Max-Ernest. "See, this one's all lemon smells —"

He nodded. "It's stronger when you brush against it —"

A discreet sign listed the rules of the restaurant. Written in Braille as well as printed, it was hung low enough on the wall for a person to touch:

Welcome to El Castillo de la Noche, The Castle of Darkness

The following items are forbidden:

Lighters and matches

Illuminated watches

Cell phones

⠠⠉⠑⠇⠇ ⠏⠓⠕⠝⠑⠎

Pocket knives

⠠⠏⠕⠉⠅⠑⠞ ⠅⠝⠊⠧⠑⠎

Pens and pencils

⠠⠏⠑⠝⠎ ⠁⠝⠙ ⠏⠑⠝⠉⠊⠇⠎

Please leave all bags at the reception desk

⠠⠏⠇⠑⠁⠎⠑ ⠇⠑⠁⠧⠑ ⠁⠇⠇ ⠃⠁⠛⠎
⠁⠞ ⠞⠓⠑ ⠗⠑⠉⠑⠏⠞⠊⠕⠝ ⠙⠑⠎⠅

"Does a backpack count?" Cass asked their host.

Her backpack contained nearly every forbidden item. But she didn't feel secure leaving it. Especially at Hugo's restaurant.

"Normally, yes. But for you we will make an exception."

Why was he being so nice to her? Cass wondered. Was it possible he wasn't as bad as she thought?

"You are about to enter a world of darkness," said the chef to the group at large. "But it is our hope that you will not feel so much the loss of sight. Instead, you will feel as if your other senses are heightened."

Behind Señor Hugo, a pair of dark blue curtains opened and a pale man in a gray smock silently entered the room.

Señor Hugo acknowledged the newcomer without turning around. "Howard will be your waiter and your guide. Like all of us here, he is blind and has no trouble navigating in the dark." The chef bowed. "And now, if you will excuse me, the kitchen beckons —"

As Cass's mother thanked him profusely, Hugo disappeared through a side door.

"Madam," said the waiter, staring in the general direction of Cass's mother. "If you please —"

The waiter instructed Cass's mother to put her right hand on his shoulder and Cass to put *her* right hand on her mother's shoulder. Max-Ernest and Yo-Yoji were supposed to follow suit.

"Now follow me, please. And if you need to stop, say so. We don't want any collisions."

The waiter led them past the velvet curtain into a long hallway. At first, the hallway was dimly lit from the outside — but there was little to see. Only bare, gray walls. And a thick, dark carpet.

Then Max-Ernest, the last of their party, walked in and the curtains closed behind him.

Suddenly, it was pitch-black.

"What happened? It's so dark!" whispered Max-Ernest.

"It's supposed to be," said Cass. "Just keep walking."

"Yeah, but it's *really* dark. I can't see anything. Not even my hand."

"You should have practiced like me," said Cass. "I always spend at least one hour a week blindfolded. Just in case I ever get stuck in a cave and my flashlight goes out." (This was a slight exaggeration, but it was true she'd tried walking around her room with a blindfold a few times.)

"If you would all be quiet for a moment," said the waiter calmly, "I am now opening the door to the main dining room."

They could tell right away that they'd entered a much larger space. The air felt cooler and lighter. And there was more of an echo.

Other diners had already been seated and their dis-embodied voices came seemingly from all directions. *"Oops — I hope that was just water!"*

". . . I'm not sure, I think it's fish."

"Ouch — you hit my nose!"

"Don't try to seat yourselves or you may wind up on top of somebody else," the waiter warned when they reached their table.

The kids snickered.

"The theme tonight is chocolate," he continued, leading them to their chairs one by one. "Almost every dish, whether savory or sweet, contains at least a small amount of cacao. Except for Max-Ernest, who will be served an alternate menu."

"How did you know?" asked Max-Ernest, relieved.

"I believe your friend mentioned you would go into anaphylactic shock otherwise," said the waiter dryly.

He said there was an *amuse bouche* waiting in front of each of them, and after explaining what that was (of course, *you* already know), he quietly departed.

Feeling around their table, our friends ascertained that it was fully set with plates, utensils, glasses — and a few other items that were harder to identify.

"Hey, Cass, can you tell what's in this? Is it my *amuse bouche?*"

After a couple tries, Max-Ernest managed to hand Cass a small bowl. She reached in —

"Little . . . balls . . . Ugh, they're mushy and slimy and cold."

Yo-Yoji laughed. "It's like a haunted house — you know like when they put your hand in a bowl of olives and tell you they're eyeballs?"

Cass tentatively licked a finger. "Actually, it's just butter."

Exploring further, Cass discovered a warm round object on a small plate: "A roll! I think everyone's got one."

But when she tried to butter hers:

"Ow — you stabbed my hand!" complained Max-Ernest.

"Sorry."

"The *amuses* are on our plates right in front of us," said Cass's mother. "Oh, it's delicious! But don't take little bites — eat it all at once."

"Too late. Mine's dribbling all over my chin," said Yo-Yoji.

Max-Ernest gingerly prodded his *amuse bouche* with a spoon. It was soft and wet and round and jiggly and felt like a large egg yolk.

Trying to be brave, he put the whole thing in his mouth and bit down —

It squirted in all directions and he was hit with blast after blast of flavor. Like different colors of fireworks exploding one after another. First came a warm and mellow taste. Could it be . . . pancakes? Then came the cooler and juicier taste of . . . blueberries? Yes, blueberry pancakes. At the end, his senses were doused with maple syrup.

"Hey, did anybody else's taste like breakfast?" asked Yo-Yoji. "I think mine was bacon and eggs. And hot chocolate."

"Funny, mine tasted like a frittata with smoked salmon and caviar," said Cass's mother.

"Which just happens to be your favorite breakfast," said Cass in a slightly accusatory tone. "Just like my favorite happens to be waffles with mint-chip ice cream. Which is what mine was. Wow, what a coincidence, Mel!"

She'd loved her *amuse bouche* and she knew she should think it was sweet that her mother had special-ordered the food, but Cass couldn't help it: she hated the thought of her mother conspiring with Señor Hugo.

"I wish you wouldn't call me that," said her mother.

"What — you mean *Mel*? Why? It's your name, isn't it?"

Before her mother could reply, the waiter arrived with their first course: soup.

In tiny, thimble-like glasses.

Everyone sipped at the same time, but no two soups were the same. Or was it that no two sets of taste buds were the same? Each soup tasted like a well-known food item, distilled to its very essence:

"Popcorn!" (Max-Ernest)

"Pop-Tart!" (Yo-Yoji)

"Peanut butter and jelly!" (Cass)

"Potato chips!" (her mom)

All except Max-Ernest's had the barest hint of chocolate.

As the meal continued, the dishes became increasingly elaborate — and increasingly difficult to identify. But according to the waiter (who was only willing to name a dish after it had been tasted) they included: salad with cacao vinaigrette; scallops in a dark chocolate reduction; pinto beans spiced with chipotle-cocoa powder; a pork roast with an apricot-chocolate glaze; and, of course, chicken in *mole poblano*, the famous Mexican sauce made from nuts, dried chilies, and a healthy portion of Mexican chocolate.

Each new dish was harder to cut/spear/scoop than the last, and it didn't take long for the impatient eaters to give up on their forks and knives and start using their hands.

"It's a good thing Mrs. Johnson isn't here," said Max-Ernest. "She wouldn't think we were using good table manners." (He was referring to their school principal, who was a stickler for manners; the "Principal With Principles," she called herself.)

"I'd like to see her try to eat here!" said Yo-Yoji.

"Well, I hope you don't abandon manners altogether," said Cass's mom. "Your principal may not be here but somebody's mother is."

She sighed contentedly in the darkness. "You know, I think this may be the best meal I've ever had. Hugo is a genius. I could eat his food every day."

"Well, why don't you marry him, then?" asked Cass, unable to bear another positive word about Señor Hugo.

"That's ridiculous — I hardly know him!" Her mother sounded flustered. "But you make it sound like a death sentence. Would it really be so awful?"

"Yeah, pretty much."

"You know, one day I may actually want to get married, whether to Hugo or someone else," said Cass's mother stiffly. "And when I do, Cassandra, I hope you open your heart a little bit and don't hide your feelings behind cheap sarcasm."

The s-word. Cass hated it when her mom complained about her sarcasm.

"Why should I have any feelings about it?" she shot back. "You're not my real mom anyway . . . technically."

Cass bit her lip. Why had she said that? She knew how much it would upset her mother.

There was silence for a moment.

"Cass, because your friends are here, I'm not going to respond to that right now," her mother said finally. "We'll talk about it later, OK?"

"OK."

Cass could feel her ears reddening in the dark.

A few minutes later, their waiter stepped up to the table again.

"Hello, Cassandra. If you don't mind, I'm going to reach over you so I can put this plate in front of you. It's a quadruple fudge layer cake, compliments of the chef. He calls it Chocolate Death."

Max-Ernest coughed up the water he was drinking. "That's exactly how I always thought I would die!"

"Uh, thanks," said Cass. "I think."

"My pleasure," murmured the waiter, and he disappeared without another word.

"So — what do you think they do when it's somebody's birthday?" asked Yo-Yoji. "No candles, right?"

"They probably just sing," said Max-Ernest quite sensibly.

"Seriously, aren't you guys curious to see what would happen if you lit a candle in here?" Yo-Yoji persisted.

Cass giggled, then felt in her backpack. "Actually, I have one. And matches . . ."

"Cool. Let's light it, yo!" whispered Yo-Yoji, excited.

Max-Ernest tensed. "We can't, it's not right —"

"Ah, come on — don't you just want to see for a second? The waiters will never know — they're blind."

Cass turned to her right. She was certain her mother would say No. At the same time, her mother loved birthday candles. On Cass's last birthday, she made Cass blow her candles out three times, so Cass would get three wishes.

"Mel, what do you think?"

There was no response.

Was she getting the silent treatment? Cass wondered.

"Sorry about what I said before," she said softly. "I understand if you're mad but . . . can't you at least say something?"

Silence.

"Mel, are you there?" she asked more loudly. "It's not funny." She felt the chair next to her. It was empty. How strange.

Had her mother been so upset that she had to leave the room?

"Hey, you guys, where's my mom? Did she go to the bathroom?"

"Wouldn't she have to ask the waiter? I mean, unless she tried to go by herself," said Max-Ernest. "But then she probably would have bumped into something or —"

Before he could finish his thought, Cass lit a match, her hand trembling. Suddenly illuminated, Max-Ernest and Yo-Yoji looked back at her in blinking astonishment.

"Whoa, look what a mess we made!" said Yo-Yoji.

He pointed at Cass. "There's sauce all over your shirt." Then he pointed at Max-Ernest. "And your face is like totally covered."

"Where's my mom?" Cass repeated.

Her friends looked around: not only was Cass's mother's chair empty, so was the rest of the room.

They were the only ones there.

CHAPTER EIGHT

The opposite of OK

The match flickered out.

But not before the commotion had drawn the attention of their waiter. They could hear him running toward their table.

"Can I help you with something?"

"Yeah, where's my mother?" Cass demanded. "And what about everybody else —?"

The waiter said he had no more idea where Cass's mother was than they did. He was certain she wasn't in the bathroom; he had just finished cleaning it. As for the other customers being gone, that was no mystery; they'd finished dinner and gone home, naturally.

"I'm sure your mother is fine — she probably needed some air. Although if a customer can't be bothered to ask for help, we really can't be held responsible . . . Now, if you'll excuse me, I'll just go get the check . . ."

He scurried out without waiting for a response.

"The check? How are we going to pay if your mom doesn't come back?" asked Max-Ernest, distressed. "Do you think they'll make us wash dishes?"

"Forget the check — we have to find her!" Cass stood up, reaching into her backpack. "Come on —"

Quickly, she struck another match, and with this one lit a candle.

From what they could see, the restaurant looked much like any other. With the distinction that there were no windows. Nor were there any pictures on the walls. Nor any color or decoration whatsoever. It could almost have been the dining hall in a prison.

"How did they clean up so fast?"

Yo-Yoji gestured toward the tables spread out around the room. They were immaculate. Place settings gleamed. Folded napkins stood at attention. It looked as though the restaurant were just about to open. You'd never guess that minutes ago it had been full of diners.

In contrast, their own table was covered with food and spilled drinks.

Cass's face turned angry in the candlelight. "I know where my mom is — the kitchen!"

She pointed to the double doors at the far end of the room.

"I'll bet she went to talk to Hugo. She's so in love, she couldn't wait to tell him how good dinner was . . ."

The double doors turned out to be double-double; that is, behind them was another pair of double doors.

As soon as Cass pushed through this second pair of doors, they were blinded by light. Compared to the darkness of the dining room, the kitchen seemed as bright as a hospital.

As their eyes adjusted our three friends turned pale:

A man in a chef's coat held a cleaver high in the air.

As they watched, he brought it down and chopped —

a carrot.

The three kids exhaled in relief.

"Who's there?" he asked spinning around, knife in hand.

It wasn't Hugo; it was his *sous-chef.** But evidently, he too was blind.

"We're customers," said Cass. "Have you seen my mom? I mean — did anybody else come in here?"

The sous-chef shook his head sternly. "No. And this room is strictly off limits," he growled.

"What about Hugo? Where is he?" Cass persisted.

"Gone for the night. As you should be." He chopped another carrot for emphasis.

Yo-Yoji silently motioned to his friends: *Let's get out of here.*

"Why do you think the kitchen is so lit up if all

---

*A KITCHEN STAFF HAS A HIERARCHY LIKE THE CREW ON A SHIP. *SOUS-CHEF* MEANS "UNDER-CHEF." HE OR SHE IS THE SECOND IN COMMAND.

the chefs are blind?" whispered Max-Ernest as they headed back into the dining room.

"Beats me — the whole place is creepy," said Yo-Yoji.

Cass didn't say anything — just hurried forward holding the candle in front of her.

They found the entry room deserted. Even the scent bouquets were gone.

"Do you think she left with him?" asked Yo-Yoji. "Would your mom do that?"

"I dunno," said Cass, growing increasingly distressed. "It's so weird."

The waiter came out of the hallway looking harried.

"Cassandra? Is that you?"

"Yeah, we're right here. Did you find my mom?"

"I just spoke to Señor Hugo. He said not to worry about the bill — it's on the house. And he left you this —"

The waiter held out an envelope, which Cass anxiously accepted.

"Good-bye, we have to close up now," he said, ushering them toward the front door. "I hope you enjoyed your dinner."

The blind waiter bowed and walked quickly back in the direction of the main dining room.

As soon as they got outside, Cass tore open the envelope. There was a handwritten note inside.

"What does it say?" asked Max-Ernest.

"Is it from your mom?" asked Yo-Yoji.

"Not really," said Cass after a moment, shoving the note in her pocket. "I mean, yeah, it's from her, but she says the dark was making her too nervous and she went home."

"Really? Without saying good-bye?" asked Max-Ernest, surprised. "How are we supposed to get back?"

"Uh, bus. She said to take the bus. . . ."

Max-Ernest looked at his friend. "Why are you acting so weird?"

"I just . . . realized I don't have any bus money," Cass stammered.

"Well, I do. So we're cool," said Yo-Yoji. "But you sure everything's OK?"

"Totally," said Cass, forcing a smile. "Why wouldn't it be?"

But it wasn't OK. It was the opposite of OK.

Although Cass didn't share the note in her pocket with her friends, I will share it with you here. I believe it's too late now for it to make any difference. The penmanship, I think you'll agree, is remarkably neat for somebody who couldn't see:

Cassandra —
If you value your mother's life, bring me the Tuning Fork in two days' time. Tell no one — not even those two boys with you. If I learn that you have shared this note with anyone, the deal is off and you will never see your mother again.

H.

PART TWO

THE MAIN COURSE

CHAPTER NINE

HOME ALONE

By the time Cass got home, it was very late.

After bidding a hasty good night to her friends, she lingered on her doorstep, reluctant to face her empty house. If she never entered, she could maintain hope that her mother was inside.

You're not my real mom anyway.

Those were virtually the last words she'd said to her mother. What if she never had a chance to unsay them?

What if she never saw her mother again?

Quietly, she started to cry, shedding the tears she'd had to hold back in front of Max-Ernest and Yo-Yoji.

Stop that! she chided herself. Crying isn't going to help anything. You are not a little kid. You are a survivalist. You are trained to tackle emergencies. Treat this situation as you would any other disaster. A kidnapping is nothing compared to a tsunami or a tornado.

With tremendous effort, she wiped her eyes and made herself focus on the task at hand: finding the Tuning Fork.

She knew what her first step should be: reading the Tuning Fork file in the Terces Society archives. But should she go now or wait for daylight?

She held her key in the door lock, debating the question.

On the one hand, she had very little time to save her mother. What had the note said? Two days?

On the other hand, Cass had to admit, she was very sleepy. And she knew from all of her survivalist training that she would not be very effective in her mission without sufficient rest. Serious sleep deprivation could impair her mental functions as well as her ability to handle stress. It could also affect her emotions and her immune system. If she went for too many days without sleep, she might even start to hallucinate.

Not to mention: if she got caught by Pietro or Mr. Wallace, how would she explain being in the archives in the middle of the night?

Perhaps she should go to bed after all, she thought, turning the key.

It was the first time Cass had spent the entire night alone in an empty house, and she checked and rechecked every room, making sure all her alarm systems were in place:

✓ the glass vase situated so it would crash to the floor if the front door opened

✓ the crunchy pile of cereal in the hallway leading to her bedroom so she would hear footsteps before they reached her

✓ the rubber bands wrapped around her bedroom window locks so they would snap if the
windows opened

✓ and a few other smaller and more secretive
security measures.

Unfortunately, under the circumstances, she still
did not feel very secure.

She lay on her bed with her shoes on, afraid even
to get under the covers; her blankets might slow her
jumping out of bed. Unable to sleep, her mind racing, she counted the minutes until — finally — it was
morning.

Cass was almost out the door and on the way to
the Terces Society archives before she realized that
she hadn't brushed her teeth and that she was wearing her T-shirt inside out. Her teeth could wait. But
she decided she had to put on her shirt properly. If
Mr. Wallace or Pietro saw her looking so untidy they
might wonder whether something was wrong.

By the time she was ready to leave again, there
was a knock on the front door.

She got a lump in her throat: could it be her mother? Had Señor Hugo had a change of heart? Or was the evil chef here to collect the Tuning Fork ahead of schedule?

As she tried to decide whether or not to open the door, the knocking grew louder and more insistent:

"Cass, open up!" "Time for homework, yo."

Max-Ernest and Yo-Yoji. She'd forgotten that they'd rescheduled their "homework" session for that morning.

For a second, Cass's heart lifted. Her friends were here! They would help her through this awful time. Together, the three of them would save her mother just as they'd accomplished so many dangerous feats before.

Then Cass remembered Hugo's note and her heart sank. She couldn't tell them what was happening. Hugo had made that clear. Cass knew her silence was a betrayal of sorts. Max-Ernest especially considered himself her partner. As far as he was concerned, he and Cass shared everything; they had no secrets from each other. But, Cass told herself, as hard it was, this mission was hers and hers alone.

How was she going to get rid of them?

Trying to look normal — but was it more normal for her to smile or look annoyed? — she opened the door.

"Surprise!" said Max-Ernest. "I mean, not really, but —"

"Hey, guys," said Cass carefully, not moving from the doorway. "Sorry, you can't stay. My mom, um, had to leave early for work. And now I'm supposed to . . . go to my grandfathers'."

"But it's Sunday," said Max-Ernest. "Why's she going to work?"

"I dunno, she . . . had a meeting."

Max-Ernest studied Cass. "Did you guys have a fight — 'cause of what you said to her? You know, about her not being your real mom. Is that why she left last night?"

Cass looked back at him, trying not to let her alarm show. Or even to blink. Max-Ernest's astuteness had caught her off guard.

"Um . . ."

As painful as it was to think about, she had to admit his story was more plausible than hers. She decided to go with it.

"Yeah," she said with unfeigned discomfort. "That's pretty much what happened. We had a fight this morning and she went to go shopping or something."

"Well, can't we come in anyway?" asked Yo-Yoji. "Now we don't even have to pretend we're doing homework for school. And we have to start researching the Tuning Fork *some*time . . ."

Cass debated in her head again:

On the one hand, Hugo's note had been very clear about not telling them what was happening.

On the other hand, how would it hurt for them to know where she was going? After all, they *were* supposed to be looking for the Tuning Fork. They didn't have to know she was looking for it for Hugo, rather than for Pietro.

"Actually, I was on my way to the circus," she said finally. "To read about the Tuning Fork in the archives."

"Without us?" asked Max-Ernest. "You weren't going to wait?"

"I know it's kind of silly, but I thought maybe I would find out something first, then surprise you guys with it."

"Oh," said Max-Ernest, who didn't look quite satisfied with her answer.

"Well, now that the surprise is ruined, we'll come with you!" said Yo-Yoji.

"Um, OK . . . ," Cass said hesitantly, unable to think of a good reason to say No.

"Here, your mom forgot this —" said Max-Ernest, picking up a newspaper off the front stoop. "You know, you're not supposed to leave stuff outside because then burglars think nobody's home —"

Annoyed with herself for the oversight, Cass took the paper from Max-Ernest. She was really going to have to think ahead, she realized, if she didn't want anybody to figure out that her mom was missing.

"Hey, what's that on the paper?" asked Yo-Yoji.

Cass eyed the newspaper in her hand: "Ugh —!"

Apparently, a dog had relieved himself on top of it.

Max-Ernest laughed. "Don't worry — it's plastic. I got it from the clowns."

Cass forced a smile. "Ha! That's really funny!"

Max-Ernest looked at her strangely. "Now I *know* something is wrong! You never think I'm funny. Least not when I'm trying to be . . ."

Cass hid her face as she locked the door behind her.

Having friends who knew you well was supposed to be comforting, but right now it only made her more uneasy.

CHAPTER TEN

CACA BOY

Clearly, carnies were not morning people. When Cass and her friends arrived, the circus was so quiet it could have been the middle of the night.

Through a trailer window they saw Mickey and Morrie playing checkers with some locals — no doubt the clowns were cheating the "rubes" out of their hard-earned money — but from the looks of it, the clowns hadn't woken up; they'd never gone to sleep.

The only noise came from the Big Top. As they approached, they heard a man shouting inside. "Come on, you big stubborn cat — are you a lion or a mule? You think you don't want to jump now — what are you going to do when this hoop is on fire?!"

"I didn't know there were still lions in this circus," said Max-Ernest nervously. "I thought they were all gone."

When they peeked inside they saw an old man in a tattered satin suit holding a long tent rope in his hand. The kids recognized him as the "The Amazing Alfred, King of the King of Beasts."

"Welcome, children. Don't be frightened — I promise you, this fierce animal is totally under my control!"

He waved his rope in the air, attempting to crack it like a whip.

Years ago, they'd been told, Alfred had been a great lion tamer. Rather than a lion, however, the only beast in the tent this morning was a bored house cat, currently licking his paws and not paying Alfred the least bit of attention.

A bright pink hula hoop was positioned in the center of the ring, but the cat wouldn't even look at it.

"Of course, there's a simple rule about what to do if you run into a lion — whether you're at the circus or in the African savanna," Alfred continued. "Would you like to hear it?"

"Sure, Alfred — sorry, I mean, Mr. Amazing," said Max-Ernest, who was feeling it was just as well they weren't facing a real lion at the moment. Or a real whip.

"First of all, never run — that triggers their predatory instincts. Instead, spread your arms out so you look like a big animal who's too much trouble to kill." Alfred demonstrated — tearing his old suit as he did so.

"That's just like with a bear," said Cass impatiently. Although she'd never faced a bear in real life, she regularly included bear attacks as part of her survivalist training. "Now can we go?" she whispered to her friends.

"Precisely!" declared the lion tamer with a crack of his whip. "Why don't you try it on that bear there —?"

The lion tamer pointed to the side of the tent where a rather heavy and hirsute (which you may recognize as a polite way of saying *fat and hairy*) woman was now standing with her arms folded. This was Myrtle, the circus's bearded lady.

"Alfred!" Myrtle scolded. "What are you doing with that poor kitten? Kids, what are you doing here so early? Pietro didn't say anything . . ."

"They're here to keep me company," said Yo-Yoji quickly. "You know Lily. She likes me to start practicing before the sun comes out."

Myrtle snorted. "You won't have any fingers left by the time that woman gets done with you!"

"Oh great!" Cass moaned a moment later.

She hadn't anticipated the CAT FOOD trailer being padlocked. But right there, hanging from the door handle, was a large combination lock. Compared to other devices employed by the Terces Society it looked crude, but no doubt it was effective in keeping out intruders. The one exceptional feature of the lock was that there were letters rather than numbers on its face.

"Chill," said Yo-Yoji. "We can always find Pietro or Mr. Wallace to let us in."

"No, no, we can't because . . . ," Cass stammered. How to explain that they were the last people she wanted to see right now? She was hoping desperately not to run into them.

"Don't worry," said Max-Ernest. "I know where Pietro keeps the riddle."

"What riddle?" asked Cass.

"The one that tells you what the new combination is every day."

"Oh," she said, relieved that he knew about the combination but also a bit peeved that she hadn't been privy to this information.

Max-Ernest returned with a slip of paper pulled out from under an abandoned cotton candy machine.

"'What do you call a lion bite that doesn't hurt?'" he read.

"A LION LICK?" Yo-Yoji offered.

"A LION KISS?" guessed Cass.

Max-Ernest shook his head in disgust. "No. Those are totally wrong. The answer has to be more . . . you know, like a pun."

"How about LION GUM?" asked Cass. "Like all you're getting is his gums, not teeth? That's a pun. Sort of."

Max-Ernest shook his head again. "You guys are hopeless. It's so obvious."

"Oh, yeah — then what is it?"

"Easy. CATNIP. A lion is a kind of cat — that's why it says CAT FOOD on the trailer. That's probably where Pietro got the idea. And a nip is like a little bite that doesn't hurt. But it's a pun because catnip is also that stuff that makes cats go crazy. How 'bout that?"

"Pretty good, but I'll save my applause until I see you open the door," said Cass.

"Yeah, man, we still don't know if you're right," said Yo-Yoji.

But of course Max-Ernest was right. And the door opened with ease.

The Terces Society archives were notoriously esoteric and equally extensive, going back many generations.

Inside the trailer, file boxes were stacked to the ceiling. The space was crammed tighter than Cass's grandfathers' antiques store. But here everything was in order, nothing out of place.

Every box, every file, every photo, every scrap of paper had been meticulously labeled by Mr. Wallace:

Dogs, Talking
Dogs, Telekinetic
Dogs, Two-headed

Underwater Cities: Atlantis and Others

The Emerald Tablet:
Stories, Legends, Facts

Ceiling Walkers of India
1850–1917

Weevils and:
Brain Implantation
Medieval Dentistry
Prehistoric Eating Habits

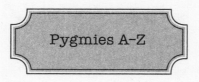

Pygmies A–Z

Cass found the Tuning Fork file wedged between *Tunes, Celtic* and *Tunnels, Rumored Under Pyramids.*

Unfortunately, she discovered, there wasn't much in it. Just the drawing of the Tuning Fork that Mr. Wallace had shown them and a long hand-written manuscript on yellowed paper. The manuscript was in Spanish, but there was an English translation attached.

While Yo-Yoji and Max-Ernest looked through other file boxes to see if they could find anything else that would be helpful in their quest, Cass sat down on the speckled linoleum floor and started reading aloud:

25 October, 1597

I write this journal sitting on a beach, I know not where.
New World or Old World or some Other World altogether.

After six weeks at sea, I have washed ashore on a desert island and I am alone but for the lizards and my thoughts.

Next to me is the fatal object that caused a great ship to sink. Yes, that small silver tool lying there so innocently on the sand killed the crew of the <u>Santa Xxxxx</u> as surely as if it stabbed each sailor in the back — and yet it never so much as touched their fingers.

Myself, I am the only survivor.

My story begins on another island, Teotihuacan, grand capital of the Aztec people. The island city that rises out of the Lake of the Moon.

In Teotihuacan, there lived a boy of twelve or thirteen or so. The son of farmers, he worked in the royal granary, and every day he carted baskets of food and grain to the palace of the great emperor, Moctezuma.

He was known as Caca Boy — a name that thankfully does not have the same meaning in the Aztec language that it has in ours! — because he carried so many of the seeds the Aztecs call the <u>cacahuatal</u>.

You cannot imagine the importance the Aztec people place on this shriveled little seed. It is the coin of the realm. They trade the seeds for all manner of goods just as if the seeds were bits of gold.

But it is the strange brown drink they make from the cacahuatal seeds that gives the seeds their true value. This is a frothy and spicy concoction that is quite delicious when sweetened. I would go so far as to say it is addictive. Soon, I predict, it will be all the rage in Europe.

The Aztecs call the drink <u>chocolatl</u>.*

Moctezuma had millions and millions of cacahuatal seeds stored in enormous bins of straw and clay. To scoop up the seeds, Caca Boy climbed inside the bins, sometimes sinking all the way to his chin. He spent so much time surrounded by the seeds that his skin was stained a dark brown, and his hair, his very pores, his whole body, stank of cacahuatal.

This would not have been so terrible, for he loved the smell, save for one thing: sadly, he had never tasted chocolatl.

Among the Aztecs, the drinking of chocolatl is restricted to the noble classes: royalty, priests, and warriors. Commoners are considered unfit for such a luxurious elixir. At the palace, the rules were even more strict: only the emperor could drink the chocolatl prepared in the royal kitchen.

If Caca Boy took so much as a sip he would be sentenced to death.

Every day, after making his delivery, Caca Boy would linger outside the palace kitchen and torture himself by watching the emperor's cooks prepare the emperor's chocolatl.

Cup after cup they made, pouring and re-pouring until the chocolatl was whipped into a delicious froth. There was red chocolatl. White chocolatl. Black chocolatl. They served it with honey.

*YES, *CHOCOLATL* WAS THE AZTEC WORD FOR *CHOCOLATE*. OR AT LEAST WHAT THE SPANISH THOUGHT THE AZTEC WORD WAS. NOBODY REALLY KNOWS WHERE THE NAME CHOCOLATE CAME FROM.

With vanilla. With flowers. All for the emperor. Always in the
emperor's special golden goblets.

One day, instead of frothing the emperor's chocolatl herself, a cook nervously placed his goblet in front of a mysterious and strangely ageless man in a shimmering robe.

In his gloved hands, the man held a silver fork that ended in two long prongs. While Caca Boy watched, mesmerized, the man carefully lowered the prongs into the emperor's chocolatl. Then he rubbed his palms together, rolling the handle of the silver fork back and forth, causing the prongs to spin faster and faster until you could barely see them.

Soon, the chocolatl was whipped into the biggest head of foam Caca Boy had ever seen. It grew and grew until there was a frothy white mountain ten times the size of the goblet beneath — and yet the goblet never overflowed onto the table.

The aroma was so strong it nearly threw Caca Boy backward.

Afterward, Caca Boy asked the cook who the man was.

"He is a sorcerer. They say his silver fork will make your food taste like anything in the world so long as it is something you have tasted before — or even that your ancestors tasted before."

"So if I had the fork, could I turn dirt into chocolatl?" asked Caca Boy, wide-eyed. "My father tasted it once. He said it was like drinking gold."

"Remember your place, Caca Boy! The drinking of chocolatl is forbidden to your kind," said the cook sharply.

"Besides," she added, lowering her voice, "magic like that always comes with a price."

Caca Boy didn't see the sorcerer's silver fork again for three years.

By then, the Spanish had arrived. War had broken out and the city was in chaos.

Even the emperor's palace was looted. From the shadows by the kitchen, Caca Boy watched the Spaniards carting away the treasures of his civilization like so much trash.

While Caca Boy silently cursed the Spanish, he saw something silver drop out of a soldier's arms. Caca Boy couldn't believe his luck. In a flash, he darted into the street and pocketed it. And then he ran.

He knew the emperor's guards would kill him if they caught him with the silver fork. If he was lucky, he might be sacrificed to Huitzilopochtli.*

The Spanish were even more vicious. If he were caught by the Conquistadors, he would be sacrificed to their greed — and much more quickly.

There was only one place to hide.

He flew down the familiar streets, flung open the doors to the granary, and dove headfirst into one of the giant vats of cacahuatal seeds. He hid there, buried, for hours. Seeds wedged between his toes and even up his nose.

Finally, when he was sure it must be the middle of the night, he

*THE AZTECS BELIEVED THEY MUST SACRIFICE A BRAVE MAN TO THE SUN GOD, *HUITZILOPOCHTLI*, EVERY DAY. OTHERWISE, THEY FEARED, THE SUN WOULD NOT RISE THE NEXT MORNING.

stuck his head out. And then he froze. Because he was staring into the eyes of a man. A man equally surprised.

Luckily, this man was neither Aztec warrior nor Spanish Conquistador. He was a man of peace. A Franciscan brother. A monk.

He was I.

I had come in the vain hope of stopping my Spanish kin from looting the food supplies of the Aztecs. I was too late. At the far end of the granary, Spanish soldiers were upending stores of corn. Soon, the cacahuatal seeds would spill as well.

Now my attention was focused on the young boy in front of me. So clearly frightened and alone. Thankfully, I had learned enough of the Aztec tongue to ask why he was hiding and if he needed help.

Before answering, he looked around, measuring his chances. At one end were the Spanish. At the other, the Aztecs. In either direction, peril.

"They will kill me if they find this," he whispered, showing me the silver fork with obvious reluctance.

The object itself was less remarkable than the images engraved on it. On one prong, there was a long-tailed bird, on the other a twisting snake. I thought I recognized what the images meant and they made me shiver.

Haltingly, Caca Boy told me his story about seeing the sorcerer and then finding the fork years later.

Naturally, I dismissed what he said about the sorcerer's fork as superstitious nonsense. But I agreed to take it from him if that meant saving his life.

"Wait —"

Quickly, Caca Boy scooped up a handful of cacahuatal seeds. Frowning with concentration, he stirred the seeds with the fork . . .

As I watched in disbelief, the seeds dissolved into liquid. Foaming chocolatl was now cupped in his hand.

Blissfully, he lapped up the chocolatl, licking every drop off his fingers. At last, Caca Boy had tasted chocolatl! And it was every bit as good, nay, it was better than his father had described.

Eyes glistening, he handed me the silver fork. Then he jumped out of the bin — and ran out of sight.

I never saw Caca Boy again.

It is an awkward position for a poor friar to possess a priceless object with unholy powers.

I wanted nothing to do with the fork. Yet, I did not know how to get rid of it. And so it was still hidden in my robes months later when I found myself searching for passage back to Spain.

We friars must often make our way by begging. Alas, ship captains do not always have a matching generosity of spirit.

May God forgive me, I bargained for my berth on the <u>Santa Xxxxx</u> by giving the captain the silver fork.

At first, the ship's cook was under strict instructions to use the fork only in preparation of the captain's meals. But on a ship, secrets never stay secret for long. Word of the captain's magical feasts spread. And soon he had no choice but to share or face mutiny.

There was no limit to the fork's powers. With it, the cook turned old gruel into golden broth, and rancid meat into fat roast goose. There were impossibly ripe fruits and glorious sweetmeats. Roasted peacocks and stuffed pigs.

Whatever the crew could remember, the silver fork could cook.

Forbidden to eat such rich food by my vow of poverty, I alone did not partake of the fancy feasts. I lived on stale bread.

Need I say what happened next?

The sailors grew fat and lazy and argumentative. The decks were not swabbed. The brass was not polished. The ship veered off course.

As much as I tried, I could not stop them from gorging.

"More! More!" they cried.

And "Get out of the way, you old monk!"

And other things too rude to repeat.

Soon, the chef was forced to turn hay bales into dinner. Then old sailcloth and seawater. The meals still tasted delicious, but the food no longer fattened the crew — it made them sick. It was food in taste only.

I watched in horror as daily the sailors grew more skeletal. The more they ate the more they starved.

By the time the big storm came, most of the crew were dead. The others had no strength left to fight. Only I had the will to live.

If only I had also had the will to let this cursed fork sink with the ship! What new horrors does it have in store for future generations? I shudder to imagine.

<u>Curate ut Valeatis.</u>

— Fr. Rafael de Leon

CHAPTER ELEVEN

a dry, raspy cough

Still half-lost in the Aztec world, Cass looked up from the monk's manuscript.

"Do you think the Tuning Fork is really cursed?" she asked.

"I guess it depends on what you mean by cursed," Max-Ernest responded. He and Yo-Yoji had abandoned the other file boxes long ago and were now sitting across from her. "I mean, anybody can curse anything, right? That doesn't mean the curse *works*."

"Yeah, things like that only happen in old legends and movies and stuff," agreed Yo-Yoji.

But neither of them sounded very confident. The trouble was, as members of the Terces Society, they'd already seen plenty of things that were only supposed to happen in legends and movies. It wasn't that long ago, after all, that they'd been having a picnic lunch with a two-foot tall, five-hundred-year-old man born in a bottle. (Oh, and did I mention he was a cannibal?)*

A man's cough — a dry, raspy cough — made the kids snap to attention. And made the hairs on their neck stand on end.

The worst had already happened, Cass reminded herself. Her mother had been taken from her. She was ready to face anyone, even Señor Hugo.

---

*IF YOU'VE READ *IF YOU'RE READING THIS IT'S TOO LATE*, THEN YOU KNOW I AM REFERRING TO CASS'S FRIEND, MR. CABBAGE FACE, THE HOMUNCULUS, NOW SADLY DECEASED. IF YOU HAVEN'T READ THE BOOK, WELL, THEN IT REALLY IS TOO LATE. I'VE JUST SPOILED THE ENDING.

Slowly, they all looked up.

"Cassandra, Max-Ernest, Yo-Yoji, it's a little early in the morning for clown camp, isn't it? Don't you know a circus never stirs before noon?"

It was Mr. Wallace. The gaunt man lurched over them, blocking them from standing up.

"At your age, you should be sleeping in on a Sunday," he prattled on. "Me, I couldn't get to sleep so I decided to get a jump start on my day. Then again, I hardly fit in in the circus, do I?"

"Us . . . too," Cass stammered. "I mean, we don't fit in — I mean, we got up early."

"Hard to get your story straight sometimes, isn't it?" Mr. Wallace queried.

Mr. Wallace was the oldest member of the Terces Society — not necessarily in age (Cass wasn't sure but she thought Pietro was older) but in the sense that he had been part of the society longest. According to Pietro, Mr. Wallace knew more about the history of the Secret, and more about the Midnight Sun, than any other living person. (At least more than anyone outside of the Midnight Sun. And to what extent the Masters were considered living was open to debate.) And yet, for some reason, Cass had never trusted Mr. Wallace. And she'd never felt that he trusted her.

Mr. Wallace peered over her shoulder. "Ah, the

memoirs of the monk, Rafael de Leon. A most vivid account, don't you think? I'm glad you're following your orders so assiduously."

"My orders?" Cass's heart skipped a beat. How could he know about Hugo's note? Unless . . .

"From Pietro. To investigate the Tuning Fork."

"Oh . . . right."

Relieved, Cass stood up, gripping the Tuning Fork file tight in her hand.

She tried to sound casual: "So where do you think it could be, anyway?"

"The Tuning Fork? No idea. If I had, I'd be rich. Or dead." Mr. Wallace leaned in toward the kids. "But between you and me, I've always had a hunch it's somewhere close . . ."

The way Mr. Wallace said *close*, it almost seemed the word meant something sinister — as if the Tuning Fork might be haunting them at the very moment.

"You mean near . . . here?" asked Yo-Yoji.

Mr. Wallace nodded, taking the file from Cass's hand without asking. "We know the fork made its way to Europe with Brother Rafael. And from what I can tell, it crossed the Atlantic again a hundred years later. Possibly on the *Mayflower*. Or soon thereafter."

He put the file back in its drawer, which he closed,

Cass noticed, with an air of finality. They wouldn't be opening it again anytime soon.

"You mean like with the Puritans?" asked Max-Ernest.

Mr. Wallace shrugged. "Of course this is all speculation . . . but did you know that along with all the Puritans, there were also witches banished to the New World?"

"So you think a . . . witch had it?" Cass could hardly believe they were using the word seriously. But over the past couple years, she'd learned not to discount anything — even the supernatural.

"Well, a woman believed to be a witch anyway." Mr. Wallace smiled — an occurrence so rare as to be nearly supernatural in itself. "All those stories about witches feeding children candy have to come from somewhere, don't they? And I did read a report once about a witch named Clara who was famous for her frothy cups of hot chocolate . . ."

"And now . . . ?"

"Who knows? The Tuning Fork is probably lying around in some garage or junk shop somewhere."

"A junk shop?" Cass repeated in surprise.

Mr. Wallace nodded. "People probably assume it's just a normal musical tuning fork. Or have no idea what it is at all."

A junk shop.

That meant one thing to Cass: her grandfathers. The Fire Sale was the biggest junk shop in the neighborhood.

Was it possible they would find the Tuning Fork there?

CHAPTER TWELVE

Boxes
Redux

A short time later, Cass and her friends stood with her grandfathers Larry and Wayne outside the old redbrick fire station. In the driveway was Grandpa Wayne's decrepit old pickup truck, piled high with all sorts of junk. It looked as if Cass's grandfathers were moving out.

"I think you're a little confused, Cass," said Grandpa Larry, chuckling. "Tuning forks aren't really forks. They're not for cooking or eating."

"Well, I suppose you *could* cook with a tuning fork," said Grandpa Wayne. "Maybe as a fork when you're carving meat. Or as a skewer. I sort of like that idea — you could make double shish kebabs!"

"No you couldn't," Larry responded. "The ends of a tuning fork are much too blunt."

"Well, then, you file them down, of course!"

"Never mind about that," Cass repeated. "Please —"

"Patience, Cass," said Larry. "Can't your grandfathers have a little intellectual debate now and then?"

"It's just — we were wondering whether you might have any old tuning forks lying around? It's for a school report we're doing . . . well, an over-the-summer report for school." She stumbled but recovered. "For next year."

"Homework in summer? That's terrible," said
Grandpa Larry. "It's an oxymoron!"*

"An outrage," agreed Grandpa Wayne. "We can't support it."

"I know, I agree, but please," said Cass. "It would be really helpful."

Larry surveyed the pile of junk in the truck, then looked in the window of their store. "Wayne, where's that old orange crate? You remember — with that dulcimer I made in Woodstock. Isn't there a tuning fork in there?"

"Oh, right, that's — that's against the back wall, isn't it? Left-hand side next to the washroom?" Wayne gestured inside the store. "By the fire hose."

"Orange crate. Back wall. Fire hose. Got that, guys?" asked Grandpa Larry. The kids nodded.

"Come on, Larry, we got to scoot," said Grandpa Wayne, hopping into the driver's seat of his truck.

"You bet we do!" Grandpa Larry grinned, climbing into the passenger seat of the truck. "This is the most exciting day of our lives. *Antiques Caravan* has come to town. With all our stuff we're going to be the stars of the show."

"You be the star. No way you're getting me on TV," grumbled Wayne.

---

*AN *OXYMORON*, IF YOU DON'T KNOW, IS NOT AN OX OR A MORON; IT IS A CONTRADICTION IN TERMS. HERE ARE A FEW OF MY FAVORITES: *SILENT SCREAM, LIVING DEAD, VIRTUAL REALITY, OPEN SECRET, SAME DIFFERENCE*, AND SPEAKING OF HOMEWORK IN SUMMER, *SUMMER SCHOOL*.

"You won't care when you hear how much money we can get for this telephone! Everything from the 1970s is huge right now!"

Larry held up the phone for Cass and her friends to see. It was shaped like a pair of lips. Big red lips.

"Don't forget to feed Sebastian," Wayne called out the truck window.

"And tell your mom to watch us on *Antiques Caravan*, Cass," called Larry. "They're broadcasting live!"

The truck lurched into gear and sputtered away in a cloud of smoke.

The left-hand side of the back wall next to the washroom happened to be the very most crowded section of the store. Here boxes were piled three and four deep, all the way to the ceiling. (Cass hadn't yet tackled this section in her baby box search; she'd been hoping to find her box without having to touch it.)

"OK, if you guys want to be here, you have to help. That means really help, Max-Ernest," said Cass. "The only way we're going to find that orange crate is by taking down all those boxes so we can see what's behind."

Max-Ernest applied himself a little more diligently this time. Even so, the work was slow and difficult,

and after an hour they'd moved fewer than a quarter
of the boxes out of the way.

Sebastian was lying nearby on the old beach towel known as his "magic carpet" (because Larry and Wayne used it to lift the dog and "fly" him around the room). As Cass dropped what seemed like the hundredth box of opera records onto the floor, he kept nudging her leg and barking.

"Shh. Just let me find this crate, Sebastian. I need it to save my mom. She was kidnapped," Cass whispered, grateful to be able to confide in somebody, even a dog.

She petted his head repeatedly, but Sebastian, who tended to bark very loudly because he was very nearly deaf, only barked louder.

Cass was about to go hunt for some dog food when she realized he was barking in the direction of the old fire hose Wayne had mentioned. It was coiled around a big iron wheel.

Wedged behind the wheel was a box Cass hadn't noticed earlier. Was this the cause of Sebastian's barking?

Growing excited, Cass pulled out the box. It was cardboard and about the size of a case of soda pop. It looked banged-up, as if it had been in her grandfather's store for quite a while.

Cass sighed, disappointed. One thing was certain: it wasn't an orange crate. Why had Sebastian steered her so wrong?

She was about to push the box aside with the others when she noticed a quarter-size hole cut into the cardboard. And the words **HANDLE WITH CARE** written in black marker.

Could it be . . . ?

She looked over at her friends — they were both absorbed in what they were doing — and then she nervously peeled back the layers of masking tape that kept the box closed.

The box was empty, save for a single piece of paper.

BABY GIRL - 7 LBS, 3 OZ
TIME OF BIRTH - 6:35 PM

According to the story her grandfathers had told her, those were the only words written on the piece of paper that had been taped to her chest. Yet here she found a long letter written below them.

DEAR LARRY AND WAYNE:

YOU ARE THE MESSIEST, MOST DISORGANIZED, MOST FRUSTRATING CLIENTS I HAVE EVER HAD THE DISPLEA-

SURE OF WORKING FOR IN MY ENTIRE CAREER AS AN
ACCOUNTANT. HOWEVER, I DO NOT KNOW WHO ELSE TO
TURN TO. DESPITE THE DISARRAY IN WHICH YOU LIVE,
YOU HAVE GOOD HEARTS AND YOU KNOW MANY PEOPLE.
I AM SURE YOU WILL FIND A GOOD HOME FOR THIS
BABY GIRL. IT IS EXTREMELY IMPORTANT THAT NOBODY
KNOW OF MY CONNECTION TO THE CHILD — ESPECIALLY
THE CHILD HERSELF. ANY MENTION OF MY NAME WILL
PUT HER IN DANGER.

YOUR HUMBLE SERVANT,
WWW III

WWW III.

William Wilton Wallace, the Third.

Mr. Wallace.

It had to be. It couldn't be a coincidence. Even if there were somebody else with those initials, what were the chances that he would also be an accountant?

Of all the people in the world, it was Mr. Wallace who had left her on her grandfathers' doorstep!

Cass knew she shouldn't be surprised. As she'd learned in her hunt for the homunculus, Mr. Cabbage Face, her connections to the Terces Society ran deep. The founder of the Terces Society, the

Jester, was her ancestor. Her great-great-great-great-grandfather. Or something like that. She was the Heir of the Jester. Mr. Cabbage Face had told her as much. He could tell by her ears.

And then there was the fact that she had found her birth certificate, the first clue that she wasn't exactly who she thought she was, in a Terces Society file. Mr. Wallace had claimed never to have seen the birth certificate before, but looking back, she'd been foolish to believe him.

He always seemed to disapprove of her being a member of the Terces Society. He said it was because of her age, but what if it was because of who she was?

Could Mr. Wallace be her father?! No. It was impossible. She refused to believe it. They looked nothing alike. More importantly, their personalities were nothing alike. But it was very likely that he knew who her parents were.

Correction: who her *birth parents* were. They hadn't raised her, she reminded herself. Somebody else had.

She stared at the box in front of her, eyes moistening, thinking about how her mother had been there at the firehouse with her grandfathers when she, Cass, then an orphaned baby, was delivered to their doorstep. Just as if her mother had been waiting for her.

As if it had been meant to be.

"What's that? Did you find the orange crate?" asked Yo-Yoji.

"No, just . . . nothing."

Cass quickly pushed the box behind the fire hose.

If she didn't act fast, she would be orphaned again. That was all that mattered now.

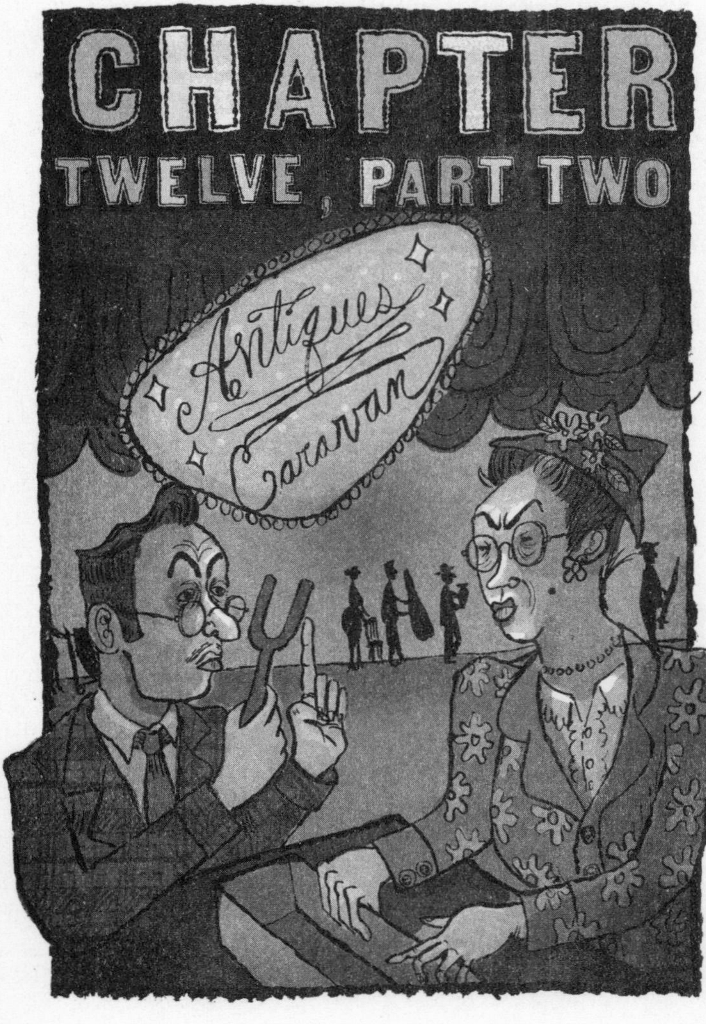
CHAPTER
TWELVE, PART TWO
Antiques Caravan

ax-Ernest was the first to spot it. It was teetering at the top of the back row of boxes. An old wooden crate with a picture of an orange shining in the sky like a sun.

Fighting his fear of heights, he climbed up to the orange crate, dislodging more than a few boxes along the way.

"This is it!" Victorious, he passed the crate down to Yo-Yoji.

They had to pry off the lid with a screwdriver, but soon they were pulling things out, making yet another pile on the floor.

At the bottom of the crate, beneath a broken thumb piano and a curiously misshapen string instrument that they guessed was the dulcimer Larry had made, was a gleaming, two-pronged metal object.

"Is *that* the Tuning Fork?" Cass asked, feeling a tingle of excitement in her ears.

"Well it's *a* tuning fork . . ." Yo-Yoji picked it up, then hit one of the prongs with a small candlestick he found nearby. "Hear that note? That's an A." (As Cass and Max-Ernest had memorably learned when they were trying to interpret the song of the Sound Prism, Yo-Yoji had perfect pitch — the musical kind, that is, not the taste-bud version.)

"But, wait — if it works, that means it can't be the right one. Because the Tuning Fork isn't really a tuning fork," Max-Ernest pointed out. "How 'bout that?"

"Oh . . . right," said Cass, crushed.

"Besides, it doesn't look very Aztec," Max-Ernest added.

Cass sat down on the orange crate, suddenly filled with an overwhelming sense of despair. "This whole thing was stupid — what were the chances my grandfathers would have *the* tuning fork we were looking for? We just wasted all this time — for nothing."

Well, not exactly for nothing, she reminded herself. But she would return to *that* box later.

"What's the big deal? We'll find the Tuning Fork," said Yo-Yoji. "Eventually."

"Well, realistically, we probably won't," said Max-Ernest conversationally. "We don't even know if the Tuning Fork is still around. For all we know, it could be just a legend, like Pietro said. Or like a myth that's partly based in fact. Or —"

Cass gritted her teeth. "Thanks, that's really reassuring, Max-Ernest. You're a big help."

"Why is that reassuring?" asked Max-Ernest, confused. "Oh wait, you were being sarcastic, huh?"

Cass was about to respond in a suitably snippy manner but she stopped herself. After all, it was definite progress for Max-Ernest to recognize sarcasm.

The question was: how to convey the urgency of their task without giving her secret away?

"Sorry. I wasn't supposed to tell you guys this but . . ." Cass struggled with her conscience: was it OK to fudge the truth in this circumstance? "Well, Pietro said if the Midnight Sun finds the Tuning Fork before we do, then this will be our last mission for the Terces Society — ever!"

"Really? He said that?" asked Max-Ernest.

Cass nodded.

"That sucks!" said Yo-Yoji. "Why would he —?"

"Actually, I think it's Mr. Wallace's fault," Cass elaborated. "You know how he doesn't think kids should be in the Terces Society? Well, they agreed this would be a test."

"But we took an oath," said Max-Ernest. "Can they un-oath us? I thought we were in for life. I mean, unless we talked about the Secret. Or something else we weren't supposed to talk about —"

Cass grimaced at this reference to secret-spilling. "Well, it's up to them, isn't it? They kind of make the rules, don't they?"

"But the Terces Society is hundreds of years old —"

"Well, it doesn't matter, anyway — nobody's going to kick us out because we're going to hunt down the Tuning Fork as fast as we can," said Yo-Yoji, determined. "But first we gotta eat. I'm starved."

"I agree — our blood sugar levels are really low," said Max-Ernest.

Cass was hardly in the mood for a relaxing lunch, but she had to acknowledge she was hungry, too; Max-Ernest was right about their blood sugar levels. Combing through her grandfathers' stuff was hard work.

She led her friends upstairs to the old firemen's galley — now her grandfathers' kitchen — to see what there was to eat.

"... You're right, it *is* Chippendale — that's the good news ..."

Sitting on the kitchen table was an old portable TV — so old it had antennae sticking out of the back. Next to the TV was an equally old VCR — a video cassette recorder left over from the days when film and television shows were recorded on video tape. A blinking red light indicated a recording in progress.

On the television screen, a dapper man in a three-piece suit was talking to a wide-eyed — and rather wide-bodied — young woman. A shiny wooden table stood beside them.

"A piece like this recently sold for $300,000 . . . ,"
said Dapper Man.

"$300,000?!" repeated Wide Woman.

"Hey, it's *Antiques Caravan!*" said Yo-Yoji. "Your grandfathers must have set it to record."

Cass and Max-Ernest gathered close to watch:

On-screen, Dapper Man nodded. *"If you'd left the table as it was, you would be a rich woman. Unfortunately, by restoring the finish you've made it totally worthless. No better than a fake."*

"Oh no! I thought I was doing the right thing . . ." Tears streamed down Wide Woman's face.

"Look — your grandfathers are in the back."

Max-Ernest pointed to the corner of the television screen where the two older men — identifiable by their exceptionally long beards — were having what looked like a heated argument with another antiques appraiser. Larry kept shaking his red lips telephone in the air.

"I guess the antiques guy didn't think the phone was worth very much money," said Cass.

After a short break for what the show called "a word from our sponsors" Dapper Man was back, now speaking to a woman in a violet pantsuit and matching hat.

Yo-Yoji stared. "Is that who I think it is . . . ? I

thought she crawled into a cave or something during the summer . . ."

Max-Ernest's jaw dropped. "What's Mrs. Johnson doing on *Antiques Caravan?*"

Indeed, Pantsuit Woman was their very own school principal — on television.

"It was my Great-Great-Great-Aunt Clara's," Mrs. Johnson was saying proudly. *"One of the original New England colonists, and a leading citizen in her time. Best cook in the county. Famous for her candies. She carried the piece with her on the* Mayflower. *The workmanship is English . . ."*

"That's weird," said Max-Ernest. "Didn't Mr. Wallace say something about the *Mayflower* and a woman named Clara?"

"Yeah, a witch," said Yo-Yoji. "How funny would that be if Mrs. Johnson's aunt was a witch!"

Dapper Man gestured toward a small object that was sitting under a bright light. *"I can't tell what it is exactly — perhaps a ritual object of some kind? What I'm certain about is that it is not English . . ."*

Mrs. Johnson looked at the antiques appraiser with outrage. *"Are you doubting that my Aunt Clara came over on the* Mayflower?"

"You know what's *really* weird —" said Cass, "how

much that thing on the table looks like a tuning
fork."

"Most of the design has worn away but it is un-doubtedly pre-Columbian — probably Mayan or Aztec," Dapper Man continued smoothly. *"Do you have proof this object is yours? It is illegal to own a pre-Columbian artifact without proper documentation."*

"Proper documentation? What are you accusing me of!? I've never been so insulted in all my life!"

Mrs. Johnson grabbed the item in question off the table and stormed out of the television picture frame, leaving the appraiser aghast.

Back at the fire station, Max-Ernest and Yo-Yoji were still staring at the television screen, unable to believe the object they'd been looking for was in their principal's possession.

Cass was already standing up and heading for the round opening in the kitchen floor.

"C'mon, follow me!"

Trying to get the Tuning Fork out of the hands of Mrs. Johnson was only slightly more appealing than cuddling up to a T. rex, but they had no choice.

And there was no time to lose.

Grabbing hold of the brass fire pole, she slid down to the floor below.

CHAPTER THIRTEEN

ATTACK OF THE KILLER GNOMES

I f you've ever run into a teacher outside of school then you know what an alarming experience that can be.

Say your teacher is at the supermarket buying groceries. Awful, right? You don't want to know what your teacher eats for dinner. Or how about seeing your teacher at the movies on a date? What could be worse than that?

Yes, in theory, we know our teachers are human. But we don't want to see the evidence up close.

Now imagine that instead of a teacher it is your principal you're going to be seeing outside of school. In fact, you're going to visit her *house*.

That, dear reader, is the terrible task Cass and her friends now undertook.

Their principal's house was the last of five identical townhouses squashed together on a short block. I say identical but in fact there was no mistaking Mrs. Johnson's for anybody else's. While the other four houses had more or less unexceptional grass and shrubbery in their tiny front yards, Mrs. Johnson's had, well —

Gnomes. Lots of gnomes.

I've never understood what possesses normally sane people to decorate their gardens with plaster-cast versions of two-foot-tall fantasy humanoids, but whatever it is it had possessed Mrs. Johnson one hundred times over.

There were short gnomes. Fat gnomes. Skinny gnomes. They had bushy beards and long beards. Pointy hats and floppy hats. Blue jackets and red jackets. Red cheeks and . . . more red cheeks.

"It looks like a theme park," said Max-Ernest. "Like we're on the gnome ride or something."

"I think they look freakin' scary," said Yo-Yoji.

Cass studied the gnomes. They did seem menacing. Like a Lilliputian army.

"Are we going to knock on the door?" asked Max-Ernest.

"No!" Cass answered immediately. "She might answer and what would we do then . . . ? Besides, I'm not sure she's home anyway. Follow me —"

Cass trudged through the ivy, past the watchful eyes of one hundred gnomes, and made her way to the side of the house.

The path was blocked by an overflowing trash can. She was about to walk around it when —

"Look —!" she whispered. "Can you believe it?"

They all made faces as they inspected their principal's garbage: it was topped by an unappetizing mix of half-eaten lasagna, used teabags, and soiled newspapers.

"Wait — it's definitely gross, but what are we looking at?" asked Yo-Yoji.

"Mrs. Johnson doesn't recycle!" said Cass, as if it were the most obvious — and most heinous — crime in the world. "Everything's mixed together."

Max-Ernest shook his head: "What happened to 'green living is clean living'? Isn't that the motto written above the trash at school?"

"And look at that —" Cass pointed to the last bit of incriminating evidence: the ugly gray contents of an ashtray dumped into a frozen-dinner tin.

Max-Ernest gaped, unable to hide his shock: "Mrs. Johnson *smokes*?!"

Yo-Yoji motioned his friends forward. "C'mon, the garbage is making me ill."

A moment later, they were standing outside their principal's bedroom window.

"We really shouldn't be doing this," Max-Ernest muttered. But he peered in all the same.

"How can she sleep in there? It's so . . . crowded," said Cass.

Indeed, every available surface in Mrs. Johnson's bedroom was covered with figurines and knickknacks. Mostly gnomes. But also a few fairies and witches — including a small fabric witch of the kind you often see in a kitchen, this one hanging from a lamp shade.

And at the foot of Mrs. Johnson's bed there was a wicker basket containing a St. Bernard puppy curled up in a ball.

"Poor puppy — he has to live with Mrs. Johnson," said Yo-Yoji.

Cass studied the puppy more closely. "What's wrong with it? It's like it's sleeping with its eyes open. Are you sure it's . . . alive?"

"It's stuffed," said Max-Ernest. "Like a plushy puppy. Just super realistic. You know, like those fake babies people get when their kids grow up and they want to keep being parents . . ."

"Hey, I think she's in the next room," whispered Yo-Yoji.

As quietly as they could, they all crouched down and made their way to the next window — Mrs. Johnson's study.

His friends pressed their noses against the glass: they could see Mrs. Johnson in profile, her face lit green by the computer screen in front of her. On the screen was a card game.

"Poker!" said Yo-Yoji. "Our principal is playing poker. Look at her — she's a full-on gambler."

Next to Mrs. Johnson, a cigarette rested in an ashtray. She picked it up and took a drag. Smoke curled like dragon's breath out of her mouth.

While Yo-Yoji and Max-Ernest stared in horrified fascination, Cass crept along to the other end of
the window.

Here, right on the other side of the glass, sitting
on top of a file cabinet, was a small metal object. Cass
couldn't see it in detail — it was half hidden by a stack
of paper — but the two prongs were unmistakable.

She turned to her friends: "OK, this is the plan: you
two go knock on the door and talk to Mrs. Johnson while
I slip in through the window and get the Tuning Fork."

"That's stealing!" said Max-Ernest in alarm.

"She doesn't have proof she owns it, remember?
For all anybody knows, it could be ours."

"It's still stealing."

Cass knew Max-Ernest was right; breaking and
entering was hardly model behavior. But her mother's life was on the line.

Unfortunately, she couldn't tell him that.

Before the kids could debate further, a high-
pitched wail sounded and the side of the house was
flooded with light.

One of the gnomes was spinning in a circle, his
eyes glowing red. Evidently, the fantasy creature hid
a very real alarm system.

"Who's there?! I'm warning you, I have a very
vicious dog!"

*   *   *

Two minutes later, the three kids were standing in the doorway facing a furious, sputtering principal.

"Not only do you barge in on my house uninvited — you have the gall to ask me to give up a precious family heirloom? Why on earth should I?"

"Well, that guy said you couldn't sell it without documentation — so what are you going to do with it? Throw it away?" asked Cass. "And not recycle it just like you don't recycle anything else," she couldn't help adding.

Mrs. Johnson stared at the kids in disbelief. "Have you been . . . rifling through my . . . my trash?!"

They shrugged.

"How very, very . . . dare you!" Mrs. Johnson exclaimed.

"Yeah, and we saw everything in it — *everything*," said Yo-Yoji, drawing out the word.

"And we're going to tell the whole school if you don't give us the Tuning Fork," said Cass, immediately catching on.

Max-Ernest nodded. "How 'bout that?"

Mrs. Johnson, still wearing her violet pantsuit, was rapidly turning a matching shade. "I see — and how do you know this trash is mine?"

"Does anybody else live here?" asked Cass. "Are

they the ones smoking the cigarettes and getting cancer?"

"It will be your word against mine," Mrs. Johnson snapped. "Nobody will believe you. You'll all be expelled!"

Yo-Yoji held up his cell phone. "What if we have pictures?"

Mrs. Johnson recoiled from the image of her un-recycled trash. "You children are horrors."

"Maybe we're horrors, but you're a hypocrite," said Cass.

"This is blackmail!"

"Hey, Cass . . . ," Max- Ernest whispered in her ear. She nodded and he reached into his pocket.

"Mrs. Johnson," Max-Ernest said, "I think your dog had an accident."

"What do you mean? What dog?"

"We saw a puppy sleeping by your bed . . ."

Mrs. Johnson nodded cautiously.

Max-Ernest pointed down to the ground where he had discreetly dropped the piece of molded brown plastic that he'd tricked Cass with earlier. It looked awfully lifelike lying in the dirt.

"But how in the world —?"

Max-Ernest shrugged. "It's only natural right? That's what dogs do."

As the distressed Mrs. Johnson puzzled over how her fake puppy could possibly have defecated on her doorstep, Cass pushed past her and ran inside —

"Where do you think you're going, young lady?!"

— and then returned with the Tuning Fork tight in her hand.

Mrs. Johnson trembled with rage. "You know what — take the fork. My mother always said it was cursed — and for your sake I hope it is."

"Great. Thanks," said Cass, already starting to run down the steps.

"I never want to see it or any of you again!" shouted Mrs. Johnson as the three kids disappeared from her view. "Don't bother coming back to school as long as I'm principal!"

Blackmail is an ugly word. And I leave it to you to judge whether it applies in this case.

Cass was trying to save her mother's life. Perhaps that excuses her. Perhaps it doesn't. I wouldn't venture to say.

All I know is that against all odds she got hold of the Tuning Fork just as instructed by Señor Hugo. And she would have brought it to his restaurant with time to spare.

Had he not come for her first.

CHAPTER FOURTEEN

Cranberry Juice

When Cass entered her house, it was quiet inside. So quiet she heard the ticking of the clock in the entry hall. And the whistle of a train half a mile away.

She'd intended to stay only five minutes — long enough for Max-Ernest and Yo-Yoji to get safely out of sight. Then she would leave for Señor Hugo's restaurant.

She knew immediately that that wouldn't be necessary.

The vase she'd left by the front door was still intact. None of her alarm systems had been triggered. There was no sign of a break-in whatsoever. But he was here — she could feel it.

She turned the corner and looked into the kitchen —

"Hello, Cassandra."

Señor Hugo was sitting at the kitchen table, just as comfortably as if he'd been invited. He was turned to face her and Cass could see herself reflected in his dark glasses.

Unaccountably, she was not afraid.

"Hello, Señor Hugo. I have it — what you wanted."

"I know."

She did not ask how he knew. She did not even ask how he got into her house.

With surprising calm, she took the Tuning Fork out of her backpack and set it on the table in front of him. The ancient object looked sorely out of place on the yellow Formica.

The blind chef showed no reaction.

"I just put it in front of you. Now, where's my mom?"

"First, let us make sure it's real. Fetch me a glass of water."

Trying not to let her impatience get the better of her, Cass went to the sink and rinsed the milk out of a glass.

"You know, the Tuning Fork is very danger-ous," she said, returning with the glass. "You really shouldn't use it."

"Thank you for the warning," said Hugo with more than a hint of what even Max-Ernest would have recognized as sarcasm. "Now sit down."

Frowning with concentration, he picked up the Tuning Fork and experimentally dipped it into the water. Then he rolled the handle of the Tuning Fork between his palms, so that the prongs twice rotated back and forth.

As Cass watched in astonishment from across the table, the water clouded, fizzed, foamed, and turned ruby red.

A ghostly smile flitted across Señor Hugo's lips.

"Is it . . . wine? Or . . . blood?" Cass asked nervously.

"Cranberry juice. Beautiful color, isn't it?"

"Uh-huh." Cass stared at him, realizing the implications of what he'd just said. "I *knew* you could see!"

Señor Hugo nodded, removing his sunglasses. "You know what they say, among the blind . . ." He paused.

One eye, his left, was dull and lifeless. The other stared directly and cruelly at Cass.

"The one-eyed is king," he finished the sentence.

Cass froze. Now she was scared.

"I trust my secret is safe with you?"

"As long as you give me back my mother," she managed to say.

"I think you mean, as long as I *don't* give you back your mother. She's my collateral, after all."

"But you . . . promised!"

"I also said you would never see her again if you told your friends."

"I didn't! I mean, I didn't tell them about you. They thought we were finding the Tuning Fork for . . . for . . . ," she stammered.

"For the Terces Society? You're splitting hairs."

Cass turned a shade paler. "How do you know about that?"

"How do you think?" He clenched and un-clenched his gloved fist in demonstration.

"You're . . . in . . . the . . . Midnight . . . Sun?" asked Cass, the full horror sinking in.

Señor Hugo laughed. "Dr. L and Ms. Mauvais told me to watch out for you. They said you were smart. I think they overestimated you."

The chef stood up, slipping the Tuning Fork into his satchel.

"Relax, Cassandra. Your mother is safe. For the moment, she's worth more to us alive. As insurance. In fact, I seem to remember her saying she worked in the insurance industry. How ironic."

As he walked out, he turned over his shoulder. "Oh, I wouldn't drink that cranberry juice if I were you. Like you said, it's very dangerous."

The front door closed behind him.

Cass slouched in her chair, drowning in despair.

She had betrayed the Terces Society.

Blackmailed her school principal.

Lied to her friends.

Put a cursed object with unlimited power in the hands of the Midnight Sun.

And she hadn't even succeeded in getting back her mother.

For the first time in her life, Cass, the survivalist, felt very little will to survive.

She stared at the glass of cranberry juice in front of her — if cranberry juice it was. Why not? she thought. What could happen that would be worse than what had already happened? She had no doubt the juice would taste extraordinary.

If it killed her, at least her last sip would be memorable.

Slowly and deliberately, she stood up, picked up the glass, and —

— marched back to the sink and poured.

The red liquid splashed angrily against the white porcelain. It circled the drain several times as if giving Cass a last chance to stick her finger in and get a taste. But when it finally went down, the liquid left no trace. As if it had been only water all along.

With a heavy sigh, Cass turned and walked over to the kitchen phone. She had a friend to visit. And a mother to save.

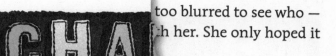

oke, she knew she was

too blurred to see who —
th her. She only hoped it

__ _____ ___ _____."

a woman. Talking to her.

to learn the language
n her cell — most of
woman was speaking

tried to make her eyes
cruciating it felt like
l.

ght. Somehow, she had
k and terrible choco-

y?" she asked. "I speak

You've been asleep for
n. "I'm Melanie. What's

t you, Simone. I'm glad to

CHAPTER SIXTEEN

FAR FROM ABIDJAN

As soon as Simone woke, she knew she was not alone.

Her vision was too blurred to see who — or what — was in the cell with her. She only hoped it wasn't the mamba.

" --, ---'-- -------! ---'-- ---- ------ --- -----."

It wasn't a snake; it was a woman. Talking to her. In English.

Simone had been trying to learn the language by reading the old newspapers in her cell — most of them were in English — but the woman was speaking too fast for her to understand.

Shakily, Simone sat up and tried to make her eyes focus. She had a headache so excruciating it felt like a drill was boring into her skull.

At least I'm alive, she thought. Somehow, she had recovered from eating that dark and terrible chocolate. That last *Palet d'Or*.

"Can you speak more slowly?" she asked. "I speak English very little."

"I said, oh, you're awake. You've been asleep for hours," answered the woman. "I'm Melanie. What's your name?"

"Simone."

"Well, it's nice to meet you, Simone. I'm glad to see you're OK."

Gradually, Simone's eyesight was returning. Her cell looked much the same as it always had. Grim and gray.

The woman — Melanie — was sitting against the wall on the opposite side of the cell. Her hair was bedraggled and her shirt was torn. She looked tired. And scared.

"Are you a supertaster, too?" Simone asked.

"A what?"

"Do they make you taste the chocolate?"

Melanie shook her head, confused. "No . . ."

"So then why are you here?"

"I've been asking myself the same question."

Now that she was fully conscious, Simone was remembering more and more about her excruciating experience eating the chocolate. And about the memories — of her past, of her family, of her home — that the chocolate had brought back to her.

A tear slid down her cheek.

"Has the bird been here?" she asked.

She didn't know why it seemed important, but it did. She could tell by the sky that it was late in the afternoon. A full day had passed. Or had it been several days? There was no way to tell.

"Bird?"

"A green bird with a long tail?"

"Oh! Yes. About an hour ago. He kept squawking. He seemed angry."

"He has hunger. He has anger if you do not feed him."

"Just like my daughter." Melanie smiled — sadly. "And they keep you here . . . to taste chocolate? Against your will?"

Simone nodded.

Melanie was silent a moment, absorbing this strange and terrible information.

"Where are your parents?" she asked finally.

"I do not know. For three years."

"They must miss you very much."

"Then why did they give me to these bad people?" Simone blurted out.

"I don't know," said Melanie. "But I bet it was because they love you and they thought you would have a better life with them. If your parents knew what it was like, I'm sure they would try to rescue you."

"You think so?" asked Simone in small voice.

Melanie crawled over and grasped Simone's hands. "Yes, I think so."

Simone smiled gratefully. "Your daughter misses you, too. I know it."

"I just hope she's OK. She's a tough girl, but she's

never been on her own for such a long time. . . ." Melanie trailed off. "The last time I saw her, we had a fight. Well, not a fight really. But we were angry at each other. She said . . . she said I wasn't her real mother . . . I adopted her, you see."

Simone nodded. "Probably she is not angry at you. Probably she is angry at her old parents. For giving her away."

Melanie looked at Simone in surprise. "I never thought of that! You may be right."

She released Simone's hands. "Where did you grow up?"

"The countryside. East of Abidjan."

"Abidjan? That's in Africa, isn't it?"

Simone laughed. Was this woman serious? "Who does not know where Abidjan is? It's the biggest city in the country."

"What country?"

"This country. The Cote d'Ivoire."

The older woman looked shocked. "We're in the Cote d'Ivoire? I had no idea we traveled so far . . ."

Simone thought about it: all this time, she'd simply assumed they were in her home country. But she'd been asleep when she arrived. She had no idea how far she'd traveled either.

"Actually, I don't know where we are," she admitted.

In truth, they could be far, far from Abidjan. They could be anywhere in the world.

"You there! Get up!" Daisy was outside their cage, turning the lock.

"Me?" Melanie asked.

"Yes, you. They want to talk to you."

"Whatever you do, don't eat any chocolate," Simone whispered.

Melanie nodded and stood shakily to her feet.

A short time later, a wretched-looking Mel was escorted out of the Tasting Room.

"Just like I thought — that woman knows nothing," said Dr. L. "Why is she here? It's her daughter we want."

"Precisely, darling," said Ms. Mauvais. "Precisely."

"I see." Dr. L smiled thinly. "Nice work, Hugo."

The chef bowed his head, his dark glasses glinting.

SECRET MESSAGE

DEAR READER:

DO NOT BE ALARMED!

WE WRITE TO YOU WITHOUT THE KNOWLEDGE OF THE WRITER OF THIS BOOK—THAT SHAMELESS CRETIN WHO CALLS HIMSELF PSEUDONYMOUS BOSCH. HOPEFULLY, YOU WILL FIND THIS NOTE BEFORE HE DOES.

PSEUDONYMOUS BOSCH IS NOT WHO HE SAYS HE IS. HE IS A LIAR AND A FRAUD. DO NOT BELIEVE A WORD HE WRITES.

THE MIDNIGHT SUN IS NOT AN EVIL ORGANIZATION OF BLOOD-THIRSTY ALCHEMISTS. WE ARE A PEACEFUL GROUP OF DOCTORS AND SPIRITUALISTS WHO HAPPEN TO SHARE A PASSIONATE LOVE OF GLOVES.

IT IS TRUE THAT WE WANT TO KNOW THE SECRET. BUT IT IS ONLY BECAUSE WE WANT TO SHARE ITS FRUITS WITH THE WORLD.

THE TERCES SOCIETY PRETENDS TO GUARD THE SECRET OUT OF PRINCIPLE, BUT IN REALITY THEY ARE SELFISH AND GREEDY AND WANT IT FOR THEMSELVES. IT IS THE TERCES SOCIETY THAT MUST BE STOPPED!

WE INVITE YOU TO COME TO ONE OF OUR MEETINGS AND FIND OUT FOR YOURSELF. YOU WILL BE SURPRISED BY HOW MUCH WE CAN OFFER A PERSON LIKE YOU.

A LONG LIFE—A VERY LONG LIFE—IS ONLY THE BEGINNING.

SECRETLY,
THE MIDNIGHT SUN

CHAPTER SEVENTEEN

Family Dinner

Family dinner. Now *that* was an oxymoron, thought Max-Ernest.

Never once in his life had he experienced anything like a family dinner.

Dinner with his parents? — yes.

Dinner as a family? — no.

For years, he and his parents had all lived in the same house. Every night, they'd all eaten at the same time and at the same table. But it was never the same dinner. Never a *family* dinner.

Rather than share, his mother had made one dinner, his father another.

Night after night, his parents sat across from each other, refusing to acknowledge each other's existence let alone each other's food. Max-Ernest, meanwhile, had been expected to eat everything: his mother's dinner *and* his father's.

The result: a lot of stomachaches.

Things had improved slightly last year when his parents had — literally — split their house down the middle, his father moving his half-house across the street. Now Max-Ernest could go back and forth between his two dinners rather than having to eat them both at once.

Tonight, though, something radical was going to

take place. He and his mother and his father were all
going to have dinner together.

As a family.

The same dinner.

That was the plan, anyway.

It all started with Max-Ernest's allergies:

Tonight, like all Tuesday nights, was supposed to be spaghetti night in both Max-Ernest's half-households. Due to his wheat allergy, Max-Ernest could eat only gluten-free pasta. Unfortunately, all the gluten-free spaghetti was gone last Sunday when Max-Ernest's mother went to the supermarket. Why? Because Max-Ernest's father had taken the last package. As Max-Ernest's mother learned when she found herself in line behind Max-Ernest's father at the checkout stand.

There was, by all reports, a brief tussle that ended in gluten-free spaghetti spilling all over the supermarket floor. Who was at fault Max-Ernest would never learn because, strangely, each of his parents blamed him- or herself:

"I don't know what came over me," said his mother. "I just grabbed at that box as if it was the last spaghetti on earth. I'm ashamed of myself. Everybody was staring!"

"I felt so foolish," said his father. "We were squabbling like two-year-olds in a sandbox. The whole store was looking at us! Why I couldn't just give that box to your mother I'll never know."

Max-Ernest had trouble imagining the conversation that ensued after the spaghetti spill; he'd never heard his parents say more than two or three words to each other. But, apparently, instead of escalating the fight, his parents had reconciled. At least to the point of agreeing to have dinner together. At a restaurant, naturally. So they wouldn't fight over who was to cook or whose half-house to eat at.

For years, Max-Ernest had dreamed of something like this. But now that it was really happening, he felt nauseous. He wouldn't be able to eat a thing, he thought. Gluten-free or otherwise.

There were simply too many obstacles to navigate.

Left undecided, for example, was whether the three of them would drive to the restaurant in one car or two. If one car, what if his parents fought on the way and they never made it to dinner? If two, whose car would Max-Ernest go in?

And that was just getting there.

At the restaurant, would he be expected to eat two dinners as he was accustomed to (but which seemed excessive under the circumstances) or would he be permitted to order just one dinner? Would he be able to talk to both his parents at once for the first time? Would one parent be offended if he talked to the other?

Family dinner.

Correction: not an oxymoron, a *nightmare*, Max-Ernest thought.

As it turned out, all Max-Ernest's worries were for naught.

Just two minutes and thirty-five seconds before they were supposed to leave — yes, he was counting the seconds — a teary-eyed Cass arrived on his mother's half-doorstep.

"It's an emergency," she whispered. "Wherever you were going, tell your mom you can't go!"

"Great!" exclaimed Max-Ernest. "That's totally . . . great!"

"Wait, now are *you* being sarcastic?"

"No, I just didn't want to have to go to dinner. . . ."

When he spoke to his parents, Max-Ernest received an even bigger shock than he'd received when his parents announced the dinner plans in the first place:

"No problem — we'll be fine without you!" said his mother, smiling at his father. "There's leftover tabbouleh in the fridge. Or your father can give you money for delivery. He's always so generous!"

"Great — enjoy your night at home!" said his father, smiling at his mother. "Order in if you want. But your mom's tabbouleh looks terrific! That's what I'd have . . ."

A moment later, they waved good-bye as cheerfully as if they'd been planning on dinner for two all along.

Overnight, his parents had gone from acting like their whole worlds revolved around their son to being completely indifferent to his presence.

What had happened?

Max-Ernest didn't know whether to be happy or sad or disappointed or relieved or grateful or angry.

So he decided to save emotions for later.

As a place for a young survivalist — or anyone else — to find comfort, Max-Ernest's mother's half-house left something to be desired. It was an elegant but cold place decorated with hard, sharp objects. More troublingly, an entire side of the half-house was boarded up with plywood where Max-Ernest's father's half-house had been sawn off. Navigating the half-house was difficult for anyone who wasn't used to it (and sometimes even for people who *were* used to it).

Nonetheless, it was in Max-Ernest's mother's living room that Cass now found herself pacing back and forth.

I won't go into detail about Cass's confession; I like her too much to embarrass her that way. To her credit, she told Max-Ernest everything. From her foolishly bringing up the Tuning Fork in Chef Hugo's class to her even more foolishly handing him the fork an hour before.

There were, however, two words missing from her long, solemn soliloquy:

"You didn't say I'm sorry," said Max-Ernest, sitting on his mother's favorite polished stone bench, his spiky hairs bristling like the quills of an angry porcupine.

"Why should I apologize?" asked Cass, who in her agitation was pacing more and more rapidly.

"You lied."

"Not really. I just didn't tell you everything. The note from Hugo said I couldn't . . . Ow!" Cass exclaimed. (Cass, pacing, had bumped her shin into the corner of a sleek glass coffee table.)

"No, you lied," said Max-Ernest, ignoring Cass's injury. "You told us the reason it was so important to find the Tuning Fork was that Pietro was testing us. But he wasn't, was he?"

"No, not really, but I had to say something . . . Ow!" Cass exclaimed again. (Cass, recoiling from the coffee table, had backed into the plywood wall behind her.)

"No, you didn't," said Max-Ernest, ignoring Cass's second injury. "You could have just said it was important and not told us why. Or —"

"OK. I didn't have to lie," said Cass, holding the back of her head and fighting tears (whether of emotional or physical pain, I couldn't say).

"And you got us all worried for nothing. How 'bout that?"

"For nothing!? — my mom was kidnapped!"

"I didn't mean nothing in that way. Anyway, that's not the point. You should have trusted me. Friendship is based on trust."

"How do you know? You didn't even have any friends until you met me!"

"Well, how many friends did you have?"

Cass paused. She wasn't sure if his question was rhetorical or if he actually wanted her to answer. Either way, he'd stumped her.*

"All right. I'm sorry."

Max-Ernest looked stricken. "Don't say that!"

"What?"

---

*Do you know what a rhetorical question is? Wait — don't answer that! A rhetorical question is a question that's not meant to be answered.

"That you're sorry."

"Why? I thought you wanted me to."

"But you never apologize."

Max-Ernest could count on one hand — really on one finger — the times Cass had apologized to him in the past. And the one thing he liked less than Cass lying to him was Cass changing.

"Everybody's . . . different now. It's so upsetting."

"OK, whatever. I take it back then."

"Good."

They were silent for a moment, each lost in thought.

"Anyway, sorry your mom was kidnapped. I don't mean sorry sorry, I mean . . . that's . . . bad."

"Yeah, it is."

That ended their argument. For now.

"I have to tell Pietro, don't I?" Cass said, sitting down on the bench next to Max-Ernest. (I can say with some certainty that Cass meant this as a rhetorical question, but he answered nonetheless.)

"Yes . . . no," Max-Ernest replied.

"What do you mean?"

"Well, yes, you have to tell him, it's your duty as a Terces member. But no, you can't tell him because there's no way to reach him," Max-Ernest explained. "Yo-Yoji told me that Pietro and Lily just left for

Africa to look for Owen. They haven't heard from him and they're worried. Lily even canceled Yo-Yoji's violin lessons. How 'bout that?"

"Well, then we have to go, too!" said Cass, standing up again. "I bet that's where Hugo's going with my mom."

"How're we going to go to Africa? That's ridiculous. You never make sense. We'll never be allowed."

"Well, my mom's not around to stop me, is she?"

"Maybe we can help from here."

"How?"

"I don't know — why don't we blow up the picture in *We* and see if there're any clues we missed earlier? For starters."

Cass opened her mouth, about to dismiss his idea. Then she gave him a small, grudging smile. "Actually, that's not such a bad idea. For starters."

Max-Ernest small-grudging-smiled back. "Hey, do you want an ice pack? My mom keeps lots of them in the freezer for when people hurt themselves."

Cass shook her head. She wanted to get on with the job at hand as soon as possible.

Cass had never been to Yo-Yoji's house before.

Under normal circumstances she would have resisted going: what if he didn't want her there? what if

his parents said something embarrassing? what if the
other kids at school found out? (Last year, a rumor had
gone around school that she and Yo-Yoji had crushes
on each other and they'd never quite lived it down.)

But these were anything but normal circumstances; and of the three young Terces members, Yo-
Yoji had by far the best computer setup.

So here they were.

At Cass's dream home.

Even as preoccupied as she was with her mission,
Cass couldn't help noticing that Yo-Yoji's house had
everything she'd ever wanted in life. (That's an exaggeration but it pretty well expresses her feeling upon
seeing the house.)

In the driveway, leaning against the side of the
house, there were mountain bikes and snowshoes
and kayaks and canoes and fishing poles and a trailer
that looked like it had seen more than its fair share of
camping trips.

When Yo-Yoji let her and Max-Ernest in, she saw
all the photos that Yo-Yoji's father had taken of snowy
mountain peaks and sandy deserts and river gorges.
And all the artifacts from around the world that Yo-
Yoji's mother had collected: six-armed goddesses from
India, carved Buddhas from Cambodia, handwoven
blankets and baskets from the American Southwest.

"Wow, your parents have been a lot of places, huh? That's so cool. Your father's a really good photographer." Her own mother never traveled (although it was true Melanie was famous among her friends for her collection of travel books).

Yo-Yoji shrugged. "I guess. He always has to use this old film camera he's had for forever. And then he can never get the pictures developed anywhere. It's kind of crazy."

"He should go to my grandfathers'. They have a ton of old cameras."

"Hey, Yoji — guess what," yelled a very young voice from across the house. "I still have my whole pudding left!"

It was a strange and unfamiliar sight that greeted Cass and Max-Ernest when they followed Yo-Yoji into the kitchen: a family sitting around a table. Yo-Yoji's parents, his little sister, Miho, and their littler brother, Gajin. The table was stained with some kind of brown and orange slop, and Gajin was jiggling a spoonful of chocolate pudding in front of his sister's nose.

Yes, it was family dinner. Just the way you see it on TV or in the movies. Well, maybe a bit more chaotic, but close.

Gajin smiled when he saw his older brother walk

into the room. "Hmm, looks good doesn't it?" he
taunted.

"Don't you just love chocolate pudding, Yoji? Isn't it the best thing in the world? Don't you wish you had more?"

"You think you're so smart waiting to eat 'til everybody finishes, but nobody cares!" said Miho in a cutting, older-sister kind of way. But the way she was looking at his pudding you could tell she wished it was hers.

Undeterred, Gajin put the spoon in his mouth and savored it slowly. "Yummmmmmmmmmmmmmmmmm," he said, drawing the sound out as long he could.

"O-M-G, you are so immature!"

Unable to take it any longer, Miho grabbed her brother's full bowl of pudding and took a big, heaping spoonful.

"Mom! Dad!" Gajin screamed. "She's eating my pudding!"

"Sorry, Gajin," said his father. "The phrase 'you asked for it' comes to mind."

"Can't you two at least pretend we're having a nice family dinner?" asked their mother. "If you haven't noticed, your brother has guests." She turned to Cass and Max-Ernest. "Sorry, guys — please excuse these monkeys."

In truth, Yo-Yoji's mother need not have apologized. Neither Cass nor Max-Ernest had anything to compare this dinner to. And it seemed normal enough to them. That was what was so *ab*normal about it.

Looking at Yo-Yoji's family, Cass felt an ache deep in her chest. Part of it, most of it, came from missing her mother. But another part, a buried part, came from missing something she'd never had.

"Have you eaten? Most of the soup wound up on the table, but there's still a little left — it's carrot lentil."

Max-Ernest hesitated. He was hungry. "Um, maybe we could —"

Cass interrupted. "It's OK, we ate already. Thanks."

"Is your mother away, Cass?" asked Yo-Yoji's mother. "She never returned my call yesterday. I need an ally if I'm going to fight all the robo-moms at the PTA."

On hearing this, Max-Ernest coughed. Cass gave him a quick kick.

"No, she's just, uh, working all the time," she said. "Can we talk to Yo-Yoji for a second?"

"*Yo*-Yoji?" repeated his father, eyebrows raised.

"Didn't you know? That's what his friends call him," said his sister. "He thinks it's cool."

Red-faced, Yo-Yoji gave his sister a threatening look, then beckoned his friends out of the room.

Yo-Yoji's bedroom looked liked it belonged in another house.

Rather than being full of ethnic artifacts, Yo-Yoji's room was a shrine to popular culture. Rock posters were taped at random all over the walls. On the floor, game consoles and musical instruments were strewn along with discarded pants and T-shirts. The only part of the room that wasn't cluttered with mess was the illuminated glass shelf that held Yo-Yoji's carefully arranged sneaker collection.

Max-Ernest pointed to a poster prominently displayed above Yo-Yoji's desk. "Was that that band you had from when you lived in Japan?"

"Yeah," answered Yo-Yoji, kicking a purple skateboard out of the way so his friends could get by. "We used to still play together online, but there's no time anymore . . ."

The poster showed a picture of Yo-Yoji, guitar in hand, next to two Japanese friends, one with a green Mohawk behind a drum kit, the other with long bleach-blond hair holding a bass guitar. It looked like they were standing on the moon.

Cass studied the poster, impressed. "You guys went on tour? Like doing concerts and stuff?"

Yo-Yoji looked embarrassed. "Kind of, not ex-

actly. I mean we did a couple concerts — but they were in my garage . . ."

"Oh." Cass stifled a smile.

"I, um, made the poster myself."

Yo-Yoji took the news about Cass and the Tuning Fork with considerably more calm and equanimity than Max-Ernest had taken it.

"So, then, that means we're all good," said Yo-Yoji.

"What do you mean?" asked Cass, confused.

"You lied to me and Max-Ernest, just like I lied to you guys . . ."

"You mean about not being in Terces? That was completely different."

"Why? We were both following instructions. At least my instructions really came from Pietro."

"Yeah, but you should have trusted us," said Cass.

Yo-Yoji and Max-Ernest both looked at her.

"OK, fine. I should have trusted you guys, too. We're all three even," said Cass. "Can we get started finding my mom now?"

"Wait, but I never lied to anybody!" said Max-Ernest.

"I'm sure you'll get your chance, yo," said Yo-Yoji.

Max-Ernest furrowed his brow. He might not have been sure how he was feeling, but if I had to describe his emotional state I might say it was confused, dissatisfied, and slightly resentful.

Within minutes, Yo-Yoji had scanned all the pictures from *We* and they were examining pixels on his laptop computer.

Apart from the cover photo showing the Skelton Sisters holding a baby, and the two-page picture of them with Ms. Mauvais and the "orphans," there was one other picture. It showed three grinning boys in gray cloaks holding a long green snake as if it were a pet.

Here is the caption:

Orphans playing with the orphanage's very own West African Green Mamba. A venomous snake known for its fast speed, the Green Mamba is normally very dangerous. But, according to orphanage officials, this one is quite tame, having been rescued as a baby in the rainforest and raised at the orphanage.*

"Do you think you can really tame a snake like that?" asked Max-Ernest skeptically. "They have really small brains."

"I don't know," said Yo-Yoji. "But I know this: if there's a West African snake, then they're in West Africa, right? That leaves out East Africa. We narrowed it down to half the continent!"

"Actually, we already knew the plantation was in the Cote d'Ivoire, which is in West Africa, so that's not really that helpful," said Cass.

"Oh, right," said Yo-Yoji, deflated. "Well, what about the rainforest part — does that help?"

*As a side note: to the best of my knowledge, it is impossible to tame a mamba. Either the snake was defanged or something else was going on in this picture.

"Maybe," said Max-Ernest. "We could start by figuring out what parts of Cote d'Ivoire have rainforest and go from there. How 'bout that?"

An online search revealed that most of Cote d'Ivoire's rainforest was in the southeastern parts of the country. However, the rainforest was so large they couldn't use that information alone to pinpoint the plantation.

"What about the bird in the other picture?" said Max-Ernest. "Maybe it's like the Northwest Southeast African Go Five Blocks and Turn left Rainforest Parrot or something?"

Yo-Yoji laughed. "That was kind of funny, dude."

"Really?" Max-Ernest smiled, gratified.

"The bird's not identified the way the snake was," said Cass, who was feeling a creeping sense of despair again.

"So maybe *we* can identify him," said Yo-Yoji. "My parents have a lot of bird books. They're into bird-watching and stuff. They call it *birding*."

"Birding? That's weird," said Max-Ernest. "Like if you collect stamps, you're *stamping*. Or if you collect tennis shoes, like you, you're *shoeing* —?"

Not bothering to answer, Yo-Yoji zeroed in on the image of the green bird and enlarged it until the bird almost filled the screen.

"His back is to us," said Cass. "How are we going to identify him from his back?"

"At least we can see he has that really long tail. And look, there's that yellow Mohawk on the top of his head. That could help."

"Sure, if he wants to join your band."

"Ha ha," said Yo-Yoji, who clearly did not find her joke funny. "Now just a second —"

Yo-Yoji left the room for a minute and returned with a stack of books with names like *The Avian Encyclopedia* and *Hello Birdie* and *Fine Feathered Friends*.

"You weren't kidding — that's a lot of bird books," said Cass.

"Maybe if we just look for African birds in the indexes that would narrow it down," said Max-Ernest. "How 'bout that?"

This approach made sense to the others, and for over half an hour, they pored over pictures of ostriches and albatrosses, falcons and flamingoes, pelicans and loons. Alas, there were many green birds, but not one with a long tail and a yellow Mohawk.

Getting frustrated, Cass started looking through a book that Max-Ernest had discarded because it was called *Birds of the Americas* (and thus unlikely to help them identify an African bird).

She froze after flipping only a few pages.

"Hey, guys," she said slowly. "What if they're not in Africa at all?"

"What do you mean?" asked Max-Ernest.

"Well, do you think it's possible Ms. Mauvais would just pretend they were in Africa?"

"You mean like in order to confuse the Terces Society and send us on a wild-goose chase all over the world? Yes. Definitely," said Yo-Yoji.

"Well, look at this —"

Cass turned the book around so they could see the photograph of the big-eyed bird she'd been staring at. The bird had a red chest and had a yellow crest atop its head. The rest of the bird was bright green. Next to the photo, there was a smaller picture of the bird from behind — showing its exceptionally long tail.

There was no mistaking it: this bird was the bird in *We* magazine.

"It's called a quetzal. It's the national bird of Guatemala," said Cass, turning the book around to face her again.

"So then they're in Guatemala?!" Max-Ernest shook his head, thinking about all the time they'd just wasted on African birds.

Cass scanned the rest of the entry on the quetzal. "It says the bird could be anywhere in Central America."

Yoji typed on the computer, pulling up information on Central America. "So that means they're in . . . ," he started reading aloud, "Belize, Costa Rica, El Salvador, Guatemala, Honduras, Nicaragua, or Panama."

"Great. Now we're worse off!" Cass groaned. "It was easier when it was just the Cote d'Ivoire."

"Wait — what about the snake? Why's there the African snake if they're in Central America? That doesn't make any sense," said Max-Ernest.

The three friends looked at each other in consternation. So much for Central America.

"Hey guys, you see that —?" Yo-Yoji pointed to the computer screen.

He'd just enlarged another section of the snake photo. Faded words were now visible — stenciled on the stucco wall behind the kids holding the snake:

PLEASE DO NOT FEED ANIMALS

And:

MONKEY CAGES 1/4 MILE ➤

"They must be at a zoo!" said Yo-Yoji. "Or at least a place that used to be one."

Max-Ernest nodded, excited. "That would explain how there could be a Guatemalan bird and an African snake."

"Yeah, but we still don't know where the zoo is," said Cass. "It could be in Africa or Central America or anywhere."

"Actually, we know it's neither of those places," said Max-Ernest.

Cass looked at him in surprise. "What do you mean?"

"First of all, the signs are in English. Not French or Spanish. And you know what else — see how it says *mile*, not *kilometer*? Most countries use metric — besides ours."

"So they're not even in Central America, they're like in . . . North America?" Cass couldn't quite absorb the rapid change of locations.

"How 'bout that?"

Yo-Yoji smiled. "Pretty smart."

Max-Ernest grinned. "Now all we have to do is figure out which zoos are big enough to hide a chocolate plantation."

"So I guess we might get to go find your mom after all, Cass," said Yo-Yoji.

Cass nodded, beginning to tear up again — but this time from gratitude, not despair. "Thanks, you guys," she whispered, feeling in a rush just how lucky she was to have such great friends.

Just then, Yo-Yoji's little brother walked into Yo-Yoji's room unannounced. He was balancing three bowls on a tray, and his face was streaked with tears.

"Mom made me make more pudding for everybody, but there wasn't any more chocolate, so we made vanilla," he said. "It's kind of lumpy."

"Uh, I'm not really hungry," said Cass, backing away from unappetizing bowls of gelatinous gray gop.

"Me neither, dude," said Yo-Yoji. "Sorry."

"Max-Ernest will eat it. He's not allergic to vanilla," said Cass.

"Yeah, but what if I don't . . . like it?" Max-Ernest protested.

"I told Mom you wouldn't want it if I made it!"

Starting to cry, Gajin dropped the tray to the floor and ran out of the room. Bowls of pudding splattered on the wall — and all over the shelf of pristine sneakers.

~A Clarification ~

I'm not anti-vanilla, just pro-chocolate. I wanted to make that clear for all the villains, oops! I'm sorry, I mean *vanillains*, out there.

You know who you are.

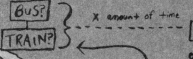

CHAPTER NINETEEN

logistics

Even with the combined Internet searching talents of three exceptionally smart young investigators, it took several hours to identify every zoo in North America. But only a few zoos were so big they might conceivably hide a chocolate plantation. By the time Max-Ernest's parents arrived to collect him and Cass, the kids had settled upon the likeliest candidate: *Wild World Wild Animal Park.*

Wild World was known for its "eco-hoods": mini artificial ecosystems that recreated various climate zones and animal habitats from all over the planet. The largest eco-hood in Wild World was their rainforest (at least they called it a rainforest), and it was there our friends hoped to find the Midnight Sun — and Cass's mother.

The question was logistical: how to get there?

THE PARENT PART

was easy.

Yo-Yoji's parents gave him a lot of freedom — especially in summertime. The next morning, when he said he was going to the beach with his friends, his parents were just glad he was going to be outside rather than spending the day on his computer.

"I think I'm going to crash at Max-Ernest's," he

said. "But if you want to talk to his parents, you should
call on my phone. 'Cause I don't know whether we'll
be at his mom's or his dad's — it's so confusing." (Yo-
Yoji was especially pleased with this last detail — it
seemed so plausible.)

The only glitch was that he had to leave wearing his bathing suit. He changed behind the trash
cans in back of his house, trading board shorts and
beach towel for a pair of jeans and his new favorite
T-shirt. (The shirt was decorated with a Japanese
character written graffiti style — the kanji, he'd been
told, for *samurai*.)

Max-Ernest's parents normally fought over every
second of his time. But they'd become so preoccupied
with each other (that morning found them having
coffee at Max-Ernest's mother's half-house; later
they'd be having an afternoon snack at his father's)
that they didn't offer a single objection when Max-
Ernest said he and Cass and Yo-Yoji were going to the
movies and that he wouldn't be home for a long, long
time because they were going to a "triple feature."

"A *triple* feature? That sounds triple-icious!" said
his mom, smiling at his dad.

"Triple-dipple-duper!" said his dad, smiling at
his mom.

Max-Ernest stared at his parents: were his eyes

deceiving him or were they holding hands? Catching his glance, they quickly let go of each other.

Max-Ernest left them with an uneasy sense that his parents' bodies had been taken over by another couple — an *alien* couple.

Cass's mother: well, that was the point, wasn't it? The upside of her having been kidnapped was that she wasn't around to forbid Cass from running off to save her.

THE HARD PART

was money.

When they pooled their resources they had only enough for the train tickets; there was no money left over for admission to the wild animal park, not to mention the trip home.

Then Cass remembered the credit card her mother kept in the drawer in the kitchen. It was for emergencies only, her mother had told her. But if her mother's very own personal kidnapping didn't qualify as an emergency, what did?

Perhaps money wasn't the hard part, after all.

THE TRAIN PART

was easy in one way, hard in another.

Destination: Xxx Xxxxx

Naturally, I can't tell you where their train was going, or how long the ride was supposed to be. To be more precise, I *can* tell you — that is, I am able to tell you if I choose — but I *won't* tell you. For reasons with which you are by now all too familiar.

However, I feel I *should* tell you about a minor, very minor, episode that occurred as they boarded the train. Only because it caused Cass so much consternation:

"After you," said Yo-Yoji.

"After me what?" asked Cass, confused.

"Um, for you to get on the train first . . ."

"Oh, right . . . You mean 'cause I'm a girl or something? That's dumb!"

"Whatever." Yo-Yoji shrugged and stepped onto the train.

Cass let Max-Ernest board before following her friends into the train car. Yo-Yoji's politeness was so weird and out of character that it had caught her off guard. But she shouldn't have snapped at him like that. He probably thought she was still angry at him. *Was* she still angry at him? she wondered.

Automatically, Max-Ernest slid over to the window, making room for Cass — just as he did on the bus every day during the school year. Cass was about to sit down next to him — just as she did every day during the school year — when she noticed out of the corner of her eye that Yo-Yoji had also slid over for her. Or started to.

Cass's ears tingled with panic. If she sat down with Max-Ernest, Yo-Yoji would *definitely* think she was still angry at him and he might even get angry at her. But if she sat down with Yo-Yoji, she would be making a big statement — after all, she sat next to Max-Ernest on the bus every day during the school year — and she knew from experience that Max-Ernest would be very hurt. She'd learned the hard way that he was more sensitive than he seemed; he might not be good at feelings, but he definitely had feelings nonetheless. Not to mention the fact that he was already sore about her lying to him about Pietro.

All things considered, she decided that sitting next to Max-Ernest was the less risky of her two options. (Of course, when I recount her thought process, it seems like she took a long time coming to this decision, but in reality it only took a second.)

If Yo-Yoji was in any way hurt or angry he didn't show it. However, let the record show that when Yo-Yoji again had the chance to offer Cass a seat — on the tram at Wild World — he didn't even glance her way.

CHAPTER TWENTY

An Invisible Chapter*

*FOR OBVIOUS SECURITY REASONS, I HAVE BEEN EXPERIMENTING WITH INVISIBLE INK. ALAS, I HAVE NOT YET FIGURED OUT HOW TO MAKE THE INK FULLY *RE*-VISIBLE.

h

not ear ove the scr ams f the   onkeys

olate plantatio   s

st

Mauv   s in h r pers nal chambers.

V   ry

un stre m d thro th curta n,   uminatin   er
gold   ress nd sign tur   diam ds.

r. L peere ver   r   oulder. "You l k lov y, my
d ling."

on th desk wa   of

ook d alarm ly lik Cas .
"Ar ou qu t cert n thos re her p ents?" he
a ked.
"   ."

"We'v b n so cl se in the   ! I don'

tt

R

erces soci

n

Midn

o squishy

99 of th m!

s

By now Ms M

r   l

said sternly.

q

z

e

nd again

ou can tell he's an African Elephant
and not an Asian Elephant by looking at his ear — see how it's shaped
just like the continent of Africa?"

The woman who said these words wore a khaki
jacket and matching pith helmet. Mosquito netting
hung over her face. She looked as though she were on
safari.

That is, aside from the microphone in her hand.
And the fact that she was standing at the front of
a tram.

She gestured to the tall gray animal standing
about twenty feet away. The elephant flapped its ears
obligingly — then spit water out its trunk, as if disgusted with the show.

"The African Elephant is officially listed as endangered. Does anyone know the difference between
a vulnerable species and an endangered species?"

The tram was silent — no one, apparently, was
able to answer the tour guide's question.

Then, in the very back, a girl with pointy ears
piped up: "Vulnerable means a ten percent chance
of extinction in the next hundred years. Endangered
means —"

The short, spiky-haired boy sitting next to her

interrupted: "Endangered means there's a twenty percent chance of extinction in twenty years."

Their taller, Asian friend, sitting across the aisle, shook his head. "I thought we said we weren't going to call attention to ourselves," he whispered. "You guys are such know-it-alls."

"Nobody can see us," said Cass defensively.

"Yeah, nobody can see us," said Max-Ernest.*

The tram had two sections hooked together like train cars; and from their vantage point the three young adventurers could see not only the elephants standing on the side of the road, but also the tram riders up front, gawking at the elephants.

The tram was painted with a camouflage pattern that suggested military maneuvers and jungle adventures, and on its sides were the words:

WILD WORLD
The World's *Wildest* Wild Animal Park
Go *WILD!* Go *WILD WORLD!*

But so far, the wildest part of the ride had been a too-close encounter with the tongue of an animal named,

---

*AS MUCH I LIKE THEM, I HAVE TO ADMIT YO-YOJI WAS CORRECT IN HIS ASSESSMENT OF HIS COMRADES. THEY WEREN'T BEING VERY CAUTIOUS. IT WAS JUST THAT CASS, THE SURVIVALIST, WAS UNABLE TO RESIST ANSWERING AN ENVIRONMENTAL QUESTION; AND MAX-ERNEST, THE FACTOID-OLOGIST, WAS UNABLE TO RESIST ANSWERING *ANY* KIND OF QUESTION.

according the tour guide, "Jerry, the Very Merry
Giraffe."

In his lap, Max-Ernest held the glossy *Welcome to Wild World* map they'd received when they bought their tickets. It showed how the animal habitats at Wild World were divided into eco-hoods — the ecological neighborhoods the kids had read about earlier — with names like *Misty Marsh*, **Dead Man's Desert**, and *Rainbow Rainforest*.

This last eco-hood, the rainforest, was by far the largest, occupying nearly half the area on the map. It was there, our heroes hoped, that they would find the hidden chocolate plantation and perhaps even the new secret headquarters of the Midnight Sun.

Currently, the tram was winding its way through the park's version of African grassland — **SERENGETI SAVANNA**. The sun was just starting to go down — this was, after all, the *SUNSET SAFARI* tram ride — and the landscape glowed gold. In the distance, a flamboyance of flamingoes was silhouetted, gathered around a watering hole.**

"It's kind of like we got to go to Africa, after all," said Max-Ernest. "How 'bout that?"

"Kind of," said Yo-Yoji, whose parents had made

(FACTOID #1: A *FACTOID* IS A USELESS PIECE OF INFORMATION. FACTOID #2: THERE'S NO SUCH THING AS A *FACTOIDOLOGIST*.)

**A GROUP OF FLAMINGOES IS ALSO REFERRED TO AS A *STAND* OF FLAMINGOES, BUT I PREFER THE WORD *FLAMBOYANCE* — DON'T YOU?

him look at one too many pictures of the real Africa. "And kind of not."

Cass looked out across the rolling, grass-covered hills of the manmade savanna. Maybe it *could* be Africa, she thought, if you ignored all the popcorn and candy strewn along the side of the road.

As they rounded a turn, an excited murmur rippled through the tram. A large yellow sign was posted on the hillside:

⚠ **WARNING** ⚠
ENTERING LION COUNTRY
KEEP ARMS INSIDE TRAM AT ALL TIMES!

But the only animal in sight was a zebra ambling away. If there were any lions nearby, he didn't seem very scared of them.

"Where are the lions? I want to see a lion!" shouted a child up front.

"Sorry — looks like they're sleeping," explained the tour guide. "Did you know the average lion sleeps over twenty hours a day? That's why they call them the king of beasts — because they're so lazy!"

The crowd tittered.

"Can you hear that ringing sound? Believe it or not, those are frogs croaking. We are now approaching Rainbow Rainforest."

This was our friends' cue to start paying attention. Cass, Max-Ernest, and Yo-Yoji all craned their necks, straining to look ahead.

Rainbow Rainforest definitely lived up to its name — at least if you weren't expecting a *real* rainbow or a *real* rainforest.

As soon as they crossed into the (so-called) rainforest, hidden sprinklers drenched the tram with water; it was like driving through a torrential downpour in the tropics. (Or maybe just like driving through a car wash.) Meanwhile, a strategically placed floodlight created a prism effect — a rainbow. Of sorts.

Unlike **SERENGETI SAVANNA**, which was wide open with views in all directions, the rainforest was dense and dark and, if you were somebody like Max-Ernest, extremely claustrophobia-inducing. The leaves were so big, and the trees so tall, that you couldn't help feeling small — as if you were looking at the world through the eyes of an ant.

"Out in the real world, more animal species live in rainforests than in any other type of environment —

and that's true here at Wild World, too. We have over twenty species of frogs, including one species that flies. And twelve kinds of monkeys — though no flying ones. You'll have to visit the Wicked Witch of the West to find those!"

As the tram drove deeper into the rainforest, the park visitors experienced a kind of sensory overload. While tropical birds cawed from every direction, the frog croaking grew louder and louder until it was almost deafening. The last rays of sunlight penetrated the trees from above, casting shadows in the shapes of vines and leaves, and creating dizzying patterns of light and dark, brown and green. The air was so pungent — with honey and cinnamon and vanilla, but also with musk and mold and much fouler scents — that they had to hold their noses.

All in all, the rainforest was not an easy place to look for a hidden chocolate plantation.

The kids heard no shouts between invisible plantation workers. They caught no whiffs of chocolate floating through the air. They saw no tractor tracks buried in the mud. No secret messages tied to tree trunks. No signs of illicit activity whatsoever.

Then again, all those things could have been there — and they still might not have been able to detect them.

Boldly, Cass walked up the tram's center aisle and asked the tour guide whether there had been an old zoo where Wild World now stood. But the tour guide said that if anything like that had ever existed, she didn't know about it. And it certainly didn't exist now.

Cass climbed back into her seat and stared out into the shadows. It was now almost completely dark in the rainforest — the only illumination coming from the lights of the tram.

"This is crazy. How're we supposed to see anything?"

"How're we even supposed to think?" echoed Max-Ernest. "It's so loud."

"Let's face it — there's nothing to see, yo," said Yo-Yoji. "We picked the wrong zoo. Or maybe it wasn't even in a zoo in the first place."

"Yeah, you're probably right," said Cass, slinking down in her seat as misery weighed down on her.

The possibility of not finding her mother was too horrible to think about; and yet she couldn't *not* think about it.

By the time the tram drove out of the rainforest, all that was left of the sun was a pinkish red tip peaking over a hill.

"Hey, what's that —?"

Max-Ernest pointed to a small gray tree — dead, by the looks of it — sticking out of the grassy hillside. A bright green bird was sitting on one of the tree's skinny, bare branches.

As the last rays of sunshine slipped away, the bird flapped its wings and lurched into the sky.

Tense with anticipation, all three kids stuck their heads out of the tram and watched the bird pass over-head. There was just enough light left to see its red belly — and then its long tail waving in the wind.

There was no doubt: it was a quetzal.

"Hey, you three in back! — heads back in the tram, please," came the order from up front.

As they watched, the bird flew straight toward the rainforest. Then veered left and entered the rain-forest directly above the point where they'd entered some twenty minutes earlier — just past the lion warning sign.

"Did you hear me? Yes, you with the backpack — and your two boyfriends. If you don't sit down in your seats I'm going to have to stop the tram!"

The kids yanked their heads back inside and sat down. Cass was so excited she didn't even get angry at the tour guide for calling Yo-Yoji and Max-Ernest her *boyfriends*.

Max-Ernest pulled a pen out of his pocket and drew an arrow on the map where the quetzal had flown into the rainforest.

They were in the right place, after all.

Somewhere, deep inside that manmade jungle, lurked the Midnight Sun.

CHAPTER
TWENTY-TWO

A Kitchen Witch,

a Fire Hose,

and a Swiss Surprise

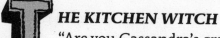

"Are you Cassandra's grandfather?"

"Who wants to know?"

Normally, Grandpa Larry was not very suspicious of strangers, but the woman standing on his doorstep looked like she'd been dropped there by a tornado. Her hair stuck out in every direction. Her lipstick was smeared across her face.

"Her principal," said the woman, breathing heavily. "You're listed as an emergency contact."

"What happened?" asked Grandpa Larry in alarm. "Is she all right?"

"As far I know. She's not home."

"So then it's *you* who's having the emergency? I didn't realize an emergency contact would be responsible for the entire school staff! What a curious system —"

"Well, that's not exactly —"

"By the way," Larry continued in a huff. "Since you're here, I'd like to have a word about assigning homework in summer. This report Cass is doing on tuning forks —"

Mrs. Johnson shrieked like a wounded animal. "Don't say that word!"

"What?"

"Tuning forks . . . Fork. That . . . dreaded thing is why I'm here," she said, gasping for air. "I . . . need it back."

Shaking, she tried to light a cigarette. It fell from her hand.

"It was my ancestor's," said Mrs. Johnson in an increasingly agitated and disjointed fashion. "She was . . . well, I never believed the rumors . . . so what if her fudge was addictive, that just makes her a good cook, right? It doesn't make her a . . . a witch."

Mrs. Johnson laughed a hoarse little laugh.

"But now I don't know what to think. She's punishing me from . . . the Beyond . . . for giving up the Tuning Fork . . . what other explanation is there? . . . I have this . . . this kitchen witch . . . you know those little cloth figures on a broom — doesn't everybody have one? It's hanging from a lamp and it keeps swinging and swinging."

"Perhaps an effect of the heat?" suggested Grandpa Larry.

Mrs. Johnson shook her head vehemently. "Sometimes I think I hear it laugh. . . . And that's not all . . . I . . . I keep losing at cards."

Grandpa Larry smiled. "Oh, we all have a bit of bad luck sometimes. That doesn't mean the ghost of a witch is seeking revenge on us."

"I'm . . . losing all my money. Soon, I'll be pen-
niless."

Larry shook his head. "Have you considered getting professional help?"

"There's only one thing that can help me!" Mrs. Johnson gripped Larry's arm. "Please. Tell Cass to get me my Tuning Fork back! I'll forgive everything. She and her horrid little friends can come back to school in the fall just like nothing happened . . ."

THE FIRE HOSE

"Lar-ry!"

When Larry reentered the fire station, Wayne was shouting at him from the most crowded corner of their crowded store.

"What's so important? I've just spent twenty minutes talking to Cass's school principal and you know how I feel about principals."

"I went outside to water and the old hose sprung a leak," Wayne explained. "So I thought, why not use a real-man's hose . . . ?"

He gestured to the big coil of fire hose at his feet.

"You were going to water the lawn with a fire hose? Isn't that a little like lighting a candle with a blowtorch?"

"That's not the point. Look what I found —"

Wayne pushed the fire hose aside, revealing the cardboard box behind it. "You recognize that, don't you?"

"How could I forget? You're talking about the birth of our granddaughter . . . her arrival, anyway," Larry amended.

"The funny thing is — I could swear it was all taped up," said Wayne, puzzled.

"Of course it was!" exclaimed Larry. "We were saving it for when Cass turned eighteen."

Wayne nodded, remembering. "And yet somebody . . ."

"But whoever comes back here?"

"Nobody . . . except Cass."

"Oh, no," said Larry, anxiously stroking his long, long beard.

Wayne shook his head, twisting the two long braids of *his* beard with his finger. "I wonder why she didn't say anything . . ."

"When would she have? This is the second day she hasn't shown up for work. And her principal said she wasn't home . . ."

"Are you thinking what I'm thinking?"

Larry nodded gravely. "The note."

He pushed the box out and opened the top. Mr. Wallace's letter was in plain view.

A few minutes later, Mr. Wallace hung up the phone.

He sat at a table in the middle of his beloved Terces Society archives, thinking. He was fairly certain he'd convinced Cass's grandfathers that he hadn't seen Cass since she was a baby, and that he barely remembered who she was. But, in truth, he was just as concerned as they were. Perhaps more so.

The question was: if Cass had found the letter, why hadn't she confronted him? Cass was so hotheaded. It was unlike her to delay something like that. Unless there was an emergency. Or there was some reason she was unable to reach him. Her grandfathers claimed she wasn't home. So where was she?

He could think of several possibilities, each more worrisome than the last.

"*Guten Tag*, Herr Wallace." A man in a pilot's uniform stepped into the trailer. The uniform was torn and muddy, but the wearer himself was no worse for wear.

"Owen?!" Mr. Wallace stared at the younger man in surprise.

"Why's everyone always so shocked to see me? Makes me feel like a ghost . . . Where are the others?"

Mr. Wallace smiled thinly. "In Africa. Looking for you."

"Ah. Well, they won't find me there. Or the Midnight Sun either."

"No?"

Owen shook his head. "I think they planted the Africa idea to divert us. I just discovered they're much closer. At the zoo, in fact."

"The zoo, huh?" Mr. Wallace looked at him thoughtfully. "Could Cass have made the same discovery?"

Owen chuckled, taking a seat opposite Mr. Wallace. "Cass? Are you kidding? She's always a step ahead of us."

"I know — to her detriment."

"Don't start on that again, Old Man," said Owen testily. He loved Cass like a sister and didn't like Mr. Wallace's tone. "The Society is much better off with her as a member. And she's better off, too."

"Oh, is that right?" Mr. Wallace snorted derisively. "She's missing, Owen."

"Missing?"

"That's what I said."

"So you think she went after them herself?"

"What I think is that I'd feel better if I knew where she was."

"Me, too," said Owen, his face serious.

"The girl must be protected at all costs," said Mr. Wallace quietly.

Owen nodded. "We agree on that at least."

He scratched his head thoughtfully. "Hmmm. Who do you think should pay a visit to the zoo? Large animal veterinarian . . . ? Concerned dad who's just lost his daughter . . . ?"

He took off his pilot's hat and started making faces in a pocket mirror, devising his new character.

CHAPTER
TWENTY-THREE
An
ANIMAL
ALPHABET

t was closing time at Wild World. Tired parents and whiny children spilled out of the park gates.

Behind them, a park worker in a giraffe suit waved good-bye.

The crowd thinned as it spread across the parking lot, some people stopping right away at cars parked in **SECTION A - ANACONDA** or **SECTION B - BOBCAT**, others drifting toward **SECTION C - CAPUCHIN** or **SECTION D - DINGO**.

"What's a *capuchin*?" asked Cass. "Is it like the color of a cappuccino or something?"

"No, that has nothing to do with it — it's an animal, not a drink," said Max-Ernest in mild disbelief. "Haven't you ever heard of a capuchin monkey?"

"Well, you don't have to be so snitty about it."

The normally talkative friends fell into a restless silence. The vast parking lot stretched in front of them.

Long after all the other park visitors had peeled away, Cass, Max-Ernest, and Yo-Yoji kept walking — all the way past **SECTIONS W - WOMBAT, X - XERUS, Y - YAK**, and **Z - ZEBRA**.

"If you're so smart, what's a *xerus*?" Yo-Yoji asked Max-Ernest, interrupting the quiet.

"Uh, I forgot, well, I mean, never heard of it," Max-Ernest reluctantly admitted. "But there are signs on the poles — it probably says." He turned around, about to go back and read about the xerus.

"No — it's not important right now!" Cass and Yo-Yoji said in unison.*

The highway that bordered Wild World was not intended for pedestrians, and for a few minutes they had to walk single file along the narrow strip of cement that passed for a sidewalk. Cars whizzed by, flattening the kids against the park's tall wrought-iron fence.

"What if somebody sees us?" worried Max-Ernest as a headlight briefly illuminated his face.

"Then they'll just think our car broke down," said Yo-Yoji.

"But we don't have a car. We're not old enough to drive."

"So then they'll think we're walking to the bus!" said Cass.

When the fence turned a corner, they turned, too. After they'd walked only a short distance, the highway noise faded away and they found themselves surrounded by darkness.

---

*SINCE WE'RE NOT ON THE SAME TIGHT SCHEDULE AS OUR YOUNG FRIENDS, PERHAPS I SHOULD TAKE THE TIME TO TELL YOU THAT A XERUS IS AN AFRICAN GROUND SQUIRREL. IT'S ALSO A GOOD WORD TO REMEMBER WHEN YOU'RE PLAYING SCRABBLE.

Cass reached into her backpack and took out a
flashlight. But when she turned it on they couldn't
see much more than the road below them, now un-
paved and lined with muddy tire tracks.

Where the road led they could not see.

Cass moved the circle of light to the right. No
longer wrought iron, the fence here was chain link
and topped with spools of razor wire. The light reflected in a yellow sign bearing a picture of a hand
struck by lightning bolts. Not a fence you'd want
to climb.

"Let's keep going," said Yo-Yoji. "There's gotta be
a back entrance somewhere."

"Yeah, but it's probably for people who work here.
Like veterinarians or whatever," said Max-Ernest.
"We'll need a pass or something —"

"Well, figuring out *something* has never been a
problem for us before, has it?" asked Cass, pushing
ahead.

The night was dark, and — except for a few moments
when the clouds parted to reveal a bright crescent
moon — they relied on Cass's flashlight to navigate.
(It was the kind that recharges whenever you move
it, so there was no danger of the battery dying.) They
each stumbled a few times — the road was dotted with

rocks and potholes — but for the most part they managed fairly well. I think eating at Hugo's restaurant must have sharpened their senses, just as he'd said it would.

They passed three back entrances to the park, but one was locked up with so many chains it would have taken Houdini himself to open it, and the other two had been welded closed. After forty minutes of hiking in the dark, they were all getting tired and discouraged, but nobody was willing to say so.

Without warning, Cass stopped and turned out her light.

"What is it?" asked Max-Ernest.

"Shh — listen."

They heard footsteps — very close by. But whose? And rustling. But from where?

Cass turned her flashlight back on and made a 360-degree turn until it landed on the park fence.

Behind the fence, terrified eyes stared out at them. Then bolted out of sight.

"Was that a deer?" asked Yo-Yoji.

"It was an antelope . . . well, I think it was," said Max-Ernest. "It could have been a gazelle. Or a —"

"At least we know we're still next to Wild World," said Cass, interrupting before he started naming every animal he knew.

They'd almost circled the entire park when a yellow light appeared in the distance ahead of them.

As they got closer, they saw that the light was emanating from a small booth next to a large gate. Behind the gate, the road turned into the park. Inside the booth, a guard was watching a football game on television.

The kids lingered underneath a pine tree about thirty feet away.

"You think we could climb over?" Yo-Yoji whispered. "I doubt the gate is electrified."

"I don't know, it looks pretty rickety. Plus, the guard would hear us," said Max-Ernest.

"Max-Ernest is right," said Cass. "I think we have to wait for it to open, then sneak in somehow."

"Is anybody else like totally starving?" Yo-Yoji grumblingly asked.

Cass pulled a bag of trail mix out from the bottom of her backpack. The trail mix — Cass's "super-chip" recipe of equal parts potato chips, banana chips, and chocolate chips — had been mashed and melted into a single lump.

Yo-Yoji made a face. "How old is that?"

"Do you want it or not . . . ? And don't take too much. That's all I've got."

Yo-Yoji broke off a handful. Max-Ernest carefully

extracted the banana chips — the only things in the trail mix he could eat. Then he put even those back.

"The chocolate might have gotten on them," he explained in a whisper.

After only a few minutes, although it felt much longer, they heard a vehicle approaching. Just in time, they slunk farther into the shadows.

A white van drove past, barely slowing as it neared the park gate. It had no back windows and no markings whatsoever. For a second, they could see the driver; he was pale and bald and expressionless, just like his vehicle.

The guard in the booth stood up straight and saluted the van driver. The gate opened with a screech.

"You think we should follow him in?" asked Cass.

"No way. The guard will see us for sure," said Max-Ernest. "He could turn on an alarm or something. Or maybe just come after us. He might even have a gun —"

"So how're we going to get in, then?" asked Yo-Yoji.

"Maybe he'll go to the bathroom," said Cass hopefully.

"I think we should make a run for it — then hide," said Yo-Yoji.

But it was too late. The gate was already closing.

"Guess we'll have to wait for the next one," said Max-Ernest.

The others gave him a look: no kidding.

In a short while, another vehicle passed by. It was a long truck with an open bed full of bales of hay. The three friends looked at each other and grinned: a hayride! Perfect.

The truck stopped at the booth. This time, the gate remained closed.

"Sign in, please." The guard handed the truck driver a clipboard.

"Thank you, don't mind if I do," said the driver, tipping his ten-gallon hat. His voice had a hint of a twang and his mouth was surrounded by a big handlebar mustache. He was a cowboy.

"Come on!" Cass whispered.

The three kids crouched down and run-walked toward the truck, keeping in the shadows by the fence.

"Don't get too lonely out here now," said the cowboy, handing back the clipboard. "G'night."

The kids climbed on just as the truck started to move.

"Ow!" Max-Ernest scraped his leg as he lifted himself over the side-rail.

"Shh!" Cass motioned for Max-Ernest to squeeze himself between hay bales beside her and Yo-Yoji.

The truck braked. The young stowaways froze. Hearts thumping in their chests.

The cowboy opened his door. "Hey, d'ya hear that?"

"Probably just an animal smelling dinner," said the guard.

"Guess so," said the cowboy uncertainly.

He paused, looking around. Then closed his door and shifted the truck back into gear.

The road was bumpy and the cowboy drove so fast it seemed the truck tires were in the air for half the ride. The kids' butts got a bit bruised, but wedged between hay bales they rode in relative safety.

The truck parked next to the van in front of a low warehouse building with three rolling garage-style doors, one of them open.

The cowboy jumped out and headed for the open door, a piece of paper in his hand. "Hello, anybody home?"

Cass, watching from behind a hay bale, was about to signal her friends to get off the truck when the bald van driver stepped out of the building, stopping the cowboy from entering. The bald man had a clear view of the truck; they would have to wait for another opportunity to escape.

"Well, howdy," said the cowboy, tipping his hat. "I got a truckload of hay for you courtesy of the friendly folks at Tapper-Perry Farms."

"I can see that," said the bald man tersely. He took the paper out of the cowboy's hand and scanned it.

"This isn't the price I agreed to."

The kids slunk farther down between the hay bales, listening.

"It's only a five percent hike. We just switched over to organic hay, so our expenses are up. All our farmin's sustainable now," said the cowboy proudly. "The alfalfa, the soy, all of it."

"Well, that's very nice for you, but I don't think our zebras give a rat's behind whether their hay is organic or mint-flavored."

"I thought this park encouraged conservation."

The bald man snorted. "I'm the operations manager. My job is to conserve money."

The cowboy peered into the warehouse. "Look at all that sugar. Is that healthy for the animals?"

"Maybe it's for people — not that it's any of your business," said the bald man, moving so that the cowboy couldn't look inside any longer. "Now you give me the price I was quoted or you just back that hay out of here. Matter of fact, I want a five percent discount."

The cowboy hesitated, fuming. Then,

"Fine. You have a forklift?"

"What's wrong with your hands? You can stack it all by the wall over there." The bald man pointed to the side of the building. "I'll cut you a check when you're done." He headed back inside the warehouse without another word.

"Jerk," said the cowboy under his breath. He started walking back toward the truck.

Cass measured the distance with her eyes. Should they try and make a run for it before he reached the truck? He would probably see them, but at least they'd have a fighting chance of escape. If they stayed on the truck, they'd be discovered for sure.

"OK, run!" she whispered.

It was the wrong decision.

She hadn't run ten feet when the cowboy grabbed her wrist with one hand and Max-Ernest's wrist with the other.

"You little rascals!"

Yo-Yoji stopped on his own a few feet ahead. "Let them go!"

"Not in your lifetime," snarled the cowboy. "No-

body sneaks on my truck and gets away with it!
Where'd you get on? The farm?"

"No, just outside the gate — honest! We're . . . animal activists," said Cass, thinking quickly. "We're here to spy on Wild World. We heard the elephants were treated badly so we came at night to see for ourselves."

"Yeah, the African Elephant is endangered," said Max-Ernest. "Do you know the difference between a vulnerable species and endangered one?"

"No, but I know you little punks are both vulnerable *and* endangered right now." He tightened his grip on Cass and Max-Ernest. They squirmed.

"But you're a conservationist," said Yo-Yoji. "Don't you want to help us?"

"Help you? I should tan your hides!" The cowboy shook his head in disgust. "But between you and me, that guy in there really ticked me off. I ain't in a mood to help this park out right now. So I'll just pretend I didn't see you."

He released his prisoners. Cass and Max-Ernest rubbed their wrists, relieved.

The cowboy chuckled. "You can set all their elephants free for all I care. Now git!"

The kids didn't need to be told twice.

*   *   *

As soon as he was alone, the cowboy spoke into his phone:

"Change of plan — I'm letting them stay to see what they find out . . . Don't underestimate those kids. You should have seen the way they handled me . . . ! You think I don't know it's dangerous, Old Man . . . ? Go ahead, call Pietro. I'm sure he would agree with me . . ."

Then he clicked off and climbed back into his truck.

As the three kids rounded the warehouse the moon came out and they could see Rainbow Rainforest looming in the distance. It was a dark mass about a half mile away, separated from them by the grassy hills of SERENGETI SAVANNA. From where they were it looked less like a rainforest and more like a storm front.

"My mom's in there somewhere," said Cass, staring. "Let's go — we've got to save her."

"We'll never be able to see in there at night," said Max-Ernest. "Remember how dark it was? — and that was when there was still a little sun left."

With Yo-Yoji's help, Max-Ernest convinced Cass they should find a place to sleep. They could enter

the rainforest early in the morning, before the park
opened.

After walking for about ten minutes, they settled on a spot nestled between two small hills. Boulders surrounded them, giving them a sense of protection.

"Do you think one of us should keep watch while the others sleep?" asked Max-Ernest. "I mean in case somebody sees us."

"That's a good idea," said Cass.

"For sure," said Yo-Yoji.

"So who . . . ?"

Max-Ernest's friends looked at him expectedly.

"Fine," he said after a moment. "But I'm waking one of you up after a couple hours. It'll be like a watch system on a boat. How 'bout that?"

Unfortunately, he didn't make it that long. He was so exhausted that he barely made it a couple minutes.

Soon, all three friends were fast asleep. As the minutes wore on, they snuggled closer together for warmth. Like puppies lying together in the grass.

Given the peaceful expressions on their faces, you'd never guess they were camping out in a wild animal park, exposed to the elements and only minutes away from the home of perhaps the most vile and villainous organization in the world, the Midnight Sun.

Shadowy forms stalked them in their sleep. But when one after another they stirred and looked briefly out at the starry night, they reassured themselves that they were dreaming, and that those shapes were only boulders.

With contented sighs, they resumed their innocent slumber.

Only when dawn came did they learn they were no longer alone.

CHAPTER
TWENTY-FOUR

CAT
FOOD

ax-Ernest's bed, like everyone's bed, sometimes got gritty. After a day of digging through stuff at Cass's grandfathers' store, for example.

Never, however, had he felt a pebble as large as the one now sticking into his thigh. It was practically a rock. In fact, it *was* a rock.

He shifted away from it, only to hit another, larger rock with his left hip.

What was going on? Where was he?

Still half asleep, Max-Ernest raised his head.

He immediately noticed two things:

First, he was not in bed. He was outside. And it was dawn.

Second, the air around him was very hot and moist. It felt almost as though there were an animal breathing down the back of his neck.

Come to think of it, it *smelled* that way, too.

Suddenly, Max-Ernest was gripped by fear. Fear worse than when Dr. L offered to operate on his brain. Fear worse than when Ms. Mauvais threatened to feed him to a shark.

Slowly, by inches, Max-Ernest turned around.

Until he faced a sight few people ever get to see. And fewer still live to tell about.

The inside of a lion's mouth.

The lion opened wider, stretching his black lips and baring his long incisors. His tongue, Max-Ernest couldn't help noticing, was just about the size of Max-Ernest's head.

The lion let out the biggest yawn Max-Ernest had ever seen. Or heard. Then the lion shook his mane and — blessedly — closed his mouth.

But Max-Ernest's relief was short-lived. Because a second later the lion was licking his lips and staring at him. It looked rather like the lion was contemplating breakfast.

"Stand up slowly," Max-Ernest heard Cass whisper from somewhere behind him. "Don't run — remember, that triggers their predatory instincts."

His heart pounding, Max-Ernest complied. He looked over his other shoulder. A few feet away from him, Yo-Yoji and Cass were already standing.

They were surrounded by lions on all sides. Six altogether. A pride. The boulders, it turned out, were seats. Thrones. For the kings of beasts.

"Now hold your arms out wide like the Amazing Alfred told us." Cass spread her arms, demonstrating. "Like you're really big, and too much trouble for a lion to chase down and eat. Like maybe you'd fight back."

Terrified, Mar-Ernest and Yo-Yoji followed suit.

"OK, start backing away — slowly."

Step by stumbling step, the three kids walked backward down the hill. The longest walk of their life.

The lions blinked at them but did not move.

Eventually, our young heroes found the courage to turn their backs on them and pick up their pace. Silently, they all thanked the Amazing Alfred for their lesson in lion safety.

Of course, it is impossible to know exactly what the lions were thinking, or whether or not the lion tamer's wide-arms trick convinced them to leave the kids alone. But, judging by their expressions, the lions didn't think the strange two-legged animals striding away from them looked very tasty.*

Most likely, the lions thought the three humans were out of their minds. The humans, after all, were walking straight toward the rainforest. And the lions knew better than to ever enter such a dangerous place.

*WHILE OUR SURVIVALIST HEROINE DESERVES CREDIT FOR GETTING HERSELF AND HER FRIENDS SAFELY AWAY FROM THE LIONS, I WOULDN'T NECESSARILY TRY THE SAME METHOD IF *YOU* EVER FIND YOURSELF FACING A LION. I SUSPECT THE REAL REASON THE LIONS HAD NO INTEREST IN EATING CASS AND HER FRIENDS IS THAT THE LIONS HAD ALREADY BEEN FED. BUT THAT'S ONLY SPECULATION.

CHAPTER TWENTY-FIVE

The garden of
of
Unearthly
Delights

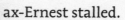ax-Ernest stalled.

There was no way to pass without getting wet. So much water rained down from the sprinklers at the entrance to Rainbow Rainforest that there was practically a waterfall.

"C'mon, if you don't hurry we might get caught!" Cass beckoned from the other side where she and Yo-Yoji were both standing drenched. "We don't know what time the first tram goes through."

"Just a second — I'm saving up my breath!"

"It's not like you have to swim . . ."

"OK, OK!" Closing his eyes, Max-Ernest sprinted through the downpour.

"Way to go, dude!" Laughing, Yo-Yoji patted Max-Ernest on the back while Cass ran ahead. "You can open your eyes now . . ."

Max-Ernest opened his eyes cautiously. Relieved, he shook his hair out like a dog.

"Darn it!"

They looked down the road: in her eagerness, Cass had slipped in the mud. She pushed herself up on her hands, sleeves dripping.

"You OK?" Yoji asked when he and Max-Ernest caught up with her.

"Fine!" said Cass, her ears tingling with embarrassment. "But look —" The remaining trail mix had spilled in the mud. There was no saving it.

"Too bad," said Yo-Yoji. "I was just going to ask for some. I'm way hungry."

"I know. Me, too."

As Cass shakily stood up, Max-Ernest pointed behind her — "Hey, is that a path?"

It was. In her fall, Cass had knocked over a bush, revealing a narrow footpath.

The kids wasted no time in following it.

At first the path was so winding and overgrown that they thought it might not be a real path at all. Or perhaps it had been made by an animal. But eventually it widened and before long they found themselves in a large, sun-filled clearing — the first time they'd seen more than a small patch of sky since they'd entered the rainforest.

"Yo, Max-Ernest — heads up," said Yo-Yoji, throwing something small and round at him. "Breakfast!"

Max-Ernest instinctively reached up to catch with both hands, not knowing what it was. But as soon as he felt the fuzzy texture, he was overwhelmed with a sense of horror. And he dropped the offending object — a peach — on the ground.

"Don't ever do that again," he said, pale and trembling.

"What? Throw fruit at you? I thought you'd be used to that after all those stand-up comedy routines of yours — just kidding."

"I have haptodysphoria."

"Don't tell me — another allergy," said Cass.

"No, it's a phobia. It's fear of peach fuzz."*

"Is that like one of your weird jokes?" asked Yo-Yoji, incredulous.

"I never joke about my conditions."

"I'll vouch for that," said Cass. "But it's too bad you won't try one, Max-Ernest — they're the best peaches I ever had."

After further investigation, they discovered the peach tree was not the only fruit tree in the vicinity; they were in an orchard. But an orchard unlike any of them had ever seen before. It was more like a botanical garden — exclusively for fruit. Each tree was labeled with the name and description of the kind of fruit the tree bore.

Most were fruits the kids had never heard of:

*UNCHARACTERISTICALLY, MAX-ERNEST'S DEFINITION IS INCORRECT. HAPTODSYPHORIA IS NOT, STRICTLY SPEAKING, A FEAR OF ANYTHING. IT IS RATHER THE UNPLEASANT SENSATION SOME PEOPLE GET TOUCHING CERTAIN OBJECTS — ESPECIALLY FUZZY ONES. LIKE PEACHES OR KIWIS.

MAGIC FRUIT

Take one bite of this mysterious fruit, and for a long moment afterward, sour things will taste sweet and sweet things sour.

STAR FRUIT

This yellow fruit originally came from Sri Lanka. When you slice it, it makes stars.

DRAGON FRUIT

Though its flesh is sweet, this fiery fruit has scales like the meanest dragon.

Cass tried to discard the hitchhiker fruit she'd picked only to have it stick to her shirt. (So that was what the sign meant about hitching a ride . . . !)

STINKY FRUIT

Known as the King of Fruits, the odor of this prickly fruit is so strong the fruit has been banished from many places in Asia.

HITCH-HIKER FRUIT

Don't brush against this fruit unless you want it to hitch a ride.

Needless to say, Max-Ernest wouldn't sample any of the fruit. "What are you guys going to do if I have an allergic reaction? You can't very well take me to the hospital," he pointed out. "So why do you think all these trees are here anyway? You think there was a fruit section in the old zoo? That doesn't really make sense."

"Wouldn't the trees be bigger then? Most of these don't look very old," said Yo-Yoji.

"Maybe Hugo planted them — and they're ingredients for chocolate, you know, like different fillings and flavors," said Cass.

Max-Ernest considered this. "Maybe. But then where are the cacao seeds? That's what you really need to make chocolate."

"What do cacao trees look like?" asked Yo-Yoji.
"You guys did all that research . . ."

"They grow kind of straight up with branches sticking straight out," said Max-Ernest. "They look kind of like cartoons. Also, they only grow in the shade. So they wouldn't be out here — hey!" Max-Ernest covered his head protectively. "Would you stop throwing things at me already?!"

"I didn't! But now I'm going to . . . !" Yo-Yoji laughed, ducking as something sailed past his head. "You threw that back so fast — who knew you could!"

"But I didn't . . ."

"Ow!" This time it was Cass who got hit — in the face. "It's neither of you, you buttheads! Look —"

A monkey was hanging by his tail from a tree limb at the edge of the orchard. In outline, he looked like a classic monkey, the kind of monkey you might see collecting coins for a street performer in an old movie. But his face was an unusually dark shade of brown and his fur was a fluffily perfect snow white.

In one hand, he held some kind of orangish red-dish fruit that resembled a deflated football. Laughing merrily, he picked seeds from the fruit. Ate one or two. Then threw the rest at the kids below.

"Hey, cut that out!" said Cass.

Yo-Yoji picked a seed off the ground — it was

purple — and threw it back at the monkey, narrowly missing him. "How do you like that, monkey-dude?!"

The monkey snorted unrepentantly. Throwing his half-eaten fruit to the ground, he dropped from his perch and caught a lower branch by one hand. With the appearance of ease, he swung himself to another tree — and disappeared into the rainforest.

Max-Ernest ran to the bottom of the tree the monkey had abandoned, and he grabbed the now squashed remains of the fruit.

"Yuck!" He held it as far away from his face as possible. Sticky white pulp oozed onto his hands. But as disgusted as he felt, he grinned with excitement. "This is it! This is a cacao pod. It looks just like the pictures."

"So those things he was throwing were cacao seeds?" Yo-Yoji scrambled to find more of the seeds on the ground.

"Forget the seeds — follow the monkey," shouted Cass. "Maybe he'll take us to the tree!"

They caught sight of the monkey almost as soon as they reentered the rainforest.

As the monkey swung effortlessly from branch to branch, the kids scrambled to keep up. Unfortunately,

the ground was covered with roots and puddles and
plenty of other less identifiable obstructions.

"I thought we were supposed to be more evolved than monkeys — I never realized walking was so slow and impractical," complained Cass, breathing hard. "Maybe in the future we'll go back to having monkey hands."

"But then we'd lose our opposable thumbs," said Max-Ernest. "That wouldn't make sense, evolution-wise."

"Yeah, but we'd have opposable tails like his — that would be cool!" She nodded to the white monkey hanging by his tail from a tree up ahead. He almost seemed to be lingering intentionally, as if he was waiting for them.

"They're called prehensile tails," said Max-Ernest. "And I don't think monkeys can write with them."

Yo-Yoji shook his head. "Don't you guys ever not talk?"

When they reached the monkey, he screeched at them — and leaped to the next tree.

"He wants us to follow," said Cass.

"That's great — as long as he takes us somewhere we want to go," said Yo-Yoji.

"Hey, is anybody paying attention in case we need to retrace our steps?" asked Max-Ernest.

But the others didn't hear him; they were already following the monkey deeper into the rainforest.

After another twenty minutes or so, their way was blocked by a huge fallen tree — with a trunk as wide as the kids were tall.

Cass and Yo-Yoji each grasped onto the tree, trying to climb over it — but they both slipped immediately. The tree bark was covered with slimy green moss. There was no way to get a foothold.

"Oh great!" Cass grumbled. "Now what?"

"I dunno," said Yo-Yoji, looking up. "And the monkey's gone."

Max-Ernest frowned in consternation. "What's this tree doing here anyway?"

"Blocking our way — what's it look like?" said Yo-Yoji.

"No, I mean — why is it here in the first place? It would have to be hundreds of years old to have such a big trunk. And they only built this rainforest like twenty years ago . . . how 'bout that?"

"So maybe it was here before," said Cass. "Anyway, the point is it's here now and we have to figure out a way to get over it."

Yo-Yoji looked closer at the tree. "Hey, Cass — give me your knife for a second."

"Why — you want to carve your initials?" she joked. "That's like polluting, you know. . . ."

"Just give it to me."

Cass dug into her backpack and handed him her Swiss army knife. Yo-Yoji dug into the bark of the tree with it.

"Here — see." He stuck his finger in where he'd carved a hole, then showed it to his friends. It was covered with white powder. Plaster.

"The tree's fake!" said Cass.

They all looked at each other, excitement on their faces.

"They must have put it here to stop people from getting through," said Max-Ernest.

"Like to a secret chocolate plantation!" said Yo-Yoji.

"Come on — there has to be a way in some-where," said Cass. "A secret passage or something."

But there wasn't. Not that they could find anyway.

On either end of the tree was dense brush. When they pushed it aside they found a hidden stone wall — topped with the familiar spools of razor wire. The wall meant they were probably right about the plan-tation being on the other side, but they were no closer to getting in.

Just as they were beginning to despair, the monkey swung into view above them. (He, obviously, had no trouble getting over the wall.) He shook his head, as if in disgust at their inability to swing from trees.

"Thanks for nothing," Yo-Yoji shouted to the monkey. "We thought you were our friend —"

Cass put her finger to her lip. "Hey, maybe you shouldn't shout so loud — somebody could be on the other side of the wall."

Yo-Yoji shrugged in annoyance, but he remained silent. Cass was right, of course.

"I think maybe he's trying to tell us something," said Max-Ernest, staring at the monkey.

Indeed, the monkey, no longer laughing, had swung down to a low branch and was pointing to the root ball of the fallen tree. That is, the fake root ball end of the fake fallen tree.

Max-Ernest was the first to make it to the tree roots, which were surprisingly large and elaborate. When you looked at them straight on, the twisting roots spread outward, creating the shape of a sun.

At the center of the roots was a large round door, and at the center of the door a large brass knob in the shape of a monkey's head.

Max-Ernest gave the knob an experimental turn. "It's locked."

"Is there a way to enter a combination or something?" asked Yo-Yoji.

Max-Ernest shook his head. "Doesn't look like it."

"Great. So there's a key then," said Cass in frustration. "How are we going to find the key?"

"Actually, I'm not even sure there's a keyhole," said Max-Ernest. "There's just a . . . mouth."

He pointed to the hole in the center of the brass monkey's face; it was exactly where a mouth should be.

"Super. Now, we're really not going to be able to open it . . . hey, cut that out!" said Cass angrily.

The monkey — the live monkey above them, that is — was throwing cacao seeds again. Cass's shouting only seemed to encourage him to throw more. She shook her fist at him.

He shook his head disdainfully, then tossed a seed into his mouth.

"Wait," said Yo-Yoji. "Here —"

He picked a cacao seed off the ground and handed it to Max-Ernest. "Put it in."

Max-Ernest looked skeptical. Nonetheless, he

carefully inserted the seed into the hole in the door-knob. It dropped like a coin in a slot.

"I think it worked —!"

He grasped the knob again. This time, it turned.

The door opened to reveal a narrow tunnel that ran the length of the tree. At the end was another round door, this one slightly ajar.

"Shh!" Cass put her fingers to her lips.

The others nodded. They didn't know exactly what dangers awaited them on the other side of that door. But that there would be dangers, of that there was no doubt.

CHAPTER TWENTY-SIX

LITTLE, BROWN PEARLS

They saw them as soon as they walked through the door.

Standing straight up. Arms stuck out to the side. Row upon row upon row.

Cacao trees.

Planted between rows of other, taller trees. For shade. (Or possibly to hide them from a passing airplane.)

They were just as Max-Ernest had described.

With one difference:

"Are they ... covered with snow?" Cass wondered aloud.

Indeed, it looked like snow had been accumulating on the trees for days, making big white mounds that weighed down the branches.

"That really wouldn't make sense," said Max-Ernest. "It's summer and it's pretty hot out."

"Duh, I just meant it looked like it —"

"Plus, there's none on the taller trees," Max-Ernest couldn't help adding. "Snow doesn't usually stick to one kind of tree and not another."

"It could be fake snow," said Yo-Yoji. "I mean, there was a fake tree, right? Maybe they're going to sell them at Christmas."

The monkey screeched at them, perhaps to say

good-bye, perhaps to tell them to stop arguing, then swung away into the cacao trees.

"C'mon," said Cass. "Let's keep going. But stay in the shade, under those taller trees. So nobody can see us."

When they got closer, they saw that the white mounds on the cacao trees were moving. There wasn't any snow at all, whether real or fake.

Rather, the trees were filled with hundreds, maybe thousands, of the white monkeys.

They chattered noisily, tossing so many cacao seeds — and the odd cacao pod — onto the ground that it seemed to be raining.

Beneath each tree was a gleaming golden pail that looked like something out of a fairy tale. Like a pail that might contain a secret potion or magic coins. Like a pail Hansel and Gretel might carry. The whole scene had a magical look about it, as if the trees were enchanted or the monkeys bewitched.

Occasionally, one of the monkeys themselves would drop onto the ground. He then would hop over to the pail and —

"Why are they sitting on those pails?" asked Max-Ernest.

"I don't know," said Cass. "It kinda looks like —"

Yo-Yoji shook his head in disbelief. "Why would anybody want to save . . . that?"

"Maybe for fertilizer?" suggested Max-Ernest, aghast.

Cass tensed. "Hey, do you guys hear voices?"

Her friends shook their heads, but they stopped talking all the same. They knew from experience that Cass's hearing was far more acute than theirs.

Quietly, they all crept farther into the shadows and flattened themselves behind the furrowed earth.

An icy voice carried in the breeze. "All our beans have been pre-digested by our specially bred capuchin monkeys. Our *mocha*chin monkeys, as we like to call them."

The three kids shivered at once. They all recognized the voice and it gave every one of them a chill.

"All these beans you see on the ground — they're the discards. The mochachins are very fussy. They insist on eating only the best and richest beans."

From their place in the shadows, the kids could see Ms. Mauvais leading a small group through the cacao orchard. She was covered head to toe in a white nun's habit — the sort with a headpiece that spreads out to either side like gull wings — but her porcelain-doll face was unmistakable. Her feet invisible beneath her robe, she seemed almost to be gliding over the mud and muck, as if she were suspended on a wire from above.

With her were the Skelton Sisters, dressed for the occasion in pink and purple camouflage as if they were part of some very girlish military operation. Montana Skelton held a video camera in her hand, Romi Skelton a microphone. The sisters were making some sort of film.*

Bringing up the rear: Señor Hugo, inscrutable as ever in his dark glasses.

Watching from the shadows, Cass stared at him, seething. This was the man who'd kidnapped her mother. Who'd manipulated her and broken his promise. She'd never hated anyone so much.

Apparently, she was making some kind of sound under her breath because Max-Ernest soon poked her. "Stop growling like that," he whispered. "They'll hear you."

Cass nodded, snapping out of it. There would be time for growling later. She had a job to do.

"When they're excreted by the monkeys, these superior beans are left perfectly intact," Ms. Mauvais continued, speaking into the camera. "But they've acquired a distinctive flavor unknown anywhere else."

---

*I PERSONALLY CANNOT TELL THE TWO GIRLS APART, BUT I HAVE IDENTI-FIED THEM RETROACTIVELY BY EXAMINING THE CREDITS ON THE FILM THEY WERE MAKING.

"So then the cocoa beans have to be, like . . . dug out?" asked Romi, making a face.

Something like a smile crossed Ms. Mauvais's frosty lips. "You don't imagine we do that ourselves! We leave it to our eager young initiates. Isn't that right, Alexander?"

She nodded in the direction of a small, unhappy-looking boy walking by with a golden pail in each hand. He wore a hooded gray tunic with a black sun embroidered on it — the insignia of the Midnight Sun.

"Oh my gosh, he is so cute!" exclaimed Romi.

She ran over to Alexander and grabbed him by the ear, causing the contents of a pail to spill out onto his leg. "Can we take this one home, Ms. Mauvais?"

"Yes, can we? Please," said Montana, grabbing the boy's other ear with her free hand and causing the other pail to spill. "We'll take very good care of him, we promise. We'll walk him and everything." She pointed the camera at her sister. "We're very good with little children, aren't we, sis?"

"Oh, yeah! We love animals," said Romi, not completely following. "That's why we're making a documentary at the zoo!"

"You mean in *Africa*," corrected her sister.

"Oh, right, *Africa*! It's so hard to remember where you are when you're on a rock tour!"

"Let the boy go, darlings!" said Ms. Mauvais through her teeth. "We'll talk about it later."

As soon as the Skelton Sisters released him, Alexander scurried over to a long trough and emptied what remained in his two pails.

More similarly uniformed — and similarly unhappy — children were bent over the trough, sifting through the monkey droppings. Whenever they extracted one of the precious cacao beans, they rinsed it clean and placed it in a special golden pail marked with the Midnight Sun insignia.

"See what diligent workers they are!" said Ms. Mauvais to the camera. "We call them our Pearl Divers because the cacao beans are like pearls — little, brown pearls. . . . Tell them about it, Señor Hugo. Señor Hugo is our master chocolatier."

He bowed, unsmiling. "Yes, they're the secret ingredient in my chocolate. *One* of the secret ingredients, I should say."

He patted the pocket of his chef's apron. As if it contained a world of secrets. Secrets he would never think of divulging to the present company.

"So all these kids in the gray dresses — well, some of them are boys but you have to admit they still look like they're in dresses — they're all orphans like from your orphanage?" asked Romi.

"Yes, but we don't think of them as orphans," said Ms. Mauvais, attempting to sound warm and kind for the camera. "They're our family. This is their home now."

Ms. Mauvais wiped her pale brow with her gloved hand; all the lying was apparently exhausting her. "And now, if you'll excuse me, I think we'll stop there . . . I trust you'll remove that unfortunate mention of the zoo."

"Then this charade is over? I may get back to work?" asked Señor Hugo, scowling.

Ms. Mauvais nodded. The chef strode away, hardly bothering to pretend he couldn't see.

During the course of the interview another person had silently joined the group. An elegant and very elderly man in a top hat. He leaned on a cane, waiting for the filming to stop.

Cass thought she recognized him as someone she'd seen over a year ago at the Midnight Sun spa.

When Ms. Mauvais's other companions had dispersed, he finally spoke up: "I'm sorry, but I don't think a nun's habit suits you, my dear. I'm used to seeing you in gold and diamonds." His voice was a throaty whisper. Even Cass had to strain to hear his words.

"Now I know why nuns are so ill-tempered," agreed Ms. Mauvais, leading him back into the shade. "Itamar, darling, you're supposed to be resting."

"I have three or four days of life left at best. Forgive me if I'd like to spend them on my feet."

"Nonsense," Ms. Mauvais protested. "You're nearly five hundred years old. They can't snatch you away that quickly."

Itamar pointed his cane at Ms. Mauvais. "I hope you're not getting sentimental, Antoinette. We chose you long ago for your heartlessness. That is what the Midnight Sun needs. Not maudlin concerns about my health."

The three eavesdroppers looked at each other. As interesting as the conversation had been thus far, perhaps the most interesting revelation was that Ms. Mauvais had a first name: *Antoinette.*

Itamar stretched his ancient mouth into a thin approximation of a smile. "I remember when your horse broke his leg. You were only ten years old. . . ."

"Not just any horse — an Arabian," said Ms. Mauvais grandly. "I trained him myself. He was my prize possession. The closest thing I had to a family after my parents died."

"And yet you killed him without shedding a tear!"

Ms. Mauvais looked for a moment as though she might object. "Don't worry. My interest in preserving your life is purely practical. I rely on your advice and counsel. No one else is sufficiently experienced . . . or sufficiently ruthless."

"Thank you. My advice now is to prepare for my death."

"But we are so close! Immortality is at hand. In a piece of chocolate, no less."

"So then it is as I suspected, Señor Hugo's secret recipe is a recipe for the Secret?"

Ms. Mauvais nodded. "Let's say it's a recipe for the recipe . . . We will save you yet."

"Perhaps. In the meantime, I am not the only one growing old. Even you, Antoinette Mauvais. Your two hundred years are beginning to show around the eyes. Or is it two hundred and fifty now?"

He touched the side of her face with his old gloved hand.

"Please don't mince words, Itamar," said Ms. Mauvais.

"I never do. If our organization is to survive, we need new members. Younger members."

"I know! Why do you think I tolerate those two

teenage trollops? Only so we can attract more fol-
lowers."

"Can you imagine kids joining the Midnight Sun?" Yo-Yoji whispered in the shadows. "What's the point if you're not old yet? I thought it was all about eternal youth."

"Well, if you have their elixirs and stuff, you never have to get old. Or it takes a lot longer anyway," replied Max-Ernest. "How 'bout that?"

"Oh yeah. So remind me then why we *don't* want to join."

"I don't know," said Max-Ernest. "Maybe because you have to wear a lot of gloves?"

"How about because they're bloodthirsty killers and they kidnapped my mom!" exclaimed Cass in an outraged whisper.

Lifting herself up slightly, Cass peered down the path Señor Hugo had taken — was that the direction in which she would find her mother? — but she couldn't see much beyond the rows of cacao trees and the fluffy white fur of the mochachin monkeys.

fter Ms. Mauvais led Itamar away, our friends stood up and took better stock of their surroundings.

About a dozen yards beyond the sorting trough, there was a large, barn-shaped warehouse sided in corrugated metal. As they watched, one of the gray-cloaked children picked up two of the specially marked golden pails and, teetering, carried them into the warehouse, leaving the door ajar.

Silently, Cass motioned that they should follow. She counted to three with her fingers, then they all walked as quickly and quietly as they could toward the warehouse. It seemed like an awfully long distance to be out in the open, but as far as they could tell nobody saw them.

Upon entering, they passed through an entryway that looked like it served as a dressing room for the children. Hundreds of the gray uniforms were stacked on shelves, and almost as many golden pails were stacked on the floor.

Once inside the warehouse proper, they found themselves gazing at dozens of gleaming stainless steel storage bins. The bins were so tall that each was equipped with a ladder to facilitate access.

"You there — pick those pails back up and follow me to the Test Kitchen!"

The kids froze. The voice was Señor Hugo's. Was he speaking to them?

No. A quick glance revealed he was down at the other side of the warehouse speaking to one of the miserable children they'd seen earlier.

But he was also walking right in their direction: in a moment, he would see them. There was no time to exit the building.

"Each of you — go jump in one of the bins!" Cass whispered, remembering how Caca Boy had hidden from the soldiers in a vat of cacao beans.

Max-Ernest started to open his mouth in protest but then thought better of it; this was obviously not the time to question a plan.

Without another word, Cass pulled herself up the nearest bin and disappeared over the edge.

Silently, Yo-Yoji and Max-Ernest climbed up the two bins on either side of hers and followed suit.

Max-Ernest looked into the well of beans and worried briefly whether the fact that he couldn't swim would be a problem. But then he closed his eyes, plugged his nose, and jumped.

He didn't immediately sink under the cacao beans and he had to squirm around and then scoop beans with his hands to cover himself. In a moment, he had burrowed down to the point where he

was almost completely surrounded by cacao beans,
only the tip of his nose sticking out. It was a strange sensation, but not entirely unpleasant.

So far, so good, he thought. Being buried alive really wasn't so bad. If only he could keep his claustrophobia from kicking in.

Max-Ernest was just congratulating himself on his success in avoiding panic when he remembered his chocolate allergy: was it the cacao beans themselves he was allergic to? And if so, would the beans have to get into his mouth to affect him, or would the allergens seep through the pores of his skin?

It was hard enough to breathe under all the beans; how would he survive if his throat started to constrict? Being captured by the Midnight Sun would almost be preferable.

Terrified, he waited for the telltale signs of an allergy attack.

There was no way to know when it would be safe to climb out.

Assuming Señor Hugo was gone, somebody else equally scary might be there. Then again, if they waited too long Hugo was likely to come back. Cass remembered that Caca Boy had come face-to-face with the monk when he emerged from hiding in the cacao beans; who would she see when she stuck her head out?

Cautiously, she shook her head from side to side, feeling the beans fall off like oversized grains of sand. Then she wriggled herself up enough to look around.

Just as she feared, there was somebody leaning over the edge of the bin, staring down at her.

"Aaah!" she shrieked. (Although thankfully not very loudly.)

Yo-Yoji smiled. "Scared much?"

"No!" said Cass, annoyed. "You just surprised me, that's all."

Next, each taking an arm, they pulled a silent and staring Max-Ernest out of the neighboring bin.

"You OK?" Cass asked Max-Ernest when they were all back on the ground.

Still closemouthed, Max-Ernest frantically shook cacao beans out of his hair. Then felt around on his face to make sure there weren't any strays.

"You can talk," said Yo-Yoji. "There's nobody here."

"Thanks. I'm fine," Max-Ernest said finally. "I just didn't want any beans to accidentally fall in my mouth."

Soon, they had all safely exited the warehouse through the back door

In front of them, a small sign pointed the way to someplace called **THE PAVILION**. They weren't sure what the Pavilion was, but since they also weren't sure where Cass's mother was, they agreed it was a reasonable place to start their search.

Rather than risking being exposed on the pathway, they chose the more difficult route of walking alongside it through the thick rainforest. After what would have been about a block and a half (if they were walking on the street rather than through mud and dense vegetation), they halted.

Peeking through the palms, they saw a round building large enough to hold an airplane or even a three-ring circus. It had a thatched roof held up by thick pillars of bundled bamboo. The building was surrounded on all sides by a wide covered porch decorated with wicker furniture and overhead fans. Silk curtains fluttered in the breeze. The whole place had the look of a luxurious tropical retreat.

The most notable thing about the Pavilion was that the entire structure was raised off the ground, like an enormous treehouse.

"That's gotta be where they are," said Cass. "This must be the Midnight Sun's new headquarters."

"It's a pretty good hideout," Max-Ernst noted. "I'll bet that roof makes it hard to see from above."

Yo-Yoji nodded in agreement. "Uh-huh . . . why do you think it's on stilts like that?"

"Probably to keep the lions out . . . or us," said Cass. "The question is, how do we get in?"

"We *could* just walk —" Yo-Yoji nodded toward the front doors, which were wide open. A steep wooden stairway led straight up to them.

Two sculptures carved from tree trunks — one of a bird, the other of a snake — stood sentry on either side of the doors. Otherwise, it looked as though nothing would keep them from entering.

The problem was: at least a hundred feet separated them from the Pavilion. The building might be camouflaged, but for them there would be no cover.

"Don't you think we should wait until dark?" asked Max-Ernest.

Cass shook her head. "I don't want my mom to have to wait that long. Plus, we're out of food . . ."

"So you really think your mother's in there?"

"Not necessarily. But we have to look . . ."

As they spoke, a plume of smoke erupted from

the Pavilion. Suddenly, the air was filled with a familiar bittersweet scent.

"Chocolate!" said Yo-Yoji. "Now we definitely have to go in."

Max-Ernest held his nose. "I hope I'm not allergic to the air . . ."

"Wait, I have an idea —"

Without telling them anything more, Cass started to retrace their steps.

An hour later, three young people wearing gray tunics and holding golden pails in their hands returned to the same spot. Anybody seeing them would have thought they were more child slaves — "eager young initiates," as Ms. Mauvais had called them.

"OK, keep your heads down and look unhappy —"

On Cass's signal, they stepped onto the lawn that surrounded the Pavilion. There was nobody around and they made it all the way to the bottom of the stairs before they were stopped.

"Can I help you?"

A tall, broad-shouldered woman hurried toward them from the side of the building. She wore a tunic similar to the children's but hers was bright white, and, as our heroes noticed immediately, she wore white gloves on her hands.

They all tensed. It had been awhile since they'd faced a full-fledged member of the Midnight Sun.

"Where do you think you're going? No initiates are allowed in the Pavilion, you must know that."

Cass's heart skipped a beat. It was Daisy. The woman who'd served as her prison guard at the Midnight Sun spa more than a year earlier. If Daisy recognized them, they were doomed.

"Señor Hugo wants this stuff in the Test Kitchen," said Cass, careful to keep her face shadowed by her hood.

"You sure he said the Test Kitchen?" Daisy hesitated, as if this were rather unusual.

"Yeah, he said to get it to him as fast as possible!"

"Ah, in that case . . . kitchen's in the back."

"Right. Thanks," said Cass.

Before Daisy could get another look at them, Cass and her friends quickly mounted the stairs.

Gold pails swinging, they passed between the snake and bird sculptures ("I think those are Aztec," Max-Ernest whispered) and entered the Pavilion.

CHAPTER
TWENTY-EIGHT

THE PAVILION

The interior of the Pavilion seemed almost to be a continuation of the rainforest outside.

Long, flowering vines dripped from a glass ceiling, and potted palms rose up to meet them. A twisting pattern of interwoven leaves and branches spread across the tile floor. In the center, a pool of water surrounded a reproduction of the famous Aztec Sun Stone.*

Apart from the luxuriant foliage, and the young interlopers themselves, the Pavilion's central room appeared empty. A deep silence pervaded the space, as if it hadn't been occupied for years.

"Where do you think everyone's gone?" whispered Max-Ernest. "It's like it was abandoned."

"I don't know," said Cass with a sinking feeling.

Including the front doors, the room had four exits: one for each point of the compass. They chose the one on the right —

Cautiously, Yo-Yoji pushed the door open. They found themselves tiptoeing into a long, curving hallway that seemed to circle the Pavilion's central room.

The outer side of the hallway was a curving glass wall overlooking a seemingly endless conveyor belt: a

---

*I ASSUME IT WAS A REPRODUCTION, ALTHOUGH I WOULDN'T PUT IT PAST THE MIDNIGHT SUN TO STEAL THE ORIGINAL FROM ITS HOME AT THE NATIONAL MUSEUM OF ANTHROPOLOGY IN MEXICO CITY. SOMETIMES KNOWN AS THE AZTEC CALENDAR, THE SUN STONE SHOWS HOW THE AZTECS MEASURED TIME (THEIR MONTHS WERE ONLY TWENTY DAYS LONG). AS I'M SURE CASS WOULD BE VERY INTERESTED TO KNOW, THE SUN STONE ALSO DEPICTS THE FOUR DISASTERS THAT THE AZTECS BELIEVED DESTROYED THE FOUR UNIVERSES THAT PRECEDED THEIRS.

chocolate factory spread out in a line. At the starting
point, a pale gooey substance (cocoa butter, although
they had no way of knowing it) poured in swirling
ribbons into vats of chocolate sludge. Then various
machines kneaded and stirred, mixed and molded,
dipped and dropped, dusted and sprinkled. There were
no human hands in sight.

It was a little like walking down the hall
alongside a car wash, but instead of seeing your
car being washed, you saw your chocolate being
made.

"Man, why did they have to put this glass here?
This is torture," said Yo-Yoji, whose stomach was
groaning with hunger.

As they watched, chocolates of all shapes and
sizes and even colors passed by.

In addition to the traditional chocolate valen-
tines and Easter bunnies, there was a chocolate
zoo filled with tiger-shaped truffles, baboon bonbons,
camel caramels, and kangaroo chews. A frosted vol-
cano erupting with molten white chocolate. A dark
chocolate lake spanned by a spun-sugar bridge. And
an entire forest of miniature chocolate trees topped
with powdered-sugar snow. (Or was the powdered
sugar supposed to represent the mochachin monkeys? Our friends weren't sure.)

More startlingly, there was a lifelike chocolate bust — the full head and shoulders — of a young boy.

"Hey, there's that kid, Alexander, that the Skelton Sisters wanted to keep," said Max-Ernest. "They made a mold out of him! How 'bout that?"

Cass remained silent. She couldn't help imagining that the next person they saw cast in chocolate would be her mother.

But there were no more busts. Pride of place was given to Señor Hugo's simple squares of chocolate. These came last, smooth dark bricks, individually tagged according to weight and purity, as if they were not just *Palets d'Or*, but actually gold bullion.

"C'mon," said Cass. "The glass isn't magically going to disappear if we wait."

At the end of the hallway, there were two doors: one marked **TEST KITCHEN**, the other **LIBRARY**.

Max-Ernest pointed to the second door. "Let's look in there first. Even if your mom's not in there, maybe there'll be some . . . information," he said, obviously overcome with curiosity to see what the Midnight Sun's library might hold.

Cass hesitated; the kitchen seemed like the more logical choice. But Max-Ernest opened the door without waiting for an answer.

There wasn't a single book in the library. Instead, the wall facing them was entirely taken up by glass vials, each on an individual white shelf. While the vials were all identical, their contents varied in color and texture.

"It looks like the Symphony of Smells," said Cass. "But times eleven."*

Max-Ernest scanned the wall, mentally counting vials. "Times twelve, actually. Well, times twelve plus twelve. The Symphony of Smells had ninety-nine vials, remember? This one has one thousand two hundred."

"So you think these are smells, too?" asked Yo-Yoji.

"I think they're flavors," said Cass. "If you read the labels — see, *sour — number ten . . . umami — number six . . .* umami is the taste of . . ."

"I know what it is," said Yo-Yoji. "It was invented in Japan."

"You mean *discovered*," said Cass, slightly miffed. "You can't invent a taste." (I'm not sure Cass is exactly right about that, but I'll let it go.)

"So then it's a *flavor* library," said Max-Ernest. "How 'bout that?"

---

*AS READERS OF A CERTAIN UNMENTIONABLE BOOK WILL REMEMBER, THE SYMPHONY OF SMELLS CONSISTED OF VIALS CONTAINING A VARIETY OF SCENTS, EACH SCENT CORRESPONDING TO AN INSTRUMENT IN THE ORCHESTRA. THE SYMPHONY OF SMELLS IS WHAT LED CASS AND MAX-

The flavor library looked like a giant vending machine, and, as the kids discovered, it operated like one, too. On an adjoining wall, a control panel allowed them to choose one or more of the vials; a mechanical arm would then retrieve the vial and pour its contents into what looked like a high-tech milkshake mixer.

In the end, a thimble-size glass of flavored liquid appeared on a tray in front of them.

The hungry kids started sampling flavors right away:

"I get kiwi-green olive seven." "I want banana-butter." "I've got dibs on cherry number six."

"What about new car smell taste?" "Why would anybody want leather flavor?" "Better than mud flavor."

"Yum." "Yuck." "Weird." "Whoa." "Hmm." "Ick!"

"Do you think you can be allergic to the flavor of something, or does the food have to actually be there?" Max-Ernest wondered philosophically as he decided against tasting the taste of plastic.

"You know what, this is kind of cool, but it kind of sucks," said Yo-Yoji, after trying at least a dozen flavors. "It's just making me hungrier."

ERNEST TO INVESTIGATE THE DISAPPEARANCE OF PIETRO, AND ULTIMATELY TO JOIN THE TERCES SOCIETY. A TRAGIC MISTAKE? ONLY TIME WILL TELL.

"OK, time's up," said Cass. "It's really lucky nobody has seen us yet."

At the far side of the room was a swinging door beneath a sign that read **TASTING ROOM**. Cass peeked through the door window, and seeing no one on the other side, pushed the door open.

It was a bright, white, laboratory-like space.

A long marble table occupied the center of the room. On one side of the table was a low stone bench. On the other side, three tall silver chairs.

Although of course they'd never been there before, *you* will remember this as the room where Simone ate that perilous square of chocolate, the *Palet d'Or.*

As it happens, an identical square of chocolate was now sitting on a white plate in the middle of the table. To be exact, three identical squares of chocolate. The only bits of color in the otherwise all-white room.

"Finally some chocolate we can really eat!" said Yo-Yoji, immediately approaching the table. "And there's even three of them . . ."

Max-Ernest looked askance at the chocolates. "Are you sure you should . . . ?"

Cass shook her head in disbelief. "Don't tell me

you're worried about stealing from the Midnight Sun? Why is this different from the flavors?"

"I don't know, it's just strange that they're sitting out there like that. It looks like they're waiting for somebody. Whoever it is could come in any second and if the chocolate's missing, they'll know somebody's here. Plus, we don't know what's in it!"

Cass considered, then turned to Yo-Yoji. "He's right. It is the Midnight Sun after all. They could be using these to poison people or something . . ."

"I don't care, I'm starving!" Yo-Yoji popped one of the chocolates in his mouth.

His friends watched anxiously.

His eyes widened. "Oh no!" He clutched his throat and made gagging sounds. "I think I'm chok —"

Then he burst into laughter. "Just kidding. Actually, it's amazing. Usually, I like milk chocolate, not dark chocolate. But that was the best I ever had. Seriously. Kind of like the mud flavor, but in a good way."

"Well, I can't have it anyway 'cause of my allergy," said Max-Ernest, unconvinced.

"Good, more for me. Cass, you gonna have yours?" Yo-Yoji asked, licking chocolate off the corner of his mouth.

Cass eyed the chocolate, trying to resist.

Then she nodded. She was too hungry to say no.

Max-Ernest watched, torn between jealousy and concern, as Cass devoured her piece of chocolate. She looked blissful.

"Wow, that was really . . . good."

"Man, I wish there were more," said Yo-Yoji, finishing Max-Ernest's piece.

"Me, too. Maybe if we look —" Cass spun around, scanning the room.

Yo-Yoji nodded. "Yeah . . . *Hai!*"

"What?" Cass turned back to him, staggering a bit. "Whoa — that made me kind of dizzy."

"*Hai!*" Yo-Yoji repeated.

Eyes rolling up into his head, he lurched forward and raised his right hand, clutching at the air.

"Yo-Yoji . . . are you OK?" asked Cass, still struggling to stand up straight. "Or are you joking around again?"

Yo-Yoji responded with more guttural sounds.

His eyes now closed, he kept moving his arm around as if he were wielding a weapon. He seemed to be in some kind of combat stance.

"I think he's speaking Japanese," said Max-Ernest, staring at their friend. "And maybe having a samurai sword fight . . . ?"

"But Yo-Yoji doesn't know Japanese. He only lived in Japan for a year . . ." She trailed off, her eyes glazing. She teetered on her feet.

Distressed, Max-Ernest reached for her. "Cass?"

"Mmm." She murmured to herself, barely conscious. Max-Ernest had to use all his strength to hold her up.

"Yo-Yoji, help me!"

But far from being able to help, Yo-Yoji was groaning and clutching his side, as if fatally wounded.

Max-Ernest was becoming frantic. "Cass, wake up! You, too, Yo-Yoji!"

"Wake up . . . wake up . . . ," Cass repeated vaguely.

"If you guys are playing a joke, I think you should stop now," said Max-Ernest. But they took no notice.

As Max-Ernest watched in horror, Yo-Yoji fell to the floor, writhing in pain.

Meanwhile, Cass continued to babble incoherently. Until Max-Ernest could hold her no longer, and she, too, fell to the floor, unconscious.

Before Max-Ernest could decide what to do, he heard the sound of footsteps approaching. Wildly, he looked around: there was only one exit — and it

was in the direction the footsteps were coming from.
There was no way he would be able to get out in time,
let alone hide his friends.

Just over his head, sticking out of the wall, was
a large grate. Gritting his teeth, he pried it open
with his fingernails, revealing a dark air shaft. He
pushed the grate into the air shaft, then pulled his
gray tunic over his head and tossed it in with the
grate; he didn't think he'd be able to fit through
the opening otherwise.

Using all his strength, he was just able to pull
himself up into the air shaft and replace the grate
before Señor Hugo, Dr. L, and Ms. Mauvais strode
into the Tasting Room. Three white-tunic-and-white-
glove-wearing Midnight Sun acolytes followed in
their wake.

Oh no, Max-Ernest despaired. He could see the
room's new occupants only in bits and pieces — but
those bits and pieces were more than enough.

Cass and Yo-Yoji were still moaning on the floor,
Yo-Yoji murmuring in Japanese, Cass in some older,
Renaissance-sounding version of English. Oddly, the
newcomers didn't appear very surprised to see them.

"It seems the boy must have some samurai in his
blood," said Dr. L. "But what of the girl? Is that her
awful ancestor speaking through her?"

Ms. Mauvais smiled one of her almost-smiles. "Let us hope so."

Max-Ernest shivered, but was uncertain himself whether it was from hearing Ms. Mauvais speak, or from the whoosh of the air being sucked in through the vent.

With a chill he realized where he was: in an air filtration system. Forget the chocolate particles. All the dust in the room would be sucked through the grate in front of him. Horrified, he imagined hundreds of thousands of dust mites flying into his nostrils . . .

Unfortunately, there was no getting out at the moment. He lifted his shirt to cover his nose; it was all he could do to protect himself from the army of invading allergens.

Dr. L leaned down and felt each of the kids' pulses in turn. He lifted their eyelids and opened their mouths, examining their reaction to the chocolate.

"I expect they will survive," he said over his shoulder. "But in what condition I don't know."

"Where is the other one? The boy with two names?" asked Señor Hugo.

Ms. Mauvais snorted. "Max-Ernest? There's no need to worry about him. He's helpless on his own."

Listening through the grate, Max-Ernest grimaced, insulted.

"Besides, his chocolate is gone. Wherever he is, he'll lose consciousness soon. Somebody will find him. It's the girl we want."

"Maybe what you and I want are not the same," said Señor Hugo.

"Who cares what you want?" Ms. Mauvais snapped. "If we do not find the Secret today, a great man will die!"

Ms. Mauvais motioned to her white-gloved henchmen. "Take the Japanese boy out of here — but leave the girl on the table."

While Yo-Yoji was carried out, the unconscious Cass was laid out on her back on the marble table, as if she were about to be carved up and eaten for dinner.

Ms. Mauvais approached, and with her gloved hand pushed another square of chocolate between Cass's lips.

"The Secret — what is the Secret?" Ms. Mauvais whispered. "We know you know it . . ."

As she spoke, Ms. Mauvais's breath fell on Cass like a morning frost. Cass's face grew paler and paler, and her ears turned a purple that bordered on blue.

* * *

Up in the air shaft, Max-Ernest frowned. Was it possible Cass knew the Secret and had never told him? How could she keep something like that to herself? Then again, she hadn't told him about her mother being kidnapped. What other secrets might she hold?

He stared down at her, wondering if his best friend had just become a stranger.

CHAPTER
TWENTY-NINE

THE JESTER'S TENT

She was in a tent. An old canvas tent that had been mended one too many times. Moonlight shone through the rips in the fabric, and a cold wind blew in from some faraway place, freezing the tips of her ears.

An oil lamp sat on the earthen floor, its weak flame flickering in the wind. Next to the lamp, an old man lay on a bed of hay. He wore a fraying old cap from which hung tarnished silver bells.

He coughed. She leaned down and touched his cheek.

"Grandfather, you are cold. I must get you out of this . . . this carnival tent and take you somewhere where there is a proper bed and a fire."

Grandfather? Why had she called him that? He wasn't one of her grandfathers — he was much older. . . . Unless . . . was she in . . . the future . . . ?

Whoever he was, he raised his head in anger. "Carnival tent? What you call a carnival, I call my castle. Though its walls be ripped, I would not be ripped from it! We fall together, the tent and I."

His head fell back into the hay; he had exhausted himself.

"Let me at least remove this old hat and wrap you in something warm. I have a scarf . . ."

She started to lift his hat, revealing his pale,

pointy ears, remarkably similar to Cass's own (save for the long, gray hairs sticking out of them). He stopped her with a brush of the hand.

"But this is my jester's cap, the crown of my jokingdom!" said the old man. "I would die without it. And I must die within it!"

"Very well," she said wearily. "But please. No more talk of death, Grandfather. I will not listen."

The Jester. The old man was the Jester . . . So then she was in the past . . .

Or dreaming of it anyway . . .

But then who was she . . . ? The Jester's granddaughter. That would make her what . . . her own grandmother? No. More like great-great-great-grandmother.

"Do not try to protect me, my love," said the Jester. "Death is like an old dog. He always knows when you are at his door."

"And no more of your riddles either! I cannot bear them now."

"You think it best that I do not jest. Yet I cannot be grave. How then should I behave?"

"I think it best . . . that you rest. I do not want you to catch plague. It is all over this wretched country."

"You and your disasters. Hurricanes. Earthquakes. Plagues. You cannot be prepared for every-thing, you know."

"And what is the harm in trying?"

"Enough — I do not want to argue. You are what I treasure most, so it is to you I must give my treasure."

She started to cry, shedding the tears she had been holding back. "But I do not want your gold. I want only for you to live."

"Oh, there is no gold, I speak of something you cannot hold."

"What is it?"

"Something that cannot be told."

"Grandfather!" she groaned. "Tell me what it is. Or go to sleep."

"I just told you. It is something that cannot be told."

"It is a secret?"

He nodded, pleased. "Very good, my child. It is indeed a secret."

Now they were outside. In a meadow. The sun shone bright in the sky, turning the tall grass gold.

Although it was midday, her skin felt cool, as if it were evening. A breeze ruffled her hair, but she did not feel it.

The Jester was still with her. But now his hat was plush and plum-purple, its silver bells bright and sparkling like diamonds. Curly hair sprung out from under the hat and bounced around his pink cheeks and mischievous grin.

Behind them was his tent, also looking shiny and new, its red and white stripes rippling, its gold flag waving.

"What secret, Grandfather?"

"Grandfather?" The Jester laughed. "But I have yet no children! Would you have me miss being a father altogether, and skip to the grand finale?"

He did a back flip in the grass, showing off his youth and vigor. The bells on his hat tinkled merrily.

"What secret, Jester?"

"*The* Secret. The secret of secrets . . ."

They were at Cass's school now. On the schoolyard. She recognized the handball courts. And Mrs. Johnson's School Clean-Up Campaign posters. But they were alone; the school must have been closed.

The Jester was an old man again, but not yet bedridden. He was standing with his arm over her shoulder, supporting himself. His tent, once more in tatters, stood lopsided beside them on the asphalt.

"The Secret of the Terces Society?"

"The Secret does not belong to the Terces Society."

"You know what I mean," she said impatiently. "Is that the secret you're talking about?"

He shrugged. "Is that the secret you wish to know most in the world?"

"Yes. No. What I want to know most is . . . who are my parents . . . ? No, forget that — where is my mother? That's what I need to know now. Is she OK? Can you help me find her?"

"Ah, but I cannot help you with that. She is of your time. To find your mother, you must wake up."

"Then can you at least tell me . . ." She didn't know how to phrase it.

"You wish to know who you are?"

"Yes. Who am I?"

"Ah, that is the question, isn't it? To learn *the* Secret you must first learn *your* Secret."

Cass tossed and turned, thrashing around on the hard cold surface, between wake and sleep.

Who am I? Who am I? What had the Jester just said? It was right there in the back of her head but she couldn't hold on to it.

"Drink, Cassandra! Drink!" said a rough and

unfriendly voice. *Señor Hugo.* "This is the antidote.
Without it, you may never regain consciousness."

His gloved hand poured some kind of milky liquid down her throat. It was chalky-tasting and made her cough, but she managed to drink most of it.

"Allow me." Still barely conscious, Cass felt a familiar chill coming from the other side of the table. *Ms. Mauvais.*

"I have a more old-fashioned remedy. But perhaps more effective . . . Cass, wake up!" Ms. Mauvais's gloved hand slapped her in the face — it stung.

"The Secret. Tell it to me. Quickly —"

"I can't remember . . . ," Cass moaned. The milky liquid dribbled down her chin.

"You must remember."

Cass opened her eyes.

She had a piercing headache and her stomach was in revolt. But it was the sight of Ms. Mauvais leaning over her that caused Cass to regurgitate Señor Hugo's antidote — right onto Ms. Mauvais's pristine white glove.

"Disgusting!" exclaimed Ms. Mauvais. "You are as rude as the Jester."

Cass gasped. "How do you know about the Jester?"

Ms. Mauvais was about to pull off her soiled glove, then seemed to think better of it. She put out her hand and one of her henchmen handed her a towel.

"Never mind how I know," she said, wiping furiously. "You were with him just now, weren't you? Don't lie — I can see it in your eyes. What did he tell you —? He told you the Secret, didn't he?"

"Where's my mother? I want to see my mother."

"Tell me the Secret and you will see your mother."

"I don't know the Secret!"

"Liar!"

Cass retched again in answer.

"Darling, please," said Dr. L, resting his own gloved hand on her bony shoulder. "Give the girl a second."

"Very well. I will wait until she collects herself."

Ms. Mauvais motioned to the henchman to mop up the mess.

"You disappoint me, Cassandra — I thought you'd be harder to catch. Those little chocolates — like cheese in a mousetrap. To think you'd fall for something so simple!"

"The chocolate was . . . a trap?" Cass asked feebly.

"Naturally. You didn't think you could step onto

this plantation without our knowing, did you? Or
did you think my monkey was just being friendly?"

"You mean, you sent him for us?" She was still feeling too sick to be very upset.

"The mochachins are very highly trained, if you hadn't noticed."

"So you saw us enter the rainforest?"

"The rainforest?" Ms. Mauvais laughed her icy laugh. "Yes, we saw you enter the rainforest. We saw you enter the park. We saw you get on the train. We've been watching from the beginning. Did you not remember that we know where you live?"

"So you . . . wanted us to come?"

"Who do you think left the *We* magazine on your grandfathers' doorstep? You should know by now there are no coincidences — especially lucky ones. Although, I admit, your acquiring the Tuning Fork for us was an unexpected bonus. We would have found it eventually, but you certainly helped. Thank you."

"You're not welcome."

"You, Cassandra — you've been a thorn in my side since I first laid eyes on you. But now you're going to be the solution to all my problems. There's a kind of poetic justice to it, don't you think?"

"How am I the solution?"

"Because of who you are . . ."

"What do you know about me?"

"Only everything. What do you think I've been doing since our last precious moments together? Once I realized who you were I started learning all I could . . . Would you like to know who your parents are? Tell me the Secret, and you'll find out."

Cass hesitated, beginning to remember snippets of her conversation with the Jester. "I don't care who they are," she said, not quite honestly. "Just let my mother go."

"Very well, as you wish. We'll release that poor woman you call your mother — when you tell me the Secret."

"I told you — I don't know the Secret. I can't even remember what he said . . . And even if I knew, I wouldn't tell you!" said Cass, finally feeling strong enough to sit up.

Was that true? she wondered. She wasn't sure. Perhaps it was best that she didn't know the Secret after all.

"I think I'll put you in one of the old animal cages for a while," said Ms. Mauvais. "Let's see if sleeping on a cement floor helps you remember . . . Hugo, work on your recipe. The chocolate is not strong enough!"

She nodded to one of her acolytes, who then threw Cass roughly over his shoulder and followed Ms. Mauvais and Dr. L out of the room. Clenching his fist, Hugo exited as well.

After the Tasting Room had been empty for a few minutes, Max-Ernest, his T-shirt still covering his nose, pushed the grate out. Before he could grab it, the grate dropped out of the opening and fell noisily to the floor.

Max-Ernest froze, ready for the worst. But when nobody came he gingerly let himself out of the air shaft.

Standing alone in the room, he pulled his shirt off his nose and allowed himself to breathe freely again.

Now that he knew the Midnight Sun knew they were there, he wasn't sure how useful a disguise the slave tunic would be. Nonetheless, he threw it back on. He found his golden pails where he'd stashed them under the table, but when he saw Cass's backpack lying next to them he picked that up instead.

And then he proceeded to walk out of the Tasting Room.

Alone.

As dire as the situation seemed, luck was with

him; he felt it. His allergy to chocolate had saved his life. Or nearly. He had plenty of other allergies. Perhaps they would protect him from any other dangers he would face.

What alarmed him most was the prospect that Cass might be keeping a secret as important as the Secret from him. But before confronting her, he would have to rescue her.

Now: how to get out of the building? Leaving the way they'd come in was out of the question. But there wasn't an exit at the rear. Not that they'd seen anyway.

The Midnight Sun would never leave themselves without an emergency exit plan, Max-Ernest reasoned. That meant there must be some kind of escape hatch — probably in the floor somewhere.

Trying to hold on to the lucky feeling he'd had just a moment ago, he headed out of the room.

PART THREE

DESSERT

CHAPTER THIRTY

A SAMURAI IN THE RAINFOREST

A mask of brown glop covered the entire left side of Yo-Yoji's face. It looked like molten chocolate. Alas, it was not. He lay on the ground where he'd been tossed an hour earlier. In a big pool of mud.

Above and around him: the dark, green gloom of the rainforest.

He blinked one muddy eye, then jerked awake.

He was not alone.

Moving with surprising speed, he pushed himself up — and threw himself into a backward roll. As he came vertical, he kicked both feet high — doing the splits in the air — and landed in a crouch.

A samurai warrior ready for combat.

In a flash, he picked up a long stick off the ground and pointed it at the neck of a big, menacing . . . shrub.

With glazed eyes, Yo-Yoji uttered a string of Japanese epithets, then struck the bush so hard that he chopped off the top, leaving the leaves on the bottom shaking.

He then bowed his head and started murmuring in Japanese. A haiku, honoring the life of the mighty enemy he'd just slain.*

---

*THE SAMURAI, YOU UNDERSTAND, WERE POET WARRIORS, MASTERS OF BUN AND BU, "PEN AND SWORD, IN ACCORD," AS THE SAYING GOES.

A HAIKU, AS YOU PROBABLY KNOW, IS A JAPANESE POETIC FORM THAT CONSISTS OF THREE LINES: THE FIRST LINE HAS FIVE SYLLABLES, THE SECOND HAS SEVEN, AND THE THIRD HAS FIVE. THE THEME OF A HAIKU

For those with a penchant for poetry, the haiku, in rough translation (my Japanese is only so-so) went like this:

> OH BRAVE WARRIOR,
> A TREE FALLS IN THE FOREST,
> YOU LIVE IN MY SWORD.

Note: Chapter 30 continues on page 313. You may skip to that page if you like, but I suggest reading Chapter 31 first.

USUALLY CONCERNS NATURE. IF YOU'VE NEVER WRITTEN A HAIKU, I SUGGEST YOU TRY. HAIKUS ARE ESPECIALLY FUN WHEN YOU'RE ANGRY AT SOMEONE AND YOU WANT TO WRITE MEAN THINGS ABOUT THEM — IN PRIVATE, OF COURSE.

pair of large gloved hands threw Cass onto the cement floor of an old animal cage and closed the iron bars with an angry clang.

Blearily, Cass recognized her large lumbering jailer as Daisy, Ms. Mauvais's toughest and most loyal servant. Had Daisy recognized Cass earlier after all? Had she just been playing her part in conspiring to get Cass to eat the chocolate?

The answer, judging by Daisy's smug and self-satisfied expression, was YES.

What a sucker I am, Cass thought bitterly. She had come to rescue her mother, and she'd succeeded only in getting imprisoned herself!

Without saying anything, Daisy took up position as guard in front of Cass's cage. A ring of keys hung from Daisy's hip, tantalizingly out of reach.

Thinking of ways she could possibly snatch it, Cass fell back asleep.

An hour or so later, she stirred.

A girl of about her own age was hovering over her.

"Hi, you eat the chocolate, yes?" she asked in a thick French accent.

"Yeah, how did you know?"

"Your eyes. They do this —"

She rolled her eyes in the back of her head, so only the whites of her eyes showed.

"That's a good trick," said Cass, pushing herself up. "You could really make somebody think you were unconscious or crazy or something. Could be useful in an emergency or if somebody took you prisoner."

"But I am a prisoner," said Simone, not fully understanding. "My name is Simone."

"Hi, I'm Cass."

Simone looked at her in surprise. "Cass? Like Cassandra?"

"Yeah, why is that so weird?"

"You are the daughter of Melanie?"

Suddenly, Cass was sitting bolt upright.

"You know my mom?"

Simone nodded. "She is a very nice lady. For one day, she lived with me. She helped me speak English. Then they moved her because they do not want us to be friends."

Cass grabbed Simone's wrist. "Where is she now?"

"She is in jail also. There —" Simone pointed with her free hand to the cement wall next to them.

"She's next door?" Cass couldn't contain herself any longer. She moved over to the bars and shouted as loud as she could.

"Mom?!"

For a moment, there was no response. Then a tentative voice:

"Cass?"

"Yeah, I'm right next door!"

A tear rolled down Cass's cheek. She was so relieved her mother was alive. And so sad they were both prisoners.

"What are you doing here, sweetheart? Did they take you, too? Are you OK?" Her mother sounded sick with worry.

"I'm fine, Mom!"

Mom. She'd said it without thinking. As if it were all she'd ever called her. And, Cass decided right then and there, it was all she would ever call her in the future.

"Quiet!" Daisy shouted, hitting their cage doors as she walked past them. "I'm going to eat my lunch now. If I hear another word, I'm putting my mamba in there with you. You'll survive just long enough for your mother to hear you scream."

Well, at least she's learned something from Ms. Mauvais, Cass reflected: how to issue a good threat.

Simone muttered something in French that Cass took to mean she should do what Daisy said.

"Oh, I can handle Daisy — I have before," Cass boasted.

Simone shrugged, pointing across the yard —

Daisy, now sitting down on a bench with her back to the cages, was adorned with a long green snake. Hissing, it slithered up her shoulder and around her neck. It glared menacingly at Cass.

Daisy nuzzled the back of the snake's head, then offered it her sandwich. "Do you want a little yum yum, Peaches?" she asked loudly.

Peaches bared her fangs, then darted forward and swallowed the entire sandwich in a single bite.

"OK, maybe you're right," said Cass, slinking back against the stone wall.

"Your mother, she loves you very much," whispered Simone. "You are very lucky."

"Thanks, Simone," said Cass, meaning it.

She closed her eyes. If Daisy looked over, she would think Cass had fallen back asleep. Meanwhile, her mind was racing. At last, she'd found her mother! There was some comfort just knowing they were so close. But how to communicate when Daisy was only twenty feet away? She could try tapping on the wall. But it looked so thick, she doubted her mother would hear. Besides, she was fairly certain her mother didn't know Morse code.

She was awakened from her reverie by the sound of tapping — not on the wall next to her, but on the

iron bars in front of her. It was the quetzal, the green
bird who'd proven so helpful in locating the chocolate plantation. He was perched on the edge of the
cement slab, tapping on the end of a bar.

Simone held out a small, broken piece of chocolate — the bird pecked it away.

"You are going to get very fat, my friend," said
Simone to the bird. She turned to Cass, explaining,
"Now because I am here, and your mom is there — he
thinks he can eat and eat and eat!" She spoke softly
so as not to attract attention.

"You mean my mom feeds him, too?"

"Yes. He flies back and forth, back and forth."

Cass thought about this for a minute, then
glanced over at Daisy: luckily, she was still sitting on
the bench, stroking her green mamba.

"Hey, do you have a pencil?"

Simone looked confused, so Cass picked up a
piece of newspaper off the floor and mimed writing
on it.

Simon smiled. "Ah, yes — for writing. Sorry, I
have nothing . . . oh, wait, maybe this?" She handed
Cass another small lump of chocolate. "Do not worry.
It is the old chocolate. Not the kind that makes the
dreams."

"I'm not worried — I'm not going to eat it."

Using the chocolate as a crayon, Cass wrote a note to her mother as quickly as possible. She was trying to finish before the chocolate melted in her hand.*

Dear Mom,

Sorry about what I said. You are my real mom and always will be. I love you.

Love, Cass

P.S. Simone gave me this chocolate. After you write back, give the bird the rest of it and hopefully he will bring the note back.

After she finished writing, she rolled up the piece of chocolate in the newspaper and placed it in front of the bird. She was afraid the bird wouldn't take the note, since she had no more chocolate to offer. But the bird took pity — or perhaps hoped there would be more chocolate to come — and he readily gripped the scroll and flapped his wings.

About five minutes later, the quetzal landed in

---

*HAVE YOU EVER TRIED WRITING IN CHOCOLATE? I CAN TELL YOU FROM EXPERIENCE THAT IT'S VERY DIFFICULT. USUALLY, THE CHOCOLATE MELTS BEFORE YOU FINISH, AND YOU HAVE TO WRITE YOUR FINAL WORDS FINGERPAINT STYLE. OF COURSE, THE CONSOLATION IS GETTING TO LICK OFF THE CHOCOLATE AFTERWARD.

front of Cass's cage with a flutter of wings. He seemed rather proud of himself.

In his claws, he clutched the roll of newspaper.

Checking again to make sure Daisy wasn't watching, Cass reached through the bars and took the newspaper.

Turning so she wouldn't be visible from the outside, she unfurled the paper. It was ripped and smudged — and, from the looks of it — nibbled by a chocolate-loving bird. But she could read most of what it said.

Cass,
Did you come to save me? That was very foolish but very typical ___. You are my hero. I'm the one who should apologize. I should ha__ __tened about Hugo. If we don'__ __t out of here, I want you t__ know how much I love you. Y____ the only __ing I care abo__ __n the world.
Love,
Mom

After reading the note three times, Cass folded it carefully, her eyes teary.

Her mother didn't hate her! Even after the terrible thing Cass had said. Her mother thought she was a hero. Cass didn't feel much like a hero — she couldn't get over the fact that it was her fault her mother was here — but heroism was something to aspire to anyway.

Obviously, the heroic thing at this moment would be to stage a daring escape and then rescue her mom. But how could she do that with Daisy and her mamba guarding the zoo-jail?

As Cass contemplated this conundrum, she heard a bloodcurdling cry. It sounded oddly like —

Note: Chapter 31 continues on page 319.

CHAPTER
THIRTY, PART TWO

THE SAMURAI STRIKES AGAIN

Continued from page 303.

Max-Ernest's hunch proved correct: the Midnight Sun had installed a trapdoor in the floor of a broom closet. He dropped down through it to the ground below, nearly spraining his ankle but not quite.

The underside of the Pavilion was nearly a full story high, and Max-Ernest could easily stand without hitting his head. Nonetheless, he walked in a crouch, trying to hide behind the pillars as much as possible.

As soon he was out from under the building he saw a line of muddy footprints leading into the rainforest — two sets going in, one going out.

Max-Ernest peered down at the smaller set. Sneakers. He didn't remember the brand of Yo-Yoji's prize pair, but he was certain these were his.

He followed the footprints, ducking branches and hopping tree roots, until he reached a large pool of muddy water.

Here Yo-Yoji's footprints died.

Max-Ernest shuddered: could they have thrown Yo-Yoji in? In his condition, he almost certainly would have drowned.

Bracing himself for the worst, Max-Ernest started looking for a stick with which to poke the water.

"*Hai!*"

Startled, Max-Ernest turned. He didn't see anyone. Who was it?

"*Hai!*"

The voice was low and deep. Almost a growl.

"*Hai!*"

It didn't sound anything like Yo-Yoji, but when Max-Ernest pushed aside a bush (or what was once a bush) he saw his friend (or what was once his friend) brandishing a stick (or what was once a stick; it was now whittled into something more closely resembling a sword).

Aside from the fact that he had pulled up his long bangs into one those short forehead-ponytails worn by sumo wrestlers, Yoji-Yoji's physical features had not changed. And yet he was utterly transformed. His facial expressions, his movements, the look in his eyes — all belonged to someone else.

"*Hai!*" said Yo-Yoji. He was facing Max-Ernest's direction but seemed to be looking at a point beside or behind him, as if he couldn't quite see Max-Ernest.

"Er, hi," said Max-Ernest.

"せっしゃの殿様はどなたじゃ?" Yo-Yoji asked. (At least Max-Ernest assumed it was a question, given the rising inflection at the end of the sentence.) "せっしゃの殿様はどなたじゃ?"

What had Dr. L said? That Yo-Yoji must have samurai in his blood. Could it be Yo-Yoji's samurai ancestor standing in front of him? It made no sense. And yet this person most clearly was *not* Yo-Yoji. Yo-Yoji didn't even speak Japanese.

"I'm sorry, Yo-Yoji, or whoever you are. I don't understand."

"せっしゃの殿様はどなたじゃ?" Yo-Yoji asked again. "せっしゃの殿様はどなたじゃ?"

Max-Ernest scratched his head in consternation. How to respond? Then — of course! He reached into his pants pocket (he was still wearing them under his tunic) and pulled out what looked like a small handheld game player.

"OK, Yo-Yoji, now say that again!"

It was unclear whether or not Yo-Yoji understood. Nevertheless he obliged:

"せっしゃの殿様はどなたじゃ?" he repeated insistently. "せっしゃの殿様はどなたじゃ?"

The translation was instant.

WHO IS MY MASTER? WHAT IS MY TASK?

Max-Ernest grinned as Yo-Yoji's words appeared

on the screen in his hand. (This was the Ultra-
Decoder II, Max-Ernest secret decoding device that
happened to contain thousands of languages in its
memory. He and Pietro had added the voice recognition software earlier that summer.) It was like having
his own private subtitles watching a Japanese movie.

Now what to say?

Max-Ernest thought about it for a moment, then
shrugged: it was a worth a try.

**I AM YOUR MASTER. YOUR TASK IS TO RESCUE OUR
FRIEND CASS.**

As soon as Max-Ernest had typed the words a
clear brisk voice emitted from the Decoder:
"われがそなたの殿じゃ。そなたの仕事は我たちの
友、キャスを救出することじゃ。"

The trouble was: it was a woman's voice.

Yo-Yoji looked at Max-Ernest in confusion.

Blushing, Max-Ernest made the necessary ad-
justments on the Decoder, and had it repeat the
words, now in a male voice.

This time, Yo-Yoji nodded in recognition and
bowed all the way until his nose was touching the
ground.

"お上様、私の刀はあなた様のもの。私の魂は
あなた様の魂です。私はあなた様に従います," he
said gravely.

MASTER-SAN, MY SWORD IS YOUR SWORD. MY SPIRIT IS YOUR SPIRIT. I SHALL DO AS YOU SAY.

Max-Ernest nodded, and typed his response.

VERY GOOD, SAMURAI-SAN. CASS IS IN THE ANIMAL CAGES. WE MUST FIND THE OLD ZOO.

After the Decoder had translated Max-Ernest's words into Japanese, Yo-Yoji bowed again. Then he proceeded to start slicing his way through the rainforest, blazing a trail back toward the Midnight Sun.

Max-Ernest followed in disbelief. It was like he was playing some kind of video game and Yo-Yoji was his samurai avatar.

End of Chapter 30.

Continued from page 312.

— a battle cry in an old samurai movie.

Daisy stood up, her face clouding with fury. "Go!" she ordered, releasing the mamba to the ground.

Faster than you would have thought possible, the mamba made a beeline through the grass. It bobbed up and down, in and out of view, as if riding across a series of invisible waves.

Watching its progress, Cass's ears turned cold.

The snake's target: Yo-Yoji and Max-Ernest.

"Watch out!" Cass yelled. "The snake's coming!"

"Too late for that!" Daisy sneered.

Running after Yo-Yoji, Max-Ernest typed furiously on his Decoder.

KILL THE SNAKE

Yo-Yoji charged forward, his sword-stick thrust out in front of him. But before he reached the snake, Max-Ernest, conscience-stricken, typed again.

NO. WAIT. KILLING BAD. TAME THE SNAKE.

Yo-Yoji stopped short.

"はいこ主人様。"

YES, MASTER.

By this time, the snake was only a foot away from

them. It reared its head like an angry cobra, its tongue darting in and out between its long fangs.

Before the snake could strike, Yo-Yoji placed the hilt-end of the stick between his teeth and pointed the other end at the snake's head. Moving with unexpected smoothness and fluidity, he lowered himself to the ground. Then, his belly in the grass, he stretched his arms backward against his sides and raised his chest upward — matching the snake's posture.*

And he hissssssssssed.

Confused, the mamba slowed to a stop and stared at Yo-Yoji. Never blinking, Yo-Yoji stared back — one snake to another.

They communed for a moment, hissssssssssssing in unison. Until, in a hushed, sibilant voice, his teeth still gripping his sword-stick, Yo-Yoji recited another haiku.

Translated by Max-Ernest's Decoder, it went as follows:

HE NEEDS NOT HIS FANGS.
AWAY THE MAMBA SLITHERS
AT ONE WITH THE GRASS

*IF YOU PRACTICE YOGA, YOU MAY RECOGNIZE THIS AS COBRA POSITION.

When he'd finished the haiku, Yo-Yoji bowed to the mamba and fell silent.

Darting out its tongue one last time, the mamba bowed to Yo-Yoji, and then took off across the grass, heading for the rainforest.

Daisy shrieked in dismay — "No!" — and started running after the only creature that she'd ever loved. "Peaches! Come back!"

"Stop her!" yelled Cass from inside her cell.

Max-Ernest snapped into action — typing.

STOP HER!

Yo-Yoji nodded in acknowledgment, then leaped in front of Daisy, blocking her way with his stick.

"Get out of my way, punk!" she shouted.

Daisy tried to brush the sword-stick aside — tearing the palm of her glove as she did so.

"Aaah! My hand!"

She staggered backward, staring at her palm.

The stick had not drawn blood. It had done something worse. It had revealed her hand.

Her old, hard, calloused hand. As for the other members of the Midnight Sun, it was the one part of her body that told the truth.

"Get the keys!" yelled Cass.

GET THE KEYS! Max-Ernest typed.

While Daisy's attention was still fixated on her

hand, Max-Ernest pointed to the ring of keys hanging from her waist.

In a single motion, Yo-Yoji sliced the key ring off
Daisy's belt loop and caught it before it dropped to
the ground.

Clutching her hand and wailing like a wounded
animal, Daisy staggered after the snake. "Pea-ches!"

Yo-Yoji bowed low before Max-Ernest, offering
the key ring as if it were a precious treasure, plun-
dered in battle.

WHAT IS MY NEXT TASK, MASTER?

But by the time Yo-Yoji looked up, Max-Ernest
was already running toward the animal cages.

Hand trembling, he unlocked Cass's cage.

She grabbed the keys from him, along with her
backpack. "Mom, I'm coming!"

End of Chapter 31.

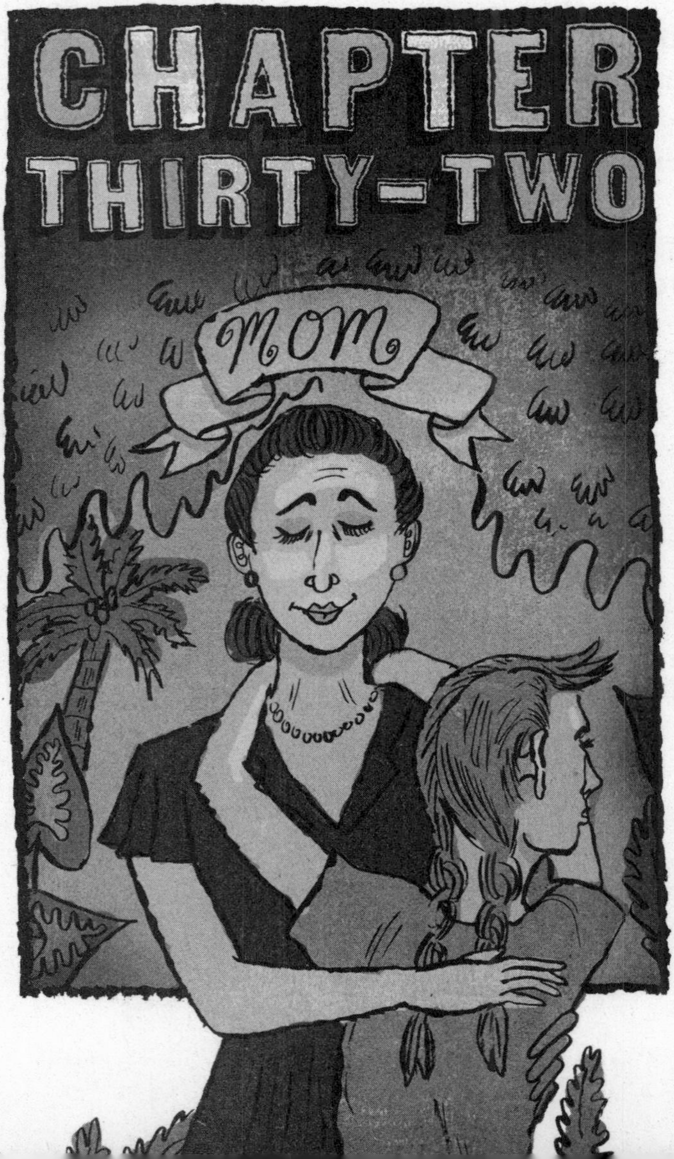
CHAPTER
THIRTY-TWO
MOM

ass buried her face in her mother's shoulder. The smells were comforting — coffee, bran muffins, printer ink, and not the slightest hint of chocolate.

"I missed you so much," said Cass.

"Well, I'm right here," said her mom. "Thank goodness you're all right . . . I have so much to tell you. I've been thinking, if you really want to find your birth parents, I'll help. It's not fair to let my fears get in the way."

Cass extracted herself from the long hug. "Thanks. But can we talk about that later?"

Her mother nodded. "You're right. First things first. You wouldn't believe what's going on here! There are child slaves, chocolate monkeys . . . I have to get to a phone!"

If she only knew, Cass thought. Part of her wanted to try to explain where they really were and what was really happening. But there were certain things mothers were just not meant to hear.

"I know, Mom. We have to get you out of here."

"Get *me* out of here? I have to get *you* out of here! I know it might not seem like it right now, but I'm the grown-up — you're my child."

"Hi, Mel," said Max-Ernest, stepping forward. Yo-Yoji stood next to him, bowing to Cass's mother.

"Max-Ernest? Yoji? You're here, too?" She had been so excited to see her daughter she hadn't noticed them when they'd sprung her from her cell.

"大后様、お足元にひざまづいて敬いまする。なぜなら私は卑しいヘビだからです。"

"Yoji? Are you speaking Japanese . . . ?" She looked at him in confusion.

"He says, 'It's an honor to meet you, ma'am,'" said Max-Ernest, glancing down at his Decoder, which in fact said,

I THROW MYSELF AT YOUR FEET, MY QUEEN. FOR I AM JUST A LOWLY SNAKE.

"That's very nice, but we've met many times . . ."

"I'll explain later," said Cass quickly. "Now, can you just wait for us here for a minute?"

"What are you talking about? You better not be thinking of going somewhere without me," said Cass's mother, indignant. "The only way I'm letting you out of my sight is if you lock me up again."

"Please. There's something I have to do," said Cass.

"What?"

"I can't tell you, Mom. But I promise, if you do what I say now, I'll do what you say for the rest of my life."

"Ha. That'll be the day." Mel turned to Simone. "What's going on here? I know my daughter. She's always up to something . . . Simone, if you know anything, you need to tell me."

"I'm sorry, I don't understand," said Simone, smiling apologetically. "My English . . ."

"Max-Ernest, Yo-Yoji, you guys are coming with me," said Cass, ignoring her mother. "Simone, you, too. I need your help."

Before her mother could stop her, she was striding away with her friends in tow.

As Mel watched in mute frustration, the quetzal emerged from the rainforest and followed the kids from above, flapping his tail in the wind.

The Tuning Fork.

As far as Cass was concerned, she couldn't leave Wild World without it. She was responsible for giving it to Hugo and she had to get it back. It was too powerful, too awful an object to leave in the hands of the Midnight Sun.

It was also, Max-Ernest had explained, the key to restoring Yo-Yoji to his old self. Max-Ernest had watched Dr. L and Hugo use the Tuning Fork to create the antidote to the *Palet d'Or*; that was how they brought Cass back. If he wasn't fed the antidote, Yo-Yoji might live the rest of his years as a samurai!

"Not that I would mind," said Max-Ernest, struggling to keep up with her. "I mean, I've never been anybody's master before, and it's kind of convenient to have somebody to boss around like that. You think I could have him fight all the bullies at school?"

"You'll have to have him fight me if you don't help me find the Tuning Fork right now," said Cass.

"OK, OK . . . where'd Yo-Yoji go, anyway?"

Simone pointed. "He is in the grass."

The others turned —

"Oh, no," said Cass. "Do you think he thinks he's a snake now?"

Yo-Yoji was on his belly, slithering toward the rainforest.

"I dunno, maybe he hypnotized himself when he was hypnotizing the mamba . . . ?"

"You better go give him his orders. Simone and I are going to go free some kids. Then I'm going to look for the Tuning Fork . . . I'll meet you in the kitchen."

Before Max-Ernest could argue, Cass was on her

way. At this rate, it would be a while before he could ask her about what he'd heard.

About the Secret.

Shaking his head, he started walking after Yo-Yoji while typing,

COME BACK. YOU'RE NOT A SNAKE.

At first glance, it could have been an explorer's hut in the most remote of jungles. But of course it was only a guesthouse hidden in the rainforest — the *faux* rainforest — behind the Pavilion.

Inside, Itamar — or what was once Itamar — lay on his back in a four-poster bed. His ancient face was so parched and shrunken he looked like the disinterred mummy of an Egyptian pharaoh.

Dr. L hovered over him, taking the measure of his skull with some kind of handheld laser. He jotted notes on a pad.

Ms. Mauvais walked in. "Is he . . . ?" She broke off, uncharacteristically hesitant.

"Yes, he's dead," said Dr. L dispassionately. "*More* dead, I should say. So much of him has been dead for centuries."

An emotion similar to grief appeared briefly on Ms. Mauvais's frozen face — a small crack in a field of ice. "If only he could have lasted another day! We are so close."

Slowly, she moved to the bedside and looked down at Itamar.

"I *did* cry over that horse," she whispered. "It's just that I never let anyone see."

Dr. L raised an eyebrow. "You? Cry? What are you talking about?"

Ms. Mauvais reeled around, snapping out of it. "Nothing! You misheard me, that is all."

"Itamar made you what you are, didn't he? Just as you made me," Dr. L reflected. "I wonder what I will feel when *you* die . . ."

Ms. Mauvais's cold eyes flashed. "I will never die."

"Doctor? Madame?" The Bald Man — the grim van driver who had identified himself earlier as the Wild World Operations manager — entered the office. "I'm sorry to have to tell you this, but the girl and her mother, they've escaped."

Ms. Mauvais glared. "Then why are you wasting your time here? Find them! I assume all the children are being rounded up?"

"Don't worry, we're on it. But there's one more thing . . ." The Bald Man hesitated. He clearly didn't like being the bearer of bad news.

"Yes, spit it out," said Dr. L.

"The police. They've been asking questions at the Wild World offices. They seem to know a lot . . ."

"The police!" scoffed Ms. Mauvais. "What do we care about the police?"

"Well, you may not care, but I don't want to end up in jail!" said the Bald Man, agitated.

"Why? What did you tell them?" asked Dr. L.

"I didn't."

"Good. Now let's make sure it stays that way."
Dr. L pointed the laser at the other man's head. "How
lucky that you're bald. I hate the smell of burning
hair."

Dr. L watched beads of sweat gather on the Bald
Man's forehead, then he lowered the laser.

"Forget the police. Find the girl."

He reached down and pressed a small button on
the wall next to the bed. An alarm started to sound.

CHAPTER THIRTY-FOUR

CHOCOLATE SNOWBALLS

I t looked like the entire cacao plantation had
been deserted. The monkeys had abandoned
the trees. The slave children were nowhere to be
seen. Even the golden pails were gone.

Cass and Simone ran into the warehouse. But it,
too, was empty of life. The alarm echoed eerily.

"The Pavilion?" Cass asked.

Simone shook her head. "Kids are not allowed
there. Unless . . ." She didn't finish her sentence. It
was not hard to imagine the orphans all being fed
Hugo's chocolate en masse. Or worse, turned into so
many chocolate busts.

Chaos greeted them as they neared the once
placid building.

They watched from the edge of the rainforest as
five white-uniformed guards attempted to herd the
gray-cloaked children — all still carrying their golden
pails — in five different directions.

"Shouldn't we take them back to the warehouse?"

"No! That's where the police will look first!"

"Our orders are to hide them in the Pavilion."

"Couldn't they have at least left the buckets?!"

"Not a trace, said Dr. L!"

Finally, the guards managed to lead the children up the steps of the Pavilion. Still in their own slave tunics, Cass and Simone easily hid in the crush.

The quetzal circled above as they disappeared inside.

The crowd of children filled the central room, the loud din in complete contrast to the hush Cass and her friends had experienced when they first entered the building.

Cass surveyed her surroundings, weighing options. After a moment, her eyes alighted on one of the golden pails. She whispered something to Simone, who looked confused for a moment, then grinned in recognition.

"Pass it on —"

Simone nodded and whispered in the ear of the child closest to her. It was Alexander, the small boy whose ears the Skelton Sisters had nearly pulled off. His eyes widened, then he broke into a smile — a rusty smile that hadn't lit up his face in years. (Cass was relieved to see his reaction; apparently, being cast in chocolate hadn't done him any permanent hurt.)

"Pass it on —" said Simone.

He gladly whispered in the ear of the kid next to him. "Pass it on —"

Soon whispers filled the room.

"Pass it on —"

                                             "Pass it on —"

"Pass it on —"

The guards looked around suspiciously:

"What's going on here?"

             "OK, line up against the wall, all of you, tallest to shortest!"

"No, shortest to tallest!"

                    "No, boys on the left, girls on the right!"

"Fine, just get them to settle down!"

As the guards debated amongst themselves, Alexander reached into his pail and dug out a fistful of monkey dung. With a look of intense concentration, he drew his hand back over his shoulder and flung it — *splat!* — into the forehead of an unsuspecting guard.

Before the other guards knew what was happening, a second boy threw a dung-ball at a second guard — *splat!* It landed on the second guard's chest.

Meanwhile, Cass climbed onto the sundial in the center of the room and shouted, "OK, everybody ready? One . . . two . . . three . . . Now!"

All at once, all the kids in the room reached into their pails and, cheering, started throwing fistfuls at the guards. It was like a hailstorm of chocolate-colored snowballs.

The guards ducked, trying to defend themselves as their white tunics developed big, brown polka dots and their hair dripped with brown, oozing excrement.

"Ugh!"

"Disgusting!"

"No not my gloves!"

"Stop!"

"Let me out of here!"

"Now everybody — make a run for it!" Cass shouted.

Cheering, the kids tossed their pails in the air like college graduates tossing their hats. Then they threw their gray cloaks aside and poured out the front door.

"Simone, can you make sure they're OK?" asked Cass, stepping back onto the floor.

Simone nodded and excitedly exited with the other kids.

A moment later, Cass was tiptoeing along the Pavilion's curving outer hallway. The hallway seemed even longer than it had the first time she'd walked down it, and she kept expecting to be stopped at every turn.

She didn't hear a sound until she reached the Test Kitchen door. Voices were coming from the other side.

She identified the speakers in her head as she listened:

"What do you mean the chocolate isn't ready? We need it now!" (Ms. Mauvais)

"She's right, Hugo. We're out of time. Our cover is blown. We must burn the building down immediately." (Dr. L)

"Burn it? What about the children you've just rounded up in there?" (Señor Hugo)

"What about them? They're evidence. They must be destroyed." (Ms. Mauvais)

There was silence. Then,

"Do whatever you have to do. But not my chocolate! I've spent years developing this chocolate — I won't leave it. Not now." (Señor Hugo)

"You have ten minutes. Then we burn. With you or without you." (Ms. Mauvais)

A door swung open. Cass flattened herself against the wall, partly hidden by a potted palm. Dr. L and Ms. Mauvais strode past without so much as a glance in her direction.

Bracing herself, she walked into the Test Kitchen.

"Cassandra. Just who I was hoping to see."

"Give it to me," said Cass. She stood in the center of the room — by the stove — and held out her hand.

The Test Kitchen, she noticed, was all stainless steel and nearly identical to the kitchen Señor Hugo taught in. He must have had the room built specially.

The chef removed his dark glasses and stared at her with his one good eye. She tried her best to hold his gaze.

"Give you what?"

"You know what — the Tuning Fork."

"Oh. I thought perhaps you meant the chocolate. I have made another piece for you. I think you will find it even stronger than the last. So strong it will tell you a secret. *The* Secret."

"You told them it wasn't ready. I heard you."

"That's because I knew they would try to kill me once they had the chocolate. Now take it. I must know if it works. If it does, I will become wealthy beyond measure."

"I'm not really hungry right now. Thanks."

"Take it."

Cass hesitated, then took the chocolate from him. "Eat."

"Maybe later." She reached around and dropped the chocolate into her backpack. Perhaps Pietro will want to have it analyzed, she thought.

"Where's the Tuning Fork? I want it back. Now."

Señor Hugo laughed. "What makes you think I would ever give it back to you?"

"You act like you're this great chef, an artist — but you don't really care about food or chocolate. All you care about is the Secret. You're no better than Ms. Mauvais and Dr. L. You're a hypocrite and a liar."

"If I were you, I would think twice about crossing me."

He gestured casually to the row of knives clinging to the long magnet behind him.

Cass shuddered, remembering his classroom knife demonstration. Unconsciously, she backed up against the opposite wall, crushing her backpack.

"I thought you said a real chef only needs one knife," she said bravely. "That looks like a lot of knives."

"*Touché* . . . but I was talking about a cooking knife. These are *throwing* knives."

Without so much as a glance over his shoulder, he reached backward and pulled the first knife off the rack.

Whiz! Boing! In a fraction of a second, it flew through the air and landed in the wall next to Cass's ear. She could hear a high-pitched hum as it vibrated back and forth.

"Just like a tuning fork, no?" the chef joked.

Whiz! Boing! A second knife flew through the air and landed next to her other ear.

"Oh, I'm sorry, I just realized I was cheating. I had my eye open. Let me try again . . . blind."

Whiz! Boing! Whiz! Boing! Whiz! Boing!

His eye closed, the chef threw knife after knife, each landing closer to Cass than the last, until she was surrounded on all sides by knives —

Hugo opened his eye and grinned. "We should do a carnival act. You could be my assistant." He

looked the jeans-and-sweatshirt-wearing girl up and
down. "Of course, you'd have to wear something a little more feminine. Perhaps sequins?"

Cass gritted her teeth. "Never."

"Aiyeee!"

Yo-Yoji leapt into the room, sword-stick thrust forward.

On his head was a gleaming stock pot — his samurai helmet. In his free hand, was the lid to the pot — his samurai shield.

Max-Ernest followed, holding his Decoder aloft as if it too were a samurai weapon.

ENGAGE THE CHEF

"シェフと婚約しろ," the Decoder translated.

Yo-Yoji looked perplexed. "私は、シェフと結婚するのですか？"

YOU WANT ME TO MARRY THE CHEF?

Max-Ernest shook his head no and typed:

NO, FIGHT THE CHEF!

Yo-Yoji nodded, relieved. Then bowed to Hugo.

Never taking his eyes off his opponent, Yo-Yoji raised his sword-stick in the air.

BATTŌJUTSU — MY SWORD IS DRAWN!

Hugo shook his head, incredulous. "What the heck are you doing?"

Yo-Yoji shrugged. A long ladle was resting on the

counter next to Yo-Yoji. He picked it up and crossed it with his sword-stick, apparently thinking the ladle was another sword.

NITŌRYUU — THE TWO-SWORD METHOD!

As Max-Ernest translated, Yo-Yoji waited expectantly for Hugo to pick up his swords.

"That's all right. I'll just use one," said Hugo, pulling the longest knife out of the wall behind Cass.

Yo-Yoji growled, his honor offended.

THEN I SHALL USE NONE!

Tossing his weapons aside, Yo-Yoji jumped into the air, and karate kicked the surprised Hugo in the stomach.

"Aarargh!" He staggered backward.

On the counter there was a large open can of what looked like melted chocolate. Cass grabbed the can and threw it at Hugo. Chocolate dripped down his face, covering his one good eye.

"There — now let's see if you're really so good at being blind!"

"How dare you!" exclaimed the outraged chef, stumbling around the room. He dropped his knife and held his eye with his hand.

Max-Ernest gasped in horror at the sight.

"Don't worry — it's not hot," said Cass. "Just chocolate syrup."

Max-Ernest nodded knowingly. "You know that's what they used to use for blood in old black-and-white movies."*

Cass gestured toward Yo-Yoji. "Tell him to hold Hugo for us."

Grunting his assent, Yo-Yoji grabbed the struggling chef from behind. He picked up the soup ladle and held it to Hugo's neck.

"Now, where's the Tuning Fork?" asked Cass.

"And why would I tell you?" Hugo spat out.

"Because you have a sword pointed at your neck." (She figured he wouldn't know it was the ladle.)

"You wouldn't dare —"

Yo-Yoji made a hissing sound, and suddenly the mamba emerged out of his collar. (It seems the snake had been hidden under his shirt all along.) Hissing in response, the snake traveled from Yo-Yoji's shoulder to Señor Hugo's.

The chef's chocolate-covered eye blinked in fear.

Afraid to move a muscle, he stood stiff while the snake wrapped around his neck several times, then lazily licked chocolate syrup off his cheek.

"*Now* will you tell us?" asked Cass.

"It's . . . right . . . here," said Hugo through his teeth.

---

*MAX-ERNEST IS ABSOLUTELY CORRECT ABOUT THIS. THE MOST FAMOUS EXAMPLE BEING ALFRED HITCHCOCK'S TERRIFYING MOVIE, *PSYCHO*, WHICH I DON'T SUGGEST YOU WATCH UNTIL YOU'RE MUCH OLDER (EVEN IF YOU'RE AN ADULT ALREADY).

"Oh, there it is —" said Max-Ernest.

The end of the Fork's handle was just visible, sticking out of the chef's apron. He pulled it out.

Cass sighed with relief. "Great. Now tell Yo-Yoji to put Hugo in one of the cages and then come back," she said, handing Yo-Yoji the key ring.

"Good idea," said Max-Ernest, typing rapidly.

...AND TAKE THE SNAKE, he wrote for good measure.

Awaiting the return of her daughter, Mel paced up and down in front of the old animal cages as fretfully if she were still trapped inside.

Suddenly, a bearded face appeared over the top of the stone wall that surrounded the old zoo. The face was followed by a navy-blue uniform.

Is that a policeman? Mel wondered. I don't think I've ever been so happy to see a cop!

One after another, a dozen men and women in police uniforms climbed over the wall. Actually, they didn't all climb; some somersaulted, others catapulted, several made a human ladder. Had Cass's mother been in a less agitated state of mind, she might have noted that they were an oddly acrobatic — not to mention an odd-*looking* — group of policemen. Preoccupied with her predicament, she stepped away

from the cages and waved frantically to the bearded
officer leading the charge.

"Officer — over here! You must help me, sir."

"You mean, help me, *ma'am*," said the officer, approaching calmly.

"Oh, I'm so sorry, Officer . . . ma'am!" said Cass's mother, blushing with embarrassment.

"You can call me Myrtle. Now what seems to be the problem?"

As Cass's mother tried to explain what was happening, Officer Myrtle (as you have probably guessed, she was none other than the circus's bearded lady) was joined by a tall skinny cop, and a short squat one, officers Mickey and Morrie respectively (yes, they were none other than the clowns).

"We heard reports about some troublemaking kids breaking into the zoo after hours," said Mickey, now cleaned up (or partly cleaned up; there were still some red and white smudges around his mouth). "Do you know anything about that . . . ?"

"We think they may have escaped from juvie," said Morrie. "Buncha lowdown nogoodniks!"

Cass's mother drew herself up. "How dare you speak of my daughter and her friends that way! They're very good kids. All three of them. They came to rescue me. And you must help us all get out of here right now . . . Hey, have I seen you two somewhere before?"

"Why, you been in trouble with the law?" asked Morrie. "You didn't just break out of one of these cells by any chance . . . ?"

"You sure look like a nice lady," said Mickey. "But you know what they say about appearances . . . !"

The clowns shook their heads solemnly, as if they'd seen one too many nice-looking ladies turn out to be terrible crooks.

"Take those two, for instance — It certainly looks bad, but for all we know, there's some totally innocent explanation." Morrie nodded into the distance where Yo-Yoji was visible escorting Hugo at ladle-point, the snake still curled around the neck of the terrified chef.

CHAPTER
THIRTY-FIVE

The TUNING FORK

K, time to make the antidote," said Cass. "We have to hurry. I want to give it to Yo-Yoji as soon as he gets back."

"We need a glass of milk," said Max-Ernest.

"Milk? You're sure?"

"Well, I'm not *sure* sure, but that's what it looked like. It was white and foamy."

Cass opened the door to the walk-in refrigerator. "I don't see any milk."

Max-Ernest frowned. "Hm. Now that I think about it, maybe it just *turned* white."

"What do you mean?"

"Let's try water."

She turned on the tap and filled a glass.

"Now what?" she demanded, handing it to him.

"I don't know, they just kind of stirred . . ."

Carefully, Max-Ernest lowered the ends of the Tuning Fork into the milk and swished them around experimentally.

Nothing happened.

"Well?"

"It's not turning white."

He tried shaking the fork sideways, then up and down. He spun it clockwise, then counterclockwise. Still nothing.

"You're obviously doing it wrong."

"OK, so you tell me what to do."

"I'm not the one who saw it! Sorry — it's just that we have to figure it out. Look at him —"

Yo-Yoji had just walked back into the kitchen.

WHAT IS MY NEXT TASK?

STAND STILL AND WAIT, Max-Ernest typed.

Yo-Yoji nodded gravely.

I WILL BE LIKE A STATUE.

He immediately froze in place. Not even blinking.

"You think there's a clue on the fork?" Cass asked.

Max-Ernest pulled the fork out of the glass and held it up to the light. "There're some kind of drawings but they're really faded."

"There's supposed to be a bird and a snake."

"Like by the front door here . . . ?"

"Yeah . . . Wait — what are you thinking? I can tell by your face —"

"Nothing. I thought I remembered something, but I lost it . . ."

As Cass groaned in frustration, the door to the kitchen opened and Simone walked in. The quetzal was now sitting on her shoulder, pecking at her hair.

"Your police friends, they are here," said Simone.

"Police? We don't know any police," said Max-Ernest. "Well, we don't know know any. I mean, once or twice we met some. Like when —"

"They say they know you. A lady with a beard? A tall man and a short man?"

Cass grinned. "Oh, *those* police! Yeah, we know them."

"They are with your mother now. I come to say good-bye."

Simone whispered to the quetzal, then pulled a long green feather from its tail. The bird squawked but did not seem to mind too much.

"Here, this is for you, so you remember us," said Simone, handing Cass the feather.

"Thanks," said Cass. The feather was beautiful but she didn't know exactly what to do with it.

"No, thank *you*," said Simone. "Because of you I am free."

"Wait — that's it!" said Max-Ernest.

"What?" asked Simone.

"That —" said Max-Ernest, pointing to the quetzal.

"What about it?" asked Cass.

"Well, the Tuning Fork is Aztec, right? And what's the most famous Aztec god? Quetzalcoatl.

The bird-snake. How 'bout that? I read about him
after we figured out the green bird was a quetzal."

"So Quetzalcoatl is the key, then?" asked Cass.

"Maybe, maybe not. But it's the only thing I can think of."

"So what was he the god of?"

"The sky . . . creation . . . I think it said he invented books and the calendar."

"The Tuning Fork takes you back in time, right? That's kind of related to a calendar. Sort of."

Max-Ernest nodded hesitantly. "Yeah, but I don't know how to make a calendar out of a tuning fork."

"What about a sundial?"

"No, I think I would have noticed if that's how they made the antidote. Anyway, we're inside. There's no sun."

"Duh, I just meant . . . I don't know what I meant. Do you remember anything else about Quetzalcoatl? Think."

"I'm trying!"

They looked over at Yo-Yoji — standing so still it looked like he might fall over. Time was clearly of the essence.

Cass took the Tuning Fork from Max-Ernest. "I see two stars, one on the top of the handle — or is that the bottom? — and one right here above the bird and snake."

She showed him the engraved star, barely visible in the silver.

"I think I also read that Quetzalcoatl was considered the god of the Morning Star," said Max-Ernest. "Maybe that's what that is."

"Kind of weird that the Midnight Sun would be into him then, isn't it? And then what's the other star?"

"Well, he had a twin brother — Xolotl, who was the Evening Star . . ."

"I'll bet that's it! Like to make you go back in the past, you need Quetzalcoatl. And to go back to the present you need Xolotl. Day then night."

"Sounds good, but then what do I do with the Tuning Fork?"

Simone, who had been having trouble following the rapid-paced conversation, spoke up for the first time. "Maybe you just turn it upside down?"

It worked. Or seemed to. As soon as Max-Ernest dipped the end of the handle into the water, the water started to cloud. In seconds, there was an alarmingly large head of foam.

"Taste it," said Cass, staring.

"No. Why?"

"I don't know. To make sure."

"But I don't even know what it's supposed to taste like. Plus I could be allergic."

"To Aztec magic? OK, I'll do it."

"No! You don't know what's going to happen. It might take you back in time again."

"Let me," said Simone. "I know how to taste and not drink. It's my job."

She grabbed hold of the glass, closed her eyes, and took a tiny sip. She spit it out, making a face. Whatever the flavor was, it wasn't her favorite.

"Vanilla," she said, opening her eyes.

"Really?" asked Cass.

"Well, it makes sense doesn't it? It's the opposite of chocolate," Max-Ernest pointed out. "And we're looking for the antidote to chocolate, right? How 'bout that?"

Apparently, Yo-Yoji liked vanilla better than Simone did. He drank the antidote as readily as if it were a milk shake.

His transformation, however, was not immediate; it happened in stages. As he drank, he relaxed his military bearing and started walking in circles, a meditative expression on his face. He mumbled to himself. First in Japanese. Then, gradually, in words more intelligible to his friends.

". . . What's going on, yo?" he asked when he at last opened his eyes. He looked around, blinking, confused. "What happened? Where are we?"

"It's kind of hard to explain," said Max-Ernest. "But, in summary, you're inside a kitchen inside a chocolate factory inside a rainforest inside a wild animal park."

Quickly, Yo-Yoji's friends filled him in on the rest. Or tried to. How do you explain to someone that his mind and body has just been possessed by a seventeenth-century samurai?

As Yo-Yoji began to absorb what had happened, a big grin broke out on his face. "Hey, do you think Master Wei will let me be her apprentice now? She always says, 'To go forward you must first go back.' Well, you gotta admit, I really went back!"

"I don't know, it depends on what you mean by back," said Max-Ernest. "You didn't necessarily go back in time. At least your body didn't. Maybe your mind . . ."

"Thanks for pointing that out," said Yo-Yoji, annoyed.

Max-Ernest turned to Cass. "Guess it's time to get out of here, huh?"

"Yeah, but first we have to get my mom."

"Right." Without thinking, Max-Ernest typed:
FIND CASS'S MOM.

And held his Decoder up to Yo-Yoji. It translated as usual into Japanese.

"Dude, why are you pointing that thing at me? What's it saying?"

"Oh! Sorry. I forgot you spoke English again. I was just telling you your orders were to go find Cass's mom."

"My orders? From who?"

"Me, your mast . . . ," Max-Ernest stammered, reddening. "I mean, no one."

Yo-Yoji laughed. "When did you turn into little general man? You giving me orders? — that's hilarious! I'd really like to see that."

Max-Ernest sighed. He was going to miss having his own personal samurai servant.

As they exited the pavilion, the kids saw the Bald Man and some of the dung-covered guards chasing after the escaped children.

"What's wrong with you people? — letting these

kids get the better of you like that! You should be ashamed of yourselves," the Bald Man shouted at the guards. "Run as fast as you like, you'll never get out of the gate!" he shouted at the children.

A familiar truck pulled up in front of Cass and her friends, splattering mud all over the already-splattered guards.

Owen, still in cowboy mode, hopped out of the cab.

"Howdy!" He tipped his hat, fully revealing his face to them for the first time. "Salutations, little lady . . . gents."

Cass smiled, relieved. But also chagrined. She couldn't believe she hadn't recognized him earlier.

Before they could greet Owen and/or berate him for giving them such a hard time when they were entering the animal park, the Bald Man rushed up. "You can't be here! This area is for . . . zoo employees only!"

"I thought it was for crazy evil alchemists only!" said Owen, his twang still in effect.

"What —?" the Bald Man sputtered. "If you know what's good for you you'll leave right now."

"Funny, I was just going to ask you to leave. There's a new sheriff in town. And the old one, looks like he's not real popular with the kids around here."

The Bald Man took a step forward, fist raised. "I don't try to make myself popular."

"You know what, I think I'll give you that ride out of here myself," said Owen. "Much friendlier —"

With that, he reached between the hay bales in the back of his truck and pulled out a long rope.

"Here, catch!"

As the Bald Man put up his hands, Owen tossed the rope around him, and hog-tied him to the truck.

Smiling, Owen addressed the rest of the dumb-founded and very dirty guards. "Now who's next?"

"Ballyhoo!"

In a moment, the clearing was filled with uni-formed police doing cartwheels and back flips. Not to mention swallowing swords — which Cass thought rather unhelpful under the circumstances.

The guards took one look at the "cops," then took off running.

Myrtle, who could barely manage a slow wad-dle let alone the gymnastic feats of her colleagues, but who was nonetheless mighty strong in the arms, plunked Cass's mother in front of Cass.

"So what's all this about monkeys and child slaves?" asked Myrtle.

"You have to get them out of here," said Cass. "I think there's going to be a fire."

Beep! Beep! Beep!

Loud horns and a jaunty circus tune signaled the arrival of a rainbow-colored VW Bug that looked like it had last been serviced in the 1960s. With a great squeal of brakes and a big cloud of smoke, the Bug stopped in front of the pavilion.

An oversized bumper sticker on the back read:

I BRAKE FOR ELEPHANTS

"Transportation for fifty, right here!" said Mickey, sticking his head out of the driver's window.

"How are you going to fit everybody in there?" asked Max-Ernest. "That's impossible."

"Don't worry, we do this all the time," said Morrie, jumping out of the car. "Step right up, kids!"

He picked up the nearest child and dropped him feetfirst into the VW's open sunroof. The child appeared to disappear as soon as he landed inside. (Although somebody standing close to the car might have heard a faint "Ow!" and then a "Why is it so dark??")

The other children clamored for the chance to follow their mate.

"Me!" "No, me!" "My turn!"

As one child after another was tossed into the

seemingly magic Bug, Simone climbed aboard the back of Owen's truck with Cass and the others.

"Owen, he said he would take me to Africa," said Simone, settling onto a hay bale next to Cass. "He says he knows a pilot that flies there all the time."

"Oh, we know that pilot," said Max-Ernest.

"I want to see my mom," said Simone. "I want to go home."

"I know what you mean," said Cass, looking in the front window of the cab where her mom was talking animatedly to Owen. She couldn't wait to go home either.

CHAPTER
THIRTY-SIX

A STUFFED LION CUB AND
A PURPLE GIRAFFE STRAW

From a distance, the couple mounting the tour bus in the Wild World parking lot would not have attracted much attention. Like so many other tourists at the animal park, they wore their new *Go Wild!* Wild World T-shirts above their plaid Bermuda shorts. The man wore a heavy camera around his neck, the woman wore dark wraparound sunglasses on her head. He carried a stuffed lion cub in his hand, she drank from an oversized cup with a purple giraffe straw. They looked exactly like everyone else who'd just spent a long hot day at the zoo.

Among the other passengers on their bus, however, they created a minor stir.

They were, first of all, so good-looking. He with his perfect tan face and perfect silver hair. She with her perfect porcelain skin and perfect gold bob.

At the same time, they acted so cool and aloof. They never smiled. They never spoke to anyone — not even to each other.

Were they foreign? Were they celebrities?

"I'll bet they're royalty!" somebody whispered.

Why hadn't they been on the bus that morning? How had they gotten to the park?

"By limousine probably," somebody guessed. "But it broke down. Or else their chauffeur just ran off with their daughter!"

Everyone had a theory.

And then there was that other odd fact about them —

"Mommy, why are they wearing gloves when it's hot out?"

"Shh, honey!" The embarrassed mother shushed her son and smiled apologetically at the unnerving couple sitting two rows back. "It's rude to point," she whispered. "For all you know, they have a skin disease and they have to cover their hands. Don't make them feel bad."

Fascinated, the little boy stared at the strange couple. As he watched, the woman crumpled her kangaroo straw in half, and the man clenched the neck of his stuffed lion so tight that a seam burst in the poor lion's head.

The boy burst into tears.

CHAPTER
THIRTY-SEVEN

THE secret keeper

When she entered the **CAT FOOD** trailer three days later, Cass found Pietro and Mr. Wallace deep in conference around a small card table. They stopped speaking as soon as they saw her, leading her to believe (correctly) that she had been the subject of their discussion.

"Cassandra! *Un abbraccio, prego!*" Pietro stood, opening his arms for an embrace.

"So you have the clown camp today, eh?" he asked, releasing her.

Cass forced a smile. "Yeah, I somehow convinced my mom that it was the best way to keep me out of trouble."

"Ha!" Pietro laughed heartily.

Cass looked awkwardly from Pietro to Mr. Wallace, who was sitting in stony silence. "So can I talk to you guys for a second?"

"Of course. Anytime —" said Pietro.

Mr. Wallace appraised Cass with a grim eye. "We know what you want to know, Cassandra. And the answer is: we don't know."

"But you're the one who gave me to my grandfathers!"

"That's true. But I never met your parents. I don't know where they're living, or even if they are living.

As far as I know, the names on your birth certificate were made up."

"So why did you have me? How did you get me? I don't understand."

"Sit down, Cassandra," said Pietro. He gestured to a nearby stool, which she reluctantly took.

"Your parents, they gave you up — for your own protection. So the Midnight Sun, it would not know where you were."

"A lot of good that did!" said Cass bitterly.

"Believe me, *I* never meant for you to get involved with the Terces Soceity, let alone the Midnight Sun," said Mr. Wallace. "But Pietro thought you were ready."

"No," Pietro corrected. "I knew the Midnight Sun was going to find her whether she was ready or not. And they did. Is it not better that she is with us?"

"Who am I?" Cass demanded. "Don't talk about me in the third person."

Mr. Wallace hesitated. "Oh, how I wish your grandfathers had destroyed that box!"

"Tell her, Wilton," said Pietro.

"Can't we at least wait until she is eighteen? Cass is an . . . energetic girl, I give you that. But such responsibility . . . !"

"Tell her, Wilton. Or I will. We have no choice. She knows too much already. *They* know too much. We've talked about this —"

"Very well. Cass, I know you take an interest in disasters. What is it you call yourself again?"

"A survivalist," said Cass defensively. "And I don't just call myself that."

"Good. Because what I am about to tell you — it will demand all your survival skills and more."

"What are you talking about?"

"Cass," said Mr. Wallace solemnly, "you are the Secret Keeper. There is one every hundred years. Your job is to know what no one else knows. To keep what is hardest to keep."

"You mean, I'm supposed to know the Secret?"

"That's right."

"I thought nobody was supposed to know it. I mean, not even you know it, right?"

"Nobody but you. Let's say you are the exception that proves the rule."

Cass sat in silence for a second, trying to grasp what he was saying.

"But how can I know it if nobody knows it? Is it written somewhere?"

Mr. Wallace shook his head.

"Then how am I supposed to . . . ?"

"I think you already know the answer to that," said Pietro, putting his hand on her shoulder.

But Cass wasn't sure she did. She wasn't sure at all.

Later that day, Cass stared out the window at the raggedy half-hole that was once Max-Ernest's father's half-house.

"It's like the best day and the worst day ever at the same time."

"I know," said Max-Ernest, straddling the one-foot gap that had run down the length of his bedroom floor ever since his parents had attempted (only half-successfully) to put their two half-houses back together. "It's like . . . you feel like you don't know who you are."

"Yeah, just like that," said Cass, surprised but glad that Max-Ernest understood how she felt. As we know, he usually wasn't very good at feelings.

"Like you've been living a lie all these years," Max-Ernest continued.

"Uh-huh . . ."

"It's almost like waking up in a different body."

"Exactly!" Cass smiled gratefully.

"I mean, it was the last thing I expected . . . every-thing came back negative. Everything. How 'bout that?"

Cass looked at her friend in confusion. "Wait — I'm talking about me, you know, what Mr. Wallace told me about being the Secret Keeper and every-thing . . . What are you talking about?"

"My allergy test, of course. Haven't you been lis-tening to a word I've been saying?"

"Your allergy test?!"

"Yeah. The results came back. All negative."

"You mean you're allergic to everything?"

"Worse! I'm allergic to nothing! Look —" He turned around and pulled up his shirt so Cass could see his back. "You see anything? Like a welt or a rash?"

"Uh, not really. Just some dots."

"See. How 'bout that? They pricked my back with all these chemicals and venoms, and I didn't react to any of them!"

Disappointed, he turned back to face Cass. Now Cass was really confused.

"What's wrong with that? You should be happy."

"Happy? But it was my allergies that kept me alive. I didn't eat Hugo's chocolate 'cause of them . . .

and now my parents talk to each other! My life is
over!"

Cass laughed out loud. How could she respond to that?

"What? And now you think I'm funny, too? Everything is terrible."

"Max-Ernest, listen to me. It wasn't because of your allergies that you didn't eat that chocolate, it was 'cause you were being smart. Yo-Yoji and I were being crazy. Anyway, the good news is you can try chocolate now."

"I know," said Max-Ernest, calming down. "Actually, I bought a chocolate bar as soon as I got the test results. But I've been too scared to eat it."

"Well, where is it?"

"Frozen in a block of ice in the freezer."

"Get it now."

"Now?" Max-Ernest repeated, frightened.

"Yes, now." She pointed to the door.

The expression on Max-Ernest's face as he swallowed his first bite of chocolate can only be described as ecstatic. It was like a blind person seeing for the first time. Or like a baby discovering television.

"Now I get it!" he said. "Why didn't you ever tell me how good chocolate was?"

"I don't know. I guess I thought everybody knew."

Max-Ernest shook his head. "What do you think would happen if I only ever ate chocolate for the rest of my life?"

"You'd get sick."

"No, no, that's not true!" Max-Ernest declared with all the fervor of a religious convert. "I read that it has these antioxidants. It makes you live longer. And you don't get heart attacks. How 'bout that?"

As Max-Ernest rhapsodized about the wondrous health effects of his newfound love, chocolate, Cass thought about the strange, and possibly very *un*healthy, effects of a certain chocolate bar in her possession. She'd been carrying it around in her backpack ever since Hugo gave it to her.

Suddenly, she realized why.

She already knew how to find the Secret, Pietro had told her. She'd thought he was talking nonsense, but now she understood.

She already knew the Secret — that was the point. The Secret was inside her. It was just that she had to dig it out.

With a solemn sense of determination, she

reached into her backpack and pulled out the plastic
baggie that contained Hugo's last *Palet d'Or*.

Max-Ernest's eyes lit up. "Is that more chocolate? Can I have it?"

"It's Señor Hugo's."

"Oh. I'm not sure . . . do you think I should? I mean, it looks good . . . really good . . ." He reached for the chocolate, eyes glazed, mouth watering.

She snatched it away from him. "You can't."

"Why? You already had one."

"It's not for you."

"Why? I want it. I have to make up for all the chocolate I never ate before."

"Because *I'm* going to eat it," she said. "He made it for me."

"You are? What are you saying?! What was I saying?!" exclaimed Max-Ernest, coming to his senses. "We can't eat that chocolate! Nobody can! It's dangerous. Why would you want to do that again?"

"It's just something I know I have to do. It's like what Lily tells Yo-Yoji: to go forward you must first go back."

"So you want to become a samurai? Or just charm a snake?"

"Neither. I'll be going into my own past, remember? Or my own ancestors' past."

Max-Ernest stared at her. "You're serious, huh?"
She nodded.

"Is it to find out the Secret?"

"In a way . . . it's hard to explain."

"To find out who your parents are?"

"Yes, but no. I mean, I know who my real parent is — my mom. But I still need to know who *I* am. That's what I need to find out. Not *the* Secret. *My* secret. But it's kind of the same thing. I think."

"But what if you can't come back? We don't even have the Tuning Fork anymore."

"Yes, we do."

"I thought you gave it back to Mrs. Johnson."

"I'm going to . . . just not yet."

She pulled the infamous object out of her backpack. Her grandfathers had convinced her to return the Tuning Fork to the principal, and everyone else had agreed it would be best. But she'd been stalling as long as possible. As if she'd known she would being needing it again all along.

Max-Ernest was starting to panic. "But this chocolate is stronger, right? It could take you a hundred years to come back. What if everybody you know is old or dead and you're still the same age? Or the reverse. You could come back really old but to

everybody on Earth it will seem like only a second
has passed. Or —"

"I'm not leaving Earth. I'll be right here."

"Sure, maybe your body will be . . . but your mind will be in a different dimension!"

"I trust you."

"You . . . do?" Max-Ernest stammered. For some reason he wouldn't have been able to explain, those three small words had brought tears to his eyes.

"Uh-huh. You'll bring me back before anything goes wrong, I know you will . . . but Max-Ernest, if I do find out the Secret, I won't be able to tell it to you — you know that, right? And that doesn't mean I don't trust you. It's just because I can't. Sometimes even best friends have to keep secrets from each other."

Max-Ernest didn't say anything. But after a moment, he nodded.

"Good," said Cass, relieved. "OK, well, here goes —"

She raised the chocolate to her lips. Then paused. Like everyone, she'd often fantasized about time travel. But she'd never imagined that she'd actually do it. And certainly never like this. She was fairly confident that none of Max-Ernest's dire science-fiction predictions would come true. Nevertheless, she had a feeling that when she came back — assuming she came back — nothing would be the same.

"Hey, Max-Ernest, just in case, well, tell my mom I love her."

"No, Cass, don't —!"

But Cass had already bit down on the chocolate bar.

"OK, I'll tell her . . . ," Max-Ernest concluded.

He could tell she didn't hear him. She was lost in the taste of chocolate.

The deepest, darkest chocolate of all time. The chocolate *of* time.

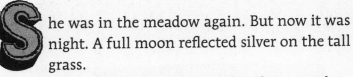

She was in the meadow again. But now it was night. A full moon reflected silver on the tall grass.

The taste of chocolate lingered in her mouth, a dim reminder of a faraway place she'd left, or so it seemed, long, long ago.

In front of her was the Jester's tent, its candy-striped sides billowing in the breeze. As she stepped closer, a cloud passed over the moon, shrouding the tent in darkness.

Holding her breath, she parted the tent flaps and looked inside, ready to meet the Jester once more —

A fiery white glow blinded her eyes. It was as if she were staring into the center of a midnight sun.

THE END

APPENDIX

379

CHOCOLOSSARY

a slightly biased glossary of chocolate terminology

Blood Chocolate: Chocolate made with the help of slave labor, usually child slaves working on African cacao plantations. The reason Cass proposed a chocolate boycott.

Cacao: The tree, pod, and seed from which chocolate is made. The root of all goodness.

Cocoa: Basically a misspelling of cacao. Also refers to Dutch process cocoa powder and a warm comforting drink sometimes topped with whipped cream.

Cocoa Butter: The oozing white fat squeezed out of cacao nibs, then later folded back in during the conching process. Sometimes rubbed on human skin.

Conching: The process whereby the thick brown sludge of early-stage chocolate is stirred and kneaded until it becomes smooth and silky.

Dark Chocolate: Heaven on Earth.

Fair Trade Chocolate: Chocolate certified not to be blood chocolate. Cass now insists that all the chocolate she eats be fair trade chocolate, made from sustainably farmed cacao.

Ganache: A soft filling or frosting made of cream and chocolate.

Midge: A tiny fly that pollinates the pink flower of the cacao tree. Without midges, there would be no cacao pods, hence no cacao seeds and ultimately no chocolate. Midges like dark moist places, one reason cacao trees grow best in the shade. Also an insulting nickname for a short person.

Milk Chocolate: Chocolate for beginners. A lesser version of dark chocolate. Very sweet. Often waxy. Eat only if you must.

Nibs: Broken bits and pieces of cacao seeds. Before chocolate as we know it is made, the nibs are crushed and pulverized, extracting the oozing white fat known as cocoa butter.

Palet d'Or: *Pillow of gold.* A chocolate square or disk. Usually a hard shell or *coverture* of dark chocolate surrounding an interior of soft, buttery chocolate or coffee *ganache.*

Vanilla: An impoverished flavor for which we should all feel sympathy.

White Chocolate: A poor excuse for chocolate. Hardly deserving the name. It is made with very little cacao or none at all. Basically cocoa butter and sugar. Bears unfortunate similarity in color to vanilla.

THE SUPERTASTER TASTE BUD TEST

Are pomelos and grapefruits as different to you as apples and oranges? Do you insist on eating sushi when everybody else is having a tuna fish sandwich? Can you distinguish between bubblegum brands without looking at their labels?

If the answer to those questions is YES, you may be a *supertaster.* Try this test to find out:

What you'll need:

• Dark grape juice or red punch or green candy or other non-poisonous material with which to color your tongue (as much as I enjoy chewing pens, I must warn you that ink tastes terrible)

• Notebook paper or some other piece of paper you have punched a hole through

• Magnifying glass

Color the tip of your tongue according to your preferred method. Place hole over tongue. Using a magnifying glass, count the pink, *un*colored dots inside the hole. (You can do this in front of a mirror, but it's easier and more fun with a friend.) These dots are *fungiform pupillae* — the little bumps on your tongue that hold your taste buds. The more pupillae you have, the more taste buds. Most people have about fifteen pupillae in that amount of space. Supertasters have thirty or more.

DARK CHOCOLATE TASTING

As you know, I like my chocolate dark — like my socks. But even if you're one of those milquetoasty types who prefers milk chocolate, you may benefit from a dark chocolate tasting — that is, a chocolate tasting *in* the dark. Also known as a blind tasting.

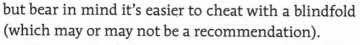

There are of course two ways to conduct a blind tasting: with blindfolds or by switching off the lights. I will let you choose between the two, but bear in mind it's easier to cheat with a blindfold (which may or may not be a recommendation).

You may include as many varieties of chocolate as you like, but five or six is probably best. Before donning your blindfolds (or turning out the lights), arrange squares of chocolate in front of each taster. I suggest going from lightest (white chocolate, if you insist) to darkest (the chocolate with the highest percentage of cacao). What is most important is that the chocolate be arranged in the same order in front of all participants — so that when somebody says he likes "chocolate number three," everybody else knows which chocolate he's talking about.

Here are the things to "look for" when you're conducting a dark chocolate tasting:

Sound
Does the chocolate snap when you break it? Or is the chocolate soft and mushy? Usually, dark chocolate is drier than milk chocolate, which makes dark chocolate snappier.

Scent
Most of what we think of as taste is scent. So before biting into your chocolate, take a whiff. What do you smell other than simply chocolate? Any fruits or spices? Maybe a dirty smell or even a bad smell?

Taste
When you take your first bite, pinch your nose. This way you'll be certain that what you're tasting you're actually tasting and not smelling. Remember, by itself the tongue can only detect five flavors: salt, sweet, sour, bitter, and umami (savoriness).

Texture
Finally, release your nose and let the chocolate melt across your tongue. What does it feel like? It should be smooth but not waxy. Hard but not grainy.

As the chocolate melts, different flavors are released. What does it taste like at first? What tastes linger afterward? Where do you taste the chocolate on your tongue?

SELECTED RECIPES FROM . . .
PB'S SECRET CHOCOLATE COOKBOOK

Remember, anyone can be a master chef. All it takes is the right ingredient — chocolate!

PB's All-Time Favorite Chocolate Recipe

- 1 bar of chocolate (preferably dark)
- 1 hand
- 1 mouth

Grasp bar in hand. Stick in mouth. Oh wait — REMOVE WRAPPER. *Then* stick in mouth. Now eat. Repeat.

NOTE: SPEED IS OF THE ESSENCE IN THIS RECIPE. OTHERWISE, SOMEBODY MAY SEE YOU AND YOU MAY BE FORCED TO SHARE.

Zuper-Rapide Mousse au Chocolat
(Super-Fast Chocolate Mousse)

- 1 cup of cream
- 1 bar of chocolate
- 1 beret
- French accent

Whip cream with blender until it makes little mountain peaks. Melt chocolate in small saucepan. (The best way to do this is to put the saucepan inside a larger pot filled with warm water.)* Then stir chocolate into whipped cream. Lick fingers. Tip beret. Say *voila*. Serve.

Caca Boy's Aztec Hot Chocolate

The Aztecs drank chocolate in all sorts of ways, with all sorts of flavorings, but usually they preferred their chocolate hot and spicy.

- Hot cocoa mix
- Hot water (or milk)
- Cinnamon
- Chili powder

Follow directions on the hot cocoa package. Then add cinnamon. And, if you're brave, a pinch of chili powder.

---

*THIS KIND OF WARM WATER BATH IS CALLED A *BAIN-MARIE*. SUPPOSEDLY, THE BAIN-MARIE WAS INVENTED BY AN ALCHEMIST IN ANCIENT ALEXANDRIA, MARIA THE JEWESS, WHO NEEDED A GENTLE WAY TO MELT HER ALCHEMICAL MATERIALS. LATER, IT BECAME A PREFFERED METHOD

Triple Chocolate Hot Fudge Sundae

Just like a normal hot fudge sundae, but in place of
vanilla ice cream, try chocolate ice cream. And in
place of whipped cream, use chocolate mousse (see
recipe above). The hot fudge part stays the same, naturally. Unless you want to triple the usual of amount
of fudge, in which case you have a Triple Triple Chocolate Hot Fudge Sundae.

Chocolate Fondue

The only thing better than cheese fondue.

• Chocolate for melting
• Things for dipping (i.e., bananas, strawberries,
  orange sections, cookies, marshmallows, fingers)

Melt chocolate in *bain-marie* or fondue pot. Dip se-
lected items. Eat until you feel sick.

FOR MELTING CHOCOLATE. AS IT TURNS OUT, THERE IS MORE TO THE
CHOCOLATE–ALCHEMY CONNECTION THAN THE ILLUSTRIOUS MEMBERS
OF THE TERCES SOCIETY INITIALLY SUPPOSED.

Indoor S'mores

A proper s'more is made beside a campfire and consists of one roasted marshmallow and two broken pieces of chocolate sandwiched between graham cracker squares. Ideally, the marshmallow is golden brown not burned (although the charred marshmallow has its supporters!) and hot enough to melt the chocolate. If you're anything like me, you spend much of your life impatiently waiting for your next s'more. But let's face it. For most of us, campfires are few and far between. After much reflection, I think I have found a solution — something to tide us over until the next campfire:

Stick a marshmallow onto a skewer or fondue fork. Dip the marshmallow in chocolate fondue. Then place it between two squares of graham cracker. Behold the *Indoor S'more*!

Important: you must tell or listen to a ghost story while eating. Otherwise, your Indoor S'more is no more a s'more than I am.

Chocolate Chocolate Chip Cookies

Chocolate chip cookies are almost perfect. This is how you correct their one minor flaw.

- 1 chocolate chip cookie recipe (see back of chocolate chip package)
- ½ cup (or a little more) cocoa powder
- extra dough for eating uncooked

Follow the instructions in your chocolate chip cookie recipe. But before spooning out your cookies, add cocoa powder. Stir.

NOTE: IF YOU FEEL YOUR COOKIES *STILL* AREN'T CHOCOLATY ENOUGH, YOU MAY ADD BROKEN PIECES OF CHOCOLATE BARS AND / OR M&M'S.

Chocolate Egg Cream

If your grandparents were raised in Brooklyn, they probably wax poetic about the joys of this classic soda fountain concoction.

- Seltzer water
- Chocolate syrup
- Milk
- Not a single egg

Like James Bond's martini, an egg cream should be shaken, not stirred.

PB's Grilled PB, B, and C

- Two slices of bread
- Peanut butter
- One banana, sliced
- One chocolate bar
- Butter
- Milk (for drinking)

Make a peanut butter, banana, and chocolate sandwich. Butter the outside. Grill in a pan or heat in a panini press. Serve with glass of milk. Inform any nearby adults that they are not allowed to taste your sandwich — it will make them fat.

Afrikaans	*Hallo*
Albanian	*Allo*
Alsatian	*Bùschùr*
Apache	*Dad'atay*
Arabic	*Salaam*
Assyrian	*Shlomo*
Balinese	*Om swastyastu*
Basque	*Kaixo*
Belorussian	*Pryvitáni*
Bengali	*Nomoskaar*
Blackfoot	*Oki*
Bulgarian	*Zdravéi*
Burmese	*Mingala ba*
Cantonese	*Néih hóu*
Catalan	*Hola*
Chaldean	*Shlama illakh*
Chechen	*Marsha voghiila*
Cherokee	*O-si-yo*
Cheyenne	*Haaahe*
Creole	*Bonjou*
Croatian	*Zdravo*
Czech	*Dobrý den*
Danish	*Goddag*
Dutch	*Hoi*
Edo	*Kóyo*

Egyptian (ancient)	*Iiti em hotep*
Esperanto	*Saluton*
Farsi	*Salaam*
Fijian	*Bula*
Finnish	*Hei*
French	*Bonjour*
Ga	*Mingabu*
Gaeilge (Irish)	*Haileo*
Gaelic (Scottish)	*Halò*
Georgian	*Gamardjoba*
German	*Guten tag*
Greek	*Yiassou*
Hawaiian	*Aloha*
Hebrew	*Shalom*
Hindi	*Namasté*
Huichol	*Ke áku*
Hungarian	*Jó napot*
Icelandic	*Góðan daginn*
Indonesian	*Selamat siang*
Inuktitut	*Asujutilli*
Italian	*Ciâo*
Japanese	*Konnichi wa*
Korean	*Annyong haseyo*
Kurdi	*Rozhbash*
Ladino	*Shalom*
Latin	*Ave*

Latvian	*Sveiki*
Lithuanian	*Labas*
Luganda	*Ki kati*
Luxembourgish	*Moïën*
Maasai	*Supa*
Macedonian	*Zdravo*
Maltese	*Bonju*
Manchu	*Ei*
Mandarin	*Nî hâo*
Maori	*Kia ora*
Mixe	*Za jiatzy*
Náhuatl	*Niltze*
Navajo	*Yá'át'ééh*
Nepali	*Namaste*
Nimo	*Nena wenao*
Norwegian	*Goddag*
Polish	*Dzień dobry*
Portuguese	*Olá*
Punjabi (Sikh)	*Sat siri akal*
Punjabi (Muslim)	*Asslaam alaikam*
Punjabi (Hindu)	*Namaste*
Romani	*Yov sasti*
Russian	*Zdravstvuite*
Samoan	*Talofa*
Sanskrit	*Namo namah*
Slovak	*Ahoj*

Slovenian	*Živijo*
Somali	*Maalin wanagsan*
Spanish	*Hola*
Swedish	*Hej*
Tagalog	*Kamusta*
Tajik	*Saläm*
Thai	*Sawatdee khrab*
Tongan	*Malo e lelei*
Turkish	*Merhaba*
Ukrainian	*Pryvit*
Urdu	*Assalam-o-Alekum*
Vietnamese	*Chào*
Walloon	*Bondjoû*
Welsh	*Dydd da*
Xhosa	*Molo*
Xucuru-Cariri	*Akakáume*
Yiddish	*Sholem aleykhem*
Yoruba	*E kú àárò*
Yucateco	*Ki'ki't'áantabah*
Zapotec	*Pa diuxi*
Zulu	*Sawubona*
Zuñi	*Keshi*

STOP RIGHT THERE!

What do you think you're doing?
You've come to **THE END** of this book.

You want to know what happens *next*, you say?
Preposterous! Outrageous! Absurd!

All right, if you insist. . . .

Turn the page for a sneak peek at my fourth book.
But proceed with caution,
and don't say I didn't warn you that . . .

THIS ISN'T WHAT IT LOOKS LIKE

In Stores Now!

How shall I put this? I must choose my words carefully.

(I know how you are. Always ready to jump on my mistakes.)

Somewhere, at some time, a girl walked down a road.

I say *somewhere* not because the where is secret, although it is.

I say *some time* not because the when is secret, although it is.

And I say *a girl* not because her name is secret, although it is.

No, I use these words because the girl herself did not know where she was.

Or when.

Or who.

She had woken standing up. With her eyes open.

It was a very strange sensation. Like materializing out of nowhere.

Her fingers and toes tingled. The tips of her ears burned (whether from heat or cold she wouldn't have been able to say).

Sunspots lingered in her eyes, blurring her vision. But when she looked up she saw there was no sun. The sky was cloudy.

Had she fainted? Did she have a concussion? (She knew that confusion and blurred vision were symptoms of concussion, but she couldn't remember how she knew it.) She touched her head, but she found no injury.

Gradually, the sunspots disappeared and her vision cleared. She looked around.

She had no idea where she was.

She seemed to be in the countryside, but of what country wasn't immediately apparent. There were fields to either side of her, but they were dry and empty. Trees dotted the landscape but in no obvious pattern. There were no signs of life.

Be systematic, she told herself. If you retrace your steps, you'll figure out where you are.

But she couldn't remember a thing that had happened before she was where she was. It was as if she had been born a moment ago.

Who am I...?

The realization that she didn't know her own name came over her belatedly, like a chill you don't notice until you see your breath clouding in the air.

She felt uneasy but not exactly frightened. Real amnesia, she knew (although she couldn't remember how she knew it), was exceedingly rare. Most likely, her memory would return in a moment.

She decided the best thing was to walk.

The walking was not easy. There were no signs or streetlights to guide the way. The road was not paved, and it was riddled with rocks and tree roots and mud holes.

She stumbled more than once, but she trudged forward. What else was there to do?

An hour passed. Or maybe two. Or was it less?

She didn't see anyone else. Until she did.

Ahead of her, just a few feet off the road, a little boy was climbing a big tree. Like a cat, he made his way on all fours out onto a long branch. Like a cat, he got stuck.

"Father...Father!"

His cries grew louder, but nobody came.

I wonder if he'll recognize me, the girl thought. He could be my little brother for all I know.

"Don't worry, I'll get you down!" she shouted.

If the boy heard her, he showed no sign. "Father!" he kept yelling.

An old hemp rope lay beneath the tree. The remains of a swing. The girl picked it up, then automatically started to climb the old and twisting tree trunk. As if it were the natural thing to do. As if she had rescued many other children before.

Remember the Three-Point Rule, she told herself. But she couldn't remember how she knew the rule.*

"You shouldn't climb up trees if you're too scared to climb down," she said when she came close to the boy.

He ignored her, continuing to yell for his father. It certainly didn't seem as though he recognized her.

"Are you deaf? I'm trying to help...."

The boy's shirt—little more than a rag—had caught on a branch. As soon as the girl started to untangle him, the boy jumped in fright—and almost fell out of the tree.

She gripped him tight. "Careful—"

He screamed, "Goat! Goat!"

At least that's what it sounded like.

"Calm down—you're OK."

She gave him a pat of reassurance, but his cries only grew louder and more hysterical.

"I'll get you down, no problem."

Expertly, she tied the rope to the tree. A *Buntline Hitch Knot*, she remembered the knot was called. But she didn't remember how she knew the name.

She tugged on the boy's shirt collar. He clung to the tree branch, refusing to move.

"Goat! Goat!"

"Is there a goat down there? Is that what's

ALWAYS CONNECT TO WHAT YOU'RE CLIMBING WITH AT LEAST TWO FEET AND ONE HAND OR TWO HANDS AND ONE FOOT. YOU MIGHT REMEMBER THIS HELPFUL RULE FROM A HIGHLY EDUCATIONAL AND FRANKLY RATHER BRILLIANT BOOK CALLED IF YOU'RE READING THIS, IT'S TOO LATE.

scaring you? Don't worry, it won't hurt you. Goats don't eat people. Tin cans, tennis balls, maybe — but not little boys. Not usually, anyways." She smiled to show she was joking, but he didn't smile back.

Eventually, she coaxed him down by gently placing his hands on the rope — then forcibly pushing him off the branch.

"Pretend it's a fire pole!" she called after him.

He slid down the rope, a look of terror on his face.

As soon as his feet hit the ground, the boy bolted.

"You're welcome," said the girl under her breath.

In the distance, a man — presumably the boy's father — waited. He wore a plumed hat, dark vest, and big, billowing sleeves. He looked like a musketeer.

He must be an actor, thought the girl. Maybe there is a theater nearby.

The boy was still crying about the goat as he jumped into his father's arms.

The girl waved. But the man didn't acknowledge her.

Gee, people are really friendly around here, thought the girl.

Shaking her head, she returned to the road — and stepped right into a puddle.

She grunted in annoyance.

As she shook water off her foot, she looked curiously at the puddle. The muddy water reflected blue sky and silver clouds and a flock of birds passing by.

But there was one reflection she could not see: her own.

Not *goat*, she thought.

Ghost.

If you're ready for more fun, read
THE SECRET SERIES

Dear Reader,

Whatever you do, do NOT read the books in my *New York Times* bestselling Secret Series. I know they are full of exciting adventures and puzzling mysteries about evil villains and a secret society—but all these things are strictly confidential—and dangerous! Oh no, have I accidentally tempted you to read them? Well, do so if you must, but remember: You've been warned!

Dastardly Yours,

pseudonymous bosch

BOB312

Book #1

Book #2

Book #3

Book #4